heart of
thorns

 BOOK ONE

VAMPIRE ROYALS OF NEW YORK

Heart of Thorns
Vampire Royals of New York: Gabriel
Book One
Copyright © 2021 by Sarah Piper
SarahPiperBooks.com

Cover design by Covers by Juan

ISBN-13: 978-1-948455-25-1

VAMPIRE ROYALS OF NEW YORK

Dorian

Dark Deception

Dark Seduction

Dark Obsession

Gabriel

Heart of Thorns

Heart of Fury

Heart of Flames

TAROT ACADEMY

Spells of Iron and Bone

Spells of Breath and Blade

Spells of Flame and Fury

Spells of Blood and Sorrow

Spells of Mist and Spirit

THE WITCH'S REBELS

Shadow Kissed

Darkness Bound

Demon Sworn

Blood Cursed

Death Untold

Rebel Reborn

THE WITCH'S MONSTERS

Blood and Midnight

CHAPTER ONE

The witch was going to be a fucking headache.

Gabriel Redthorne had known it since he'd first spied her roaming his brother's gardens at Ravenswood.

Then, he'd found her mysterious and compelling—an obsession he'd been nurturing for weeks.

Now?

"Your chances of seeing another sunrise are entirely dependent upon your cooperation, *witch*." He said it like the dirty word it was, lip curling as he took in the sight of her.

Obstinate. Ornery. Filthy.

They were secluded in one of the VIP rooms on the upper level of Bloodbath, the East Village nightclub he and his royal vampire brothers had liberated from their enemies last night. The window that overlooked the ground level offered a breathtaking view of the carnage the Redthorne allies had wrought: mutilated demons, still twitching where they lay. The wet ash of all the traitorous vampires they'd slaughtered. Broken bones, lost limbs, shattered glass, rivers of blood still gleaming in the cracks and crevices.

Luck or magic—one of them had spared the witch's life.

"You *will* answer my questions," he said.

She glared at him. Her sapphire-bright eyes stood out starkly in a face painted by death. Gabriel wore the same mask, the taste of demon blood still rancid in his throat long after it had dried on his clothing.

She wasn't the only witch they'd captured—a half-dozen of them had been working their dark magics for the enemy—but Gabriel had no use for the others.

It was Jacinda he needed. Jacinda whose intoxicating gaze held a fire that sparked in him thoughts too dangerous to voice.

"I've got nothing to say to you, Prince," she hissed. She sat on a plush velvet chair against the back wall, nursing a bottle of water one of his inconveniently compassionate brothers had given her. Clothing hung from her in tatters—dark, blood-spattered jeans, one side ripped from ankle to knee. A lacy black top missing a sleeve. No shoes, bare toes curled against the cold floor, her violet nail polish chipped.

She held herself haughtily, as though she were dressed for the runway.

"Not quite ready to grind my bones into dust, then?" Gabriel smirked, recalling her earlier taunt. To be fair, that particular threat had come *after* he'd tied her to a barstool downstairs, but still. Even without the idle threats, her crimes were severe enough to warrant a thorough questioning, followed by an even more thorough punishment.

His specialty.

She shrugged, sipped her water. "I don't like to vanquish enemies on an empty stomach."

"Is that what I am?" He prowled across the room, stopping to loom over her. "Your enemy?"

All that bravado, all that fire, yet her fingers gripped the bottle so tightly they turned white. The scent of adrenaline soured her blood.

Gabriel leaned forward, hands settling on the arms of her chair, bracketing her lithe frame. Beneath the gore of battle, her true scent lingered, like black pepper and damp earth and things that grew only in darkness.

He waited for it to turn his stomach. To inspire in him the same revulsion *all* witches inspired.

It didn't.

"Where *is* Renault Duchanes?" he demanded, his voice an icy blade sharpened over decades of interrogating enemies, making simpering victims of far more formidable beasts.

But this beast offered nothing but indifference, keeping her gaze locked on his like a dare. "Halfway around the world by now, if he's a smart bloodsucker."

"If he were smart, he wouldn't have abandoned his bonded witch to torture and…" Gabriel fingered the collar of her torn blouse and leaned in closer, breath stirring her hair. "*Ruin.*"

A shiver rolled up her spine, but she kept that hot steel

in her voice. "I'm not his keeper. He bailed on me, same as he bailed on everyone else, no forwarding address."

"You admit to working for him, then?"

She lifted a shoulder far too soft and elegant to be covered in demon blood. Gabriel resisted the urge to lick it clean.

"It's not exactly classified intel," she said. "I was the House Duchanes bonded witch."

"For how long?"

"Long… longer than I should've been." She finally turned away, a note of regret echoing behind the admission.

Again, her scent drifted to him. Lingered.

Gabriel backed off, retreating to the other side of the room. This wasn't going according to plan at all. He needed answers from her—answers that would lead him to the traitor Duchanes. Answers that would usher in the brutal end to a rivalry that'd stretched on for far too many decades.

More than answers, though, he needed her help.

Thanks to one of his late father's many indiscretions, the Redthorne line had been cursed centuries ago, damning the royal family and any new vampires they sired. Gabriel had only recently begun to feel the effects, but they were already excruciating. Extreme light sensitivity, an inability to properly synthesize blood, a fog of the body and mind that—left unmitigated—would certainly destroy him.

Along with the few vampires left on this earth he gave a single fuck about.

A dark witch had bound the curse. Only a dark witch could unbind it.

"In your capacity as the Duchanes witch," Gabriel said, forcing himself to stay focused, "you performed certain services. Correct?"

She nodded and glanced at his forearms, his sleeves rolled up past the evidence of his own witch-provided services—the spelled tattoos that enabled vampires to walk in daylight, to eat human food with the blood that sustained them, to drink good liquor and charm beautiful women and fool the world into believing they weren't immortal monsters.

Tattoos that—thanks to the family curse—were losing their potency.

"Spells, charms, minor hexes," she said with a shrug. "Sometimes he wanted his Tarot cards read."

"And the attempted murder of the vampire king?" he asked, cool tone recapturing her gaze. "Whose idea was that?"

"Not mine."

"Yet you crafted the poison, did you not?"

She closed her eyes and sighed. "Yes."

They said it couldn't be done, poisoning a vampire. Especially a royal vampire. Yet Duchanes and his witch had found a way to bring down Dorian Redthorne with the very herbs she'd collected at Ravenswood.

On her knees in the moonlight, skirt hiked up to mid-thigh, slender fingers digging in the dirt, luscious hair spilling down her back in waves…

The image snuck into Gabriel's mind, sending a pulse of heat to his balls. Had he known she was already plotting his eldest brother's murder that night, he might not have let his fantasies take root.

But he didn't, and they had, and nothing short of his demise would dislodge them now.

Bloody fucking witches.

"If not for some quick thinking on the part of Dorian's woman," Gabriel said now, "my brother would be ash in the wind, and you and I would be having a very *different* sort of conversation."

"It was the demon's doing. Chernikov and Duchanes made a plan, I got an assignment."

"What assignment, exactly?"

After a long pause, she finally opened her eyes, gaze flickering with genuine sorrow. "Devise a poison strong enough to kill a vampire, slow enough to make him suffer."

"*Any* vampire? Or a specific vampire?"

"I didn't ask questions." A shiver followed, a fresh shot of adrenaline coursing through her blood. "Nikolai Chernikov kills witches who ask questions. Hell, he'll probably kill me for talking to you."

Gabriel could've eased that particular worry for her; thanks to Dorian's newly forged alliances with the Rogozin demons, Chernikov and his hellspawn crew would be dead by sunset.

"Tell me something," he said instead. "How desperate does a witch need to be before she gets into bed with the head of the demonic Russian syndicate?"

He pictured her signing the contract. Pictured Chernikov's greasy smile, his black demon-eyes roving her body, a sheen of lust gleaming on his brow.

Anger leaked into Gabriel's chest. They were all the bloody same. Witches, vampires, humans—the dumb and the desperate never read the fine print on a demon deal.

Stupid girl.

"I'm not," she replied defensively, and Gabriel wondered if she'd read his thoughts.

"Not desperate? Or not in bed with demons?"

"Every last demon can *burn*," she ground out, and now her blood sang with something more powerful than fear—a pure, honest emotion that echoed in the darkest places of his own tarnished soul.

Vengeance.

Gabriel raised an eyebrow. Perhaps she wasn't such a stupid girl after all.

"Let me go," she demanded. "This is bullshit—I've got nothing to do with vampire politics. Especially royal ones."

"Says the witch who poisoned the king at the behest of his political rivals? Forgive me if I don't leap at the chance to cut you loose."

Gabriel paced the room, glanced back out the window. Down below, a handful of Rogozin's underlings attempted to mop the glass and blood from the floor. Slow, sticky work.

He wondered how long it would take to renovate the place. To leach the stink of death from the walls and turn it into a nightclub to rival his properties in Las Vegas. He'd have to sell his clubs and casino now that he was relocating back to New York, but it was just as well. The desert was no place for a dying vampire with cursed blood and a target on his back.

"What do you want from me, bloodsucker?" she asked. "Why am I still here?"

When he turned to face her again, genuine confusion had tempered the fury in her eyes.

Why haven't you killed me? That's what she *really* wanted to know. If one were inclined to believe the legends, the youngest Redthorne prince had parted thousands of demons from their heads just for breathing on him, staked his own kind for beating him at cards, and ate the hearts of human babies for breakfast—an entirely unfair accusation given that he hardly ever ate breakfast.

"You stand accused of conspiring against the royal family," he said. "*My* family. There are consequences."

"You got proof? Working as a bonded witch isn't a crime."

Gabriel nodded toward the window. "You were found at the scene of *this* crime, aiding and abetting."

"And you *caused* the scene of this crime."

"A defensive maneuver, I assure you."

The witch shook her head, clearly disgusted with him. Beneath the matted blood and ash, her hair was a silvery shade of blonde. He remembered it from that night at Ravenswood. It reminded him of moonlight, giving her an ethereal softness he was trying desperately not to notice.

To crave.

Fuck.

Since he'd been turned, Gabriel had lived his immortal life in hard edges and angles, clean lines, sharp knives, sharper fangs. Blood and death, ice and thorns. His world left no room for softness.

Least of all for a witch.

"Dorian found one of your grimoires," he said. "In the home of yet *another* demon working against the crown."

"*Another* demon? Wow, you guys have a lot of enemies. Maybe if your family had been less..." She curled her hands into claws and grimaced like a made-for-television monster. "...you'd have fewer people trying to murder you? Just a thought."

"We know all about your dark magic, witch. Your work resurrecting the gray vampires was particularly damning, not to mention utterly repugnant." Bile rose in his throat. He hated those fucking grays—the decay, the primitiveness, the constant reminder of what he and his kind would become without the magic of their own bonded witches. No conscience, no soul, no humanity. Just blood and bones and instinct, an endless hunger driving them to consume anything in their paths.

Thanks to Jacinda's clever spellcraft, Duchanes turned the foul beasts into a weapon. One Gabriel and his brothers needed to defuse before the human authorities figured out the real story behind a rash of so-called animal attacks plaguing the tri-state area.

"I did what I had to do to survive," she said. "Same as the rest of the freaks in this city."

"In *this* city, witch, death is a kindness. That you'd seek to defy it is nothing less than madness."

"The grays are already dead."

"No more than I." Crowding into her space once more, he ran a finger along her jawline, his touch as deceptively soft as his whisper. "Would you bring me back? Breathe your venomous words, deliver me from hell's doorstep?"

Her heart pounded with new fury, so loud and defiant he sensed the disturbance beneath her skin. The hot, sudden rush of her blood unleashed a scent that nearly brought him to his knees.

With hunger.

With desire.

His fangs burned to break free, his control slipping...

"You know nothing," she spat, jerking away from his touch and shattering his momentary trance. "Nothing about me. Nothing about my life *or* my magic."

"Resurrection is a devil's bargain—*that* I know. When Death finally claims you, be certain he'll demand a reckoning."

She lowered her eyes, cheeks darkening. With shame, frustration, or pleasure, Gabriel hadn't a clue.

Dorian thought Jacinda was innocent, forced into the work by a stronger, deadlier foe. Duchanes. Chernikov. Any number of rival vamps or demons looking to make a move, using the witch as their own personal warhead.

But necromancy wasn't a natural talent. Wasn't something a witch or mage picked up on a whim—even under threat. It was a dark, unwieldy thing, a razor-sharp skill set whose cultivation took years of study and intense dedication. Defying death went beyond even the darkest of known magics, a practice so vile it could seep into your soul and eradicate all traces of humanity.

Another beat passed. Two. No answers, no confessions, no sounds but the muted din of the cleanup crew downstairs.

With a deep sigh, the witch dragged the back of her hand across her brow, leaving a pale smudge in the grime. "Look, Prince. As much fun as this is, I *really* need a shower, and you should probably get back to pulling the wings off butterflies or whatever it is you do for fun."

"Butterflies? No, not exactly." Gabriel fingered a lock of her moonlight hair, silky as a flower petal, resisting the urge to press it to his lips.

A deep tremor rumbled through her body.

In a flash he dropped the lock of hair and grabbed her face, jerking it upward, forcing her to meet his gaze. Her breath caught, heartbeat clamoring, eyes wide.

The pressure of his touch was light enough, but they both knew he could shatter her jaw.

Gabriel hovered close—so close he could see the galaxies swirling in the blue depths of her irises. So close a breath could turn into a kiss.

In a dark whisper, he said, "Why do you insist on making this more difficult than it needs to be?"

Her gaze scorched the air between them. "Because I'm *no* one's fucking butterfly."

A twitch of his lips, a smile nearly set loose.

It wouldn't do.

Gabriel released her and turned toward the small bar at the corner of the room, spared the destruction that had decimated the main level. He reached for a bottle of bourbon, poured two glasses.

Over his shoulder, he said, "They say my brother has a tender heart."

She laughed, a sound full of nails and teeth. "Yes, you bloodsuckers are all such lovable softies."

"He's forbidden me from killing you. And while I'm not in the habit of taking orders from my brother—and I despise witches almost as passionately as I despise demons —I'm feeling sentimental today." He turned toward her and held out one of the glasses. "Lucky for you."

Daggers glinted in those bright eyes, but she took the offered beverage, downing it in a few gulps. "Unlucky for you, King Tender-Heart hasn't forbidden *me* from killing anyone."

Gabriel's laughter finally escaped. Dry and brittle, like dust blown from a long-forgotten heirloom. Crossing the room, he turned to her once more and said, "You're my prisoner, witch. Stripped of your charms and amulets. Exhausted. Easy prey. Think you can take me down? Have a go."

Without hesitation she touched her neck, lips muttering a silent hex—all part of the show. Short of a demon's hellfire, the well-aimed throw of a sharp stake, or a *very* long sword, nothing could kill a vampire at any sort of distance.

"Do you feel it, Prince?" Her husky whisper rolled over Gabriel's flesh, making him shiver.

It seemed to unleash something, that whisper. An uncomfortable itch in his chest. A flicker of doubt in his mind.

"Is it just the dryness in the air?" she mused. "Ash from one of the *many* vampires you and your friends staked last night?"

Gabriel's throat tightened. Ached.

She brought her fingertips to her lips and blew away imaginary ashes, a child wishing on dandelion seeds. Then, through a menacing grin, "Or maybe, *bloodsucker*, I'm not such easy prey after all."

CHAPTER TWO

"Need some water, Prince? A lozenge?" The witch frowned, shiny black fingernails fluttering over her collarbone like beetles. "Cherry's my favorite, but they say honey-lemon's better for a scratchy throat."

Gabriel coughed. The tightness in his chest progressed to a burn that quickly stole his breath.

He panted like a dog, hands trembling as he reached for her. "If you've… poisoned… I'll kill—"

"No. You won't." She lowered her hand and flashed a saccharine-sweet smile.

At once his throat relaxed. Breath rushed back into his lungs, clear and crisp. The tremor vanished, hands steady once again.

Gabriel blinked away the blur in his eyes. Couldn't be certain it'd even happened—already, his memory of the last few seconds was fading. He took another breath. Pressed a hand to his chest, testing his heart.

Still beating, for fuck's sake.

"Feeling better?" she cooed.

Bloody hell. He stalked toward her again, done with the games. Done with the niceties. Done with all of it. The sooner he could set her straight, the sooner he could escape her intense presence. "I need three things from you, witch."

She glanced at her fingernails, calm and collected. "You and every other bloodsucker in this city. Take a number, Prince."

"One, you'll reveal the location of your former vampire master. If you don't know his location, you'll help me discern it by any means necessary. Two—"

"I already told you, I have no idea—"

"*Two*, you'll break a blood curse—dark magic, demon-bought, definitely in your wheelhouse."

"*Excuse* me? Curses aren't—"

"Three, you'll confess your crimes and accept your punishment."

"Ah, and there it is, folks." Jacinda rolled her eyes. "The final threat of a desperate vampire. Also, a boring one. Confess your crimes and accept your punishment? Really? Did you practice that line in front of the mirror last night? I bet you did. That and the sexy eyebrow thing."

"Sexy eyebrow thing?"

"Straight out of a vampire soap opera."

Amusement stirred inside him, but he kept it in check—along with his sexy eyebrow—and swallowed another mouthful of bourbon. "I'm not prone to threats, witch. Or soap operas. Only promises."

"Why don't we just skip to the good part, then?" She made a slicing motion across her throat, then held out her glass for a refill, defeat finally settling on her shoulders. "What a fucking day *this* turned out to be. TGIF, mother-fuckers!"

Gabriel smiled. A real one, utterly unintentional.

Fuck.

He was starting to like this witch. The fire. The fight.

He poured them each another round.

"Tell you what." He downed his drink and refilled his glass again, emptying the bottle. "I'll let you pick two out of three. Player's choice."

"Is this a joke?"

"It's a kindness."

She shrugged and ran a black-tipped finger around the rim of her glass. "I thought you wanted me to work behind the bar. Isn't that what you told your brother?"

"*That* was a joke. Putting a poisons expert in charge of serving drinks to New York's supernatural elite? Not exactly good business sense."

"That's too bad, because I've got *zero* experience with curses and no clue about Duchanes."

"That *is* too bad. Choosing death, are we?"

She folded her arms across her chest, assessing. "Death by *what*, exactly?"

"Exsanguination." *Devil's balls,* how he loved the way that word rolled off the tongue.

"I see. And who's doing the drinking?" Her smile was

lighter now. Teasing. Bordering on flirtatious. "You, I presume?"

He grinned and spread his arms. *Welcome to the party, witch.*

She stood from the chair and set down her glass, the tatters of her blouse lifting to reveal the expanse of skin across her lower abdomen, smooth and unmarred. Kissable.

Gabriel's cock stirred.

Then, squaring her shoulders and lifting her chin, his bold little witch huffed out a breath and said, "Fine. Do it. Make it quick, though—I hate melodramatic endings."

She was still smiling. Still teasing.

The woman had *no* idea who she was playing with.

And that's all it was. Games and spells, smoke and mirrors. Gabriel and his cock would do well to remember it.

He set down the empty bottle. The glass.

Gave her one last look, dark and deadly.

He was on her in a flash, one hand gripping her hip, the other fisting her hair and yanking it to the side, exposing her neck.

She gasped at the roughness of his handling but didn't draw back. Didn't flinch. Not even when he pressed his mouth to her soft flesh, that tantalizing spot just below the jaw.

Jacinda trembled in his arms.

Fear? Lust? Shock? Gabriel didn't give a fuck.

A steady pulse throbbed beneath his lips. His tongue darted out to taste.

Everything about her drove him mad.

The salt of her sweat. Soft wisps of hair tickling his nose. That forbidden, dark-earth scent. The heat of her, warm and throbbing and full of life, like the very heartbeat of existence.

Blood rushed beneath her skin, darkening her neck. Singing to him once again. Begging.

His fangs barely broke through, sharp points grazing her tender flesh, and—

"Wait!" she gasped, adrenaline spiking once again. "Please... please stop."

It was nothing more than a whisper, but a concession nevertheless.

"Fear makes honest fools of us all," Gabriel said.

The words rang hollow. He should've been thrilled at his victory, but this one left a bitter taste, the reasons for which he had no interest in exploring.

Grudgingly, he released her and backed off.

Jacinda swept her hair back in front of her shoulders, hiding that delectable neck from view. Her smile was gone, eyes no longer glittering. "How long?"

"I beg your pardon?"

"If I agree to help you, how much longer will you let me live? A week? A month?"

At his obvious confusion, she continued, "Everyone was terrified of Augustus, Prince, and with good reason. But that old bloodsucker? He had *nothing* on you."

Gabriel bristled at the mention of his dead father. At the comparison. The witch was utterly clueless, and her presumptions put his lingering desire on ice.

"I know your game," she pressed. "Everyone in this city talks, and believe me, I've heard *all* the stories about the ruthless Redthorne prince."

"Have you, now? And what do the stories say?"

"People are nothing but transactions to you—even your own family members. Once they're no longer useful, they... they disappear. Usually after you torture them to death."

She lifted her eyebrows as if she were daring him to deny it.

Those blue eyes blazed right through him.

He blurred into her space once more, hand curling possessively around that delicate neck, thumb brushing the pulse point.

Jacinda sucked in a startled breath, and he thought again of her kneeling in the dirt at Ravenswood, face turned up, a pale flower blooming in the darkness.

His fangs descended in earnest. It took everything in him not to sink them into her flesh and fucking *break* her.

"Then I suggest, little moonflower," he whispered, "you find a way to remain useful."

CHAPTER THREE

Seeing no better options at the moment—not her finest, mind you—Jacinda Colburn followed her captor out of Bloodbath and into the bright Manhattan day.

Gabriel winced at the sunlight and hurried their pace, weaving them through the stumbling, post-hangover brunch crowd toward a nondescript building across the street, about halfway down the block.

If anyone noticed the fact that she and the vampire were covered in blood and looked like they'd been set on fire and run over with a dump truck six times, they kept the commentary to themselves.

A small comfort in what was otherwise a flaming-shit-sandwich of a day.

"Where are we going?" Jaci demanded, struggling to keep pace in her bare feet. She'd lost her favorite heels in the attack last night, which sucked almost as much as her current predicament.

"Home," came the prick's reply. No elaboration.

Reality, harsh and sudden, bitch-slapped her across the face.

"Wait. You expect me to move in with you?" She stopped on the sidewalk before the building's entrance, forcing him to turn around. "No. No way. That was *not* part of the deal."

Gabriel grabbed her arm, glaring down at her with those deadly green eyes that made her shiver.

Damn it. Being in such close proximity to the vampire prince was like being stuck in perpetual winter. Forget exsanguination—the first time those cold green eyes pinned her this morning, she'd nearly died of hypothermia.

Until he'd put his mouth on her skin and damn near set her on fire...

No. She wouldn't even give that thought room to grow. The prince might've set her nerves ablaze with that little stunt in the VIP room, but clearly that was some temporary Stockholm-Syndrome-induced insanity on her part, because Gabriel Redthorne was just *all* kinds of wrong.

You could see it in those eyes.

"I expect you to obey me," he growled, the threat in his gravelly voice turning an otherwise panty-melting British accent into a thing of nightmares. "If you think I'm above making a gruesome scene on a public street, feel free to push me."

Jaci didn't need to push him. Crazy eyes never lie— she'd learned *that* from her sister.

A different sort of shiver threatened to overtake her, but she fought it off.

The vampire continued his brooding glare. Out there in the daylight, his eyes were a lighter shade of green than she'd first thought, like new moss clinging to an old stone.

"Are you coming willingly, witch, or are we already renegotiating our terms? Not off to the best start, it seems."

She opened her mouth to tell him just how far *off* he could go *fuck*, but then thought better of it.

Bide your time, girl. Pick your battles.

As much as Jaci hated to admit it—hated getting stuck in this ridiculous predicament with yet *another* cocky vampire who thought witches were their personal property —she needed him. Even more than she needed a shower and a bucket of bleach and some new heels, which was saying something.

Besides, as monstrous as Gabriel Redthorne was, Renault Duchanes was worse.

Renault would *always* be worse.

Blowing out a heavy sigh, Jaci gestured toward the door. "Lead the way, Prince."

CHAPTER FOUR

The fourteenth-floor apartment was sunny, spacious, and a *serious* upgrade from the perpetually dank basement her former vampire "master" had stashed her in.

It was also *not* Gabriel Redthorne's residence. As an earth witch with a nose for magic, Jaci was good with scents. The royal vampire's was cold and mysterious, like evergreens in winter, like crushed mint on ice, like something fervently alive trapped beneath an eternal snow.

This place held no trace of it.

"Who lives here?" she asked, bracing for the answer as she eyed up the living area—spacious, pretty, fully furnished. French doors led to a balcony outside, a café table and two chairs waiting invitingly in the sunshine.

A grim smirk turned up the corner of his mouth. "A newly acquired witch eager to prove her usefulness."

"So you're paying my rent now, vampire?"

"Think of it as a bonded arrangement, only without the

actual bond, without the promise of my protection, without unfettered access to my blood for your spellcraft, and without *any* further obligation from me—aside from allowing you to keep existing."

Jaci narrowed her eyes, trying to see through his self-satisfied mockery.

It was a trap. Had to be. Gabriel believed she'd willfully tried to murder his brother, not to mention all the other crimes he'd rattled off earlier. Now he was putting her up in damn-near luxury accommodations? Without supervision?

She peered over his shoulder into a short hallway that led to the back of the apartment, half expecting it to be overrun with a writhing horde of grays. It would serve her right, getting mauled by the very ghouls she'd helped unleash on this city.

Guilt simmered in her gut, but beyond Gabriel's unnervingly motionless physique, she found nothing but white walls and gleaming hardwoods, the faint smell of fresh paint floating on the air like an invitation to a brand-new life.

An invitation witches like Jaci never received. Not without a whole lot of strings and sharp objects attached.

"The kitchen is fully stocked," he continued, gesturing around the open-plan apartment like some kind of vampire real estate agent. "Down the hall you'll find the bedroom and bath, toiletries, linens, clothing. If there's anything else you need, leave a list outside the door and one of my associates will attend to it."

"Your vampire henchmen are now my personal shoppers?" She stifled a laugh, picturing a bunch of fanged goons in black leather jackets selecting ripe mangoes from the market, picking up her feminine supplies, rifling through the half-price underwear bin at Macy's for her size.

Gabriel folded his arms across his chest but said nothing. Not unless sighs and grunts could be considered a language.

Jaci headed into the kitchen, always her favorite spot, trying to tamp down her bubbling curiosity. The cupboards were the same gleaming oakwood as the floors, the walls painted a deep olive, the countertops ridiculously spacious. A massive granite-topped island stretched across the center, perfect for making spell jars and hex bags. A bay window took up most of the far wall, a large pantry nestled in beside it. Against her better judgment, she was already picturing the shelves stocked with jars of dried herbs and other magical ingredients, the sunny window seat overflowing with her favorite plants.

The whole place was a dream.

"What's the catch, Prince?" She tried to sound more irritated than excited, but judging from the smug look on his no-right-to-be-that-handsome face, she didn't pull it off.

"*Catches*," he said. "Plural."

Jaci laughed and rolled her eyes. "Here we go."

"First, for obvious security reasons, the apartment will be monitored at all times, including the main living areas, the bedroom, the outdoor space, and the exits and exterior hallway. Your only true privacy is in the bathroom. All other rooms are fitted with cameras with a live feed."

"*Cameras*?" Jaci's excitement died in a flash, the faint taste of smoke roiling up from her lungs.

"Not in the bathroom," he repeated.

"So you'll spy on me when I eat and sleep, but not when I shower or pee? Wow, thanks for being so considerate."

"Your cell phone will also be monitored."

"Are you serious? No. That's—that's a *complete* violation." She reached into her back pocket, only to come up empty.

Gabriel removed her cell from his shirt pocket and set it on the kitchen counter, again with that maddeningly sexy smirk-and-eyebrow combo she was pretty sure had caused the spontaneous loss of more panties, virginities, and dignities than there were supernaturals in this city. And rats. And supernatural rats.

When the hell had he swiped her phone? Last night, as she'd dashed into the wine cellar to avoid the slaughter? This morning, when he'd nearly bitten her artery in the VIP room? Right in her back pocket, millimeters from her ass, and she hadn't even felt him lift the damn thing.

Not that it mattered. The only people she ever called or texted were Renault and his bloodsucking minions, and those assholes—the few that'd survived the Redthorne attack on Bloodbath—were long gone by now.

"Next," he said, "you'll have free rein of the apartment and balcony, but you're not to leave the premises without an escort—myself or one of my associates. If you attempt to leave without my permission, our deal is null and void."

"Deal. Right. You mean the part where you let me live to see another sunrise, provided I can give you what you want and obey your every command in the process?"

Gabriel cocked his head, cold eyes glittering like ice. "You're free to counter, witch, but unless your negotiating skills are as finely honed as your necromancy, you'll find yourself on the losing end."

A draft rolled over her skin, poking its cold fingers through every tear in her clothes.

Rubbing her half-bare arms, Jaci turned toward the kitchen window and peered down onto St. Mark's Place. The street was lined with bars and cafés and trinket shops, sidewalks bustling with people and dogs. Across the way, a guy with green dreadlocks stood on a plastic milk crate, waving his arms and warning about the end times.

"What if I just want to run out for a quick coffee?" she asked.

"No need. There's an espresso machine on the counter, along with several varieties of beans, a grinder, sweeteners, syrups."

"What about bagels? Pizza? Chinese?"

"Like I said, make a list. All of your requests will be accommodated."

Soft and silent, her bare feet padded across the kitchen floor, one step, then another and the next. She didn't remember telling herself to move, yet there she was, inching closer to him, swept up in his evergreen scent and the magnetic pull of his eyes and the thin line between danger and death she always found herself straddling. Balancing.

Yearning for.

"All of them?" she asked, voice thick with something that sounded annoyingly lusty.

Get it together, slut muffin!

Gabriel looked down at her again, towering a full head taller, a wall of muscle and ice. "Within reason, witch."

"And who's judge and jury on what's reasonable?" Her breasts brushed against his chest, making her nipples ache.

Gabriel's nostrils flared, heat gathering between them once more, and she wondered if he was thinking about that moment in the VIP room, just like she was. Remembering the way their bodies had melded together, however briefly. The brush of his lips on her skin, the heat of his touch on her body, two hearts banging against the walls like wild animals.

He lifted a hand to her hair, looping one of her curls around his finger like he'd done earlier. In a soft, seductive voice that belied the tension in his body, he said, "My intention isn't to starve you, Jacinda, or keep you in squalor."

"Then what *is* your intention?"

He closed his eyes. Shook his head. Breathed out her scent as though he needed to be rid of it, his deep exhale tickling her cheeks.

"Don't," he whispered.

"Why not?" She mouthed the words, not even certain he'd heard them. Not even certain she knew what she was asking, what he was warning against, what the fuck was happening between them. For whatever reason, her mind turned to mush around this man—this monster—and despite the red alert from her nipples, she didn't like it one bit.

He opened his eyes. Took a step backward, shaking his head as if his mind betrayed him too. "Ours *isn't* a social arrangement, witch. You're an acquisition, just like Blood-bath, claimed by the royal family from a lesser foe to be put to use or put to death."

Wow, tell me how you really *feel, dickhead.*

Swallowing the inexplicable burn his words left in her chest, Jaci forced a hollow laugh. "Thanks for the reminder, Prince. For a minute there, I thought you were trying to get into my pants. What's left of them, anyway."

She'd meant it as a joke, but the moment the words were out, a flash of anger rippled through his muscles, quivering beneath his blood-caked clothing. He spun around in a blur and stalked toward the exit, leaving a gust of winter in his wake.

Yanking open the door, he paused on the threshold and turned to issue one last command. "Take the day to settle in and gather your wits, Jacinda. Starting tomorrow, you'll work on locating Duchanes."

"What about the curse?"

"Priority one, Duchanes. I'll inform you when that changes."

"But I need my—"

The door slammed shut. The vampire was gone, his

sudden absence taking up even more space than his presence.

"—grimoire," she finished, then slumped against the island counter, wondering what the fuck just happened.

She hadn't imagined the fire between them, that spark back at the club, the crackling flames here in the kitchen. It was real, but it was like they'd both been entranced by some otherworldly force.

He'd snapped out of it first.

And he couldn't get away from her fast enough.

His earlier words rang in her head like a warning bell.

I despise witches almost as passionately as I despise demons…

Jaci wondered what he'd do if he knew the truth—that his "acquisition from a lesser foe" was actually a two-for-one. A witch *and* demon, born and bred, all rolled up into one fucked-up little package who couldn't, no matter how hard she tried, get her shit together.

"Jacinda Colburn," she admonished, "you are a hell-hot magical mess."

Hellfire flared once more in her chest, itching for a worthy target. She had half a mind to waltz out that door, chase him down the hall, and light his ass up like a fire-cracker. One taste of her dark flame, and that ice-cold vampire prick with his stupid smirk and eyes the color of a misty-morning forest would be incinerated from the inside out, turned to ash before he could even bark another insult.

Hell, she'd almost done it in the VIP room, just to prove her point about not being easy prey.

Thankfully, common sense won out—then *and* now.

With no coven of her own, Renault in hiding and his allies dead or scattered to the winds, and no friends or family to speak of, Jaci was on her own in every way that counted, as broke and homeless as she'd been when she'd first crash-landed in this city seven years ago.

By now the Redthornes had seized the rest of Renault's property, which included the basement she'd lived in and most of her worldly possessions. Without a place to study and practice her magic, she had no hope of surviving, let alone completing the spells she'd spent her entire adult life trying to master.

The spells that would free her father's soul from hell, reunite it with his body, and buy her that brand-new life she so desperately wanted.

She glanced around the apartment once more, acceptance settling into her heart. This was the best she could hope for right now. Whatever his true motives—and she wasn't dumb enough to think it was just a matter of locating Renault and unraveling some old curse—Gabriel clearly needed her, and that meant job security. A roof over her head and food in her belly. A chance to end her father's torment.

Besides, she'd been in worse predicaments before, and she was pretty damned sure life wasn't done fucking with her yet, either. That didn't mean it was time to curl up on the floor like a dead centipede. First of all, she had much better legs. But also, she had things to do.

Circumstances changed, but the plan was still the plan. Craft those spells, save her father, and get the fuck out of

New York. By the time hell's demons realized she'd betrayed them, it would be far too late for them to do anything about it. Jaci and her father would be off the supernatural radar for good, living the high life on some no-name tropical island, leaving all things magical in the proverbial dust. Demon dust, vampire dust, Jaci didn't care. So long as she didn't have to step in it ever again.

She took a deep, cleansing breath, feeling marginally better than she had when she'd first walked into the place. Now that the vampire was gone, she could finally think. Could finally get down to business.

Step one, take a shower.

Step two, make some coffee.

And step three?

Summon a fucking demon.

CHAPTER FIVE

Scrubbed clean and dressed in a brand-new sweatshirt and leggings from the stash Gabriel left, Jaci snapped into explorer mode, rummaging through the cupboards and shelves and taking inventory.

Food, clothing, basic household stuff—all present and accounted for.

But she found no overt magical supplies. None of her grimoires, herbal blends, or crystals. No Tarot cards, no potions, no ritual blades. Even the knives and scissors had been removed from the drawers, and she couldn't find any candles either.

Smart thinking on Gabriel's part, de-witchifying the place. But like most bloodsuckers, he lacked imagination and severely underestimated his opponent.

God, she loved when they did that.

Witch versus vampire? It's on, *dickhead.*

Absent her anointed black candles and summoning

potions, Jaci had three options for calling upon the hell realms:

Astral travel, which was risky and unpredictable, given some of the *other* entities that traveled those roads. A blood spell—messy, painful, and exhausting. Or, drumroll, please… Straight up dying, sending her own soul to the eternal pits.

Jaci huffed out a sigh. *Blood spell it is.*

She just needed something to amplify the signal. A decent herb or crystal or… apple?

Her lips curved into a wicked grin as she spotted the overflowing fruit bowl on the kitchen countertop. "Hello, lovelies."

Technically, pomegranate was the original forbidden fruit. But apples had been maligned for so long, they were just as effective in dark magic these days. It was mostly a matter of intention, and right now, Jaci had *every* intention of besting that asshole vampire.

Just thinking about him again had her shaking with rage.

Perfect—more fuel for her dark spell. All she had to do was picture his smug face and replay the sounds of his even more smug accent, and *boom*—anger, hatred, and disgust rose up at her command.

The feelings were almost certainly mutual, but the guy's emotions were encased in ice. Any time Jaci had tried to get a read on him, all she felt was that chill. That hardness.

She thought back to the battle last night. She'd spent a good portion of it hiding in the wine cellar, but from what she'd pieced together later, she was pretty sure one of the other Redthorne princes had been killed in the chaos. Yet her captor hadn't shown so much as a flicker of grief over his brother's death.

Jaci wasn't judging him—hell, if someone bumped off her sister, she'd be dancing in the streets in a sequined minidress, dousing herself in champagne and singing songs about the good times—but she *was* curious. If the royal vampire family was so fractured that the death of one of their own didn't even cause a ripple, clearly they had bigger problems than worrying about one little witch.

And that one little witch planned to take full advantage of it.

With Gabriel's spy cameras watching—and possibly listening, too—Jaci reached for an apple, trying to keep the evil gleam out of her eyes.

"Healthy choices make for healthy witches," she singsonged, pocketing the fruit and heading back down the hallway. The bedroom had a speaker on the night table, so she plugged in her phone and queued up her favorite dark techno playlist, hoping it would drown out the noise she was about to make.

Plus, summoning a demon always went better with bass.

Closed away in the gleaming white marble bathroom, she removed one of the glass shelves from the medicine cabinet and wrapped it in a towel, then smashed it against the edge of the clawfoot bathtub. She plucked out the biggest shard and used it to bisect the apple at its equator, revealing a pentagram of seeds in the center of each half.

Jaci smiled. The dark path had never been her choice, and in her twenty-five years of life, it'd caused more pain and death than she cared to think about. Mostly, she couldn't wait to leave it all behind—to burn her spellbooks and walk away from the craft for good. Still, in moments like these, she found herself marveling at the clever ways nature tucked hints of pure magic into everything it created.

Standing before the antique mirror hung over the sink, she ate the bottom half of the apple, seeds and all, picturing the demon she wanted to call.

Then, taking a deep breath and focusing on the five-pointed star in the half that remained, she sliced her palm with the glass and made a fist, letting the blood run over the fruit, binding her magic to the seeds. Energy gathered around her, hot and prickly, raising the hairs on her arms. The moment she felt the magic crest, she called on the swirl of dark emotions Gabriel had stirred inside her, held the bloodied apple in her left palm, and pressed her right palm against the mirror, chanting her spell.

> *Blood of darkness, blood of fire*
> *Heed the call of my desire*
> *I summon thee with blackened breath*
> *To part the veils of life and death*
> *The channel is open, the path made clear*
> *Now show yourself behind the mirror*

The blood coating the apple glowed as bright as an ember, then faded, the mirror darkening before her eyes. The air filled with the scent of brimstone. The scent of home.

Fear tightened her throat, an instinctive reaction she still hadn't outgrown, even though she'd been free of hell's clutches for seven years.

Some wounds just never healed.

The black mirror wavered, and a new vision appeared in its place. A demon with long purple hair and eyes like polished obsidian stared back at her.

Jaci let out a sigh of relief. "Meech, thank the devil!"

"Stole the words right out of my mouth, Jay-Jay." Her cousin Demetria glared at her, those coal-black eyes narrowed with a mix of concern and suspicion. Normally, her dimples were on prominent display, but the woman's scowl erased them now. "It's not like you to go off-grid. I've been worried sick!"

"I have a valid excuse—I swear."

"Lemme guess. You finally got some? And it was so hot and wild you've only just now awoken from the sex-induced coma? The one that landed you in the hospital for over-sexed witch-demons where they don't even allow you to call your favorite cousin?" Meech tried to deepen her scowl, but a flash of dimple peeked through anyway, and Jaci returned it with a grin of her own.

Damn, she'd missed the purple-haired bitch. Of all the residents of hell—natural-born or transplanted—Demetria was the only demon Jaci trusted. The only maternal blood relative who'd never tormented her, never waterboarded her, never poked her with needles or drugged her or set her on fire.

Meech saved those special tortures for the monsters who actually deserved them. And she was damn good at her job. Along with Jaci's father, Demetria was at the top of the list of demons Jaci wanted to bust out of hell, but her cousin loved her work, loved the darkness, loved the fire. Nothing would get that demon out save a total collapse of the realms, and even then, Meech would probably insist on going down with the proverbial ship.

Jaci admired that, though. Personally, she'd never felt such a devotion to a place. Never felt a sense of belonging anywhere.

Especially not here.

But that's why she was doing this, she reminded herself. Once she got her father's soul out, they'd find their true home. Maybe then she'd finally understand what she'd been missing.

"I ran into some bloodsucker trouble," Jaci said now. "Bad trouble."

"Is Duchanes still threatening you? I swear, when that asshole finally bites it, I'll be greeting him at the fiery pits myself and personally overseeing his eternal stay."

"And I appreciate it. Believe me. But Duchanes is M.I.A. —turned tail and ran after the Redthornes took down Bloodbath and everyone in it."

"Holy fuck. *What?*"

"Yeah, Bloodbath really lived up to its name last night."

Jaci gave Meech the update—as much as she could remember, anyway. She wasn't even supposed to be there—Duchanes had sent her on some late-night errand to drop off supplies for one of his other witches, a whole crew of them working inside Bloodbath on a project with the grays. Demons and vampires were there too—a veritable who's who of Duchanes' most vile servants.

She'd only been inside the club a few minutes when all hell broke loose. The Redthorne vampires and their allies launched a surprise attack, wiping out most of Duchanes' organization. Caring more about protecting her own ass than standing up to the Redthornes, Jaci made for the cellar, taking cover behind an old wine barrel while the battle raged overhead.

"Next thing I know," she told her cousin now, "the Redthorne witch—Isabelle? She's dragging me out of hiding and lining me up with the other witches for an interrogation. Apparently, Duchanes was working with Chernikov on some sort of plot to bust open the hell gates and flood the city with demons."

"What? Seriously? No one ever tells me anything down here!"

"I have no idea how deep this thing goes, Meech. I was working for the asshole and *I* didn't know about it—still don't, really. All I know for sure is Duchanes and Chernikov were in bed together on the big evil, and Rogozin and the vampire royals didn't like it, so they teamed up instead."

Meech pressed her fingers to her temples, taking it all in.

SARAH PIPER

"Okay, so this whole thing is crazy. But it sounds like it might have a happy ending for you, no? Duchanes is out of the picture. You're a free witch."

"Not... exactly. I'm working for the Redthornes now. One of them, anyway." Jaci shook her head, that dark swirl of rage threatening to bubble up again as she told Meech the rest of the story—Gabriel's intense questioning, the demands, the apartment.

"I'm telling you, girl," Jaci finished up with another sigh. "The world has never met a more infuriating, annoying, egotistical bloodsucker."

"Perfect! When are you gonna stake him?" Her cheeks dimpled with her bright smile, as if the idea of killing Gabriel was not only a foregone conclusion, but the pinnacle of entertainment.

"Are you insane? He's my best shot at staying safe in this city!"

"The vampire who kidnapped you, locked you up in an apartment you're not allowed to leave, and blackmailed you into doing his bidding is your best shot at staying safe? If that's your kink, Jay-Jay, you should've stayed in hell."

Jaci shivered at the thought. "Look. As long as Gabriel believes I'm following his orders, I can keep my head down and work on the spells for Dad without worrying about anyone trying to kill me, feed on me, or fuck me."

Meech cracked up. "And you think this vampire prince isn't interested in at least two out of those three?"

Exsanguination... A shiver rolled down her spine as the vampire's earlier threat echoed. Despite the hours that had

42

passed—not to mention the scalding hot shower—the ghost of his mouth still lingered on her neck.

Fear makes honest fools of us all…

"Not with me, he isn't," Jaci insisted. "He's just another cocky vampire prick, Meech. As far as Gabriel is concerned, I'm trash. The only reason he hasn't killed me is he thinks I can help him."

"Can you?"

"Doubt it, but he doesn't need to know that."

Meech just stared at her with that know-it-all smirk, black eyes glittering like she was in on some secret. One Jaci *definitely* wasn't interested in hearing.

"Anyway," Jaci said. "I didn't summon you to gossip about—"

"Sexy evil vampires doing sexy evil things to you?" Meech wriggled her eyebrows, purple like her hair.

"You are *literally* the worst. You know that, right?"

"Truth in advertising, babe. If you're looking for the best, next time summon an angel."

They both laughed, but it didn't last. The real reason for the summoning sat heavy between them.

Meech's smile faded, her eyes turning serious. "I'm sorry, Jay-Jay. No luck yet. Emphasis on yet."

Jaci nodded, no further explanation needed. Meech had been searching for Jaci's dad's soul for as long as Jaci had been working on her spells. But the realms of hell were as complicated, convoluted, and endless as the prisoners who inhabited them.

There was only one demon who knew for sure where

her father was. One demon who thrived on brutalizing him. And she'd *never* tell.

"Viansa… Have you seen her?" Jaci dreaded the answer, but she had to ask.

Meech lowered her eyes. "Your sister—"

"*Half*-sister."

"She may be your half-sister, but that bitch is *full*-on crazy." Meech glanced up again, worry tightening her brow. "She's trying to manifest, Jay."

"What? *Here*?"

"Where else?"

"But that's impossible!" Adrenaline spiked, making Jaci itchy and hot, her heartbeat shuddering in her chest.

It was the one saving grace—the thing Jaci had counted on to keep her safe from her family. Viansa could haunt her nightmares—a favorite trick for the sociopathic succubus— but that was as far as the bitch could get. She was physically bound to hell, her dark soul eternally cursed to haunt the dreams of the living, but never their realm.

"She can't take form," Jaci said. "She can't even leave hell in a vessel. It's… no. It can't happen."

"Hence the *trying* part of the equation."

"Tell me she's not close."

"I wish I could, but you know how she fixates on shit."

Dread pooled in her belly. As the subject of Viansa's particular brand of "fixation" for the first eighteen years of her life, Jaci knew it all too well.

If Viansa succeeded—if she actually manifested in the earthly realm—not only would Jaci likely lose her father and be dragged back to hell for eternal torture, but humanity itself didn't stand much of a chance either.

"It won't come to that," Jaci said, assuring herself as much as she assured Meech. "I'll figure something out. A binding spell or dream hex or… something. I know I will."

The dimples reappeared as Meech grinned again, her black eyes shining with affection. "I know you will, girl. But maybe speed it up a little? Or a lot?"

"Already on it." Jaci forced a laugh, but inside, her stomach was twisting itself into a pretzel. Finding her father's soul was a difficult enough prospect—she'd already been working tirelessly for seven years on the locator spell and still hadn't gotten it right. Extracting it from hell was another challenge. But binding her crazy sister? Stopping her from whatever path of destruction she'd set her mind to?

And how much time did she have now, anyway? How long until Viansa brought her evil from the sheets straight to the streets?

"I've got this," she said anyway.

"You've got this." Meech blew her a kiss, and with Jaci's promise to check in again soon, they said their goodbyes. She cleaned up the evidence of the summoning, hiding a few of the larger glass shards in a stack of towels in the linen closet. Thanks to the demon blood coursing through her body, her hand would heal by morning, but for now, she washed it and wrapped it in some gauze, pulling her sweatshirt sleeve down to hide the bandage from Gabriel's spy cams.

Back in the kitchen, armed with a fresh mug of cinnamon-vanilla tea and some spicy dark chocolate she'd found in the pantry, Jaci recalibrated her mission.

Save Dad. Bind Viansa. And… fast-forward to the part where she's sipping strawberry daiquiris on the beach, her old life nothing but a fading memory.

The plan was still the plan, just like she'd said.

But now it was a little more complicated.

And it had to happen a *hell* of a lot faster.

CHAPTER SIX

Three days. That's how long Gabriel had managed to avoid the witch. Three days and three sleepless nights, torturing himself with the memory of those vexing blue eyes, of his hands on her body, his lips on her neck…

With every breath, he swore he could still smell the woman on his skin.

Fucking witches.

Why he'd *ever* thought this was a good idea was beyond him. Perhaps he'd suffered a head injury in battle.

He flipped open his laptop, queuing up the video feeds from Jacinda's apartment, situated just one floor below his new penthouse. He'd purchased the fifteen-story building a couple of weeks before the attack on Bloodbath, already planning his relocation from Nevada. That he'd be using it to house a prisoner—a witch, of all things—had never occurred to him.

In the centuries since he'd become a vampire, none of

Gabriel's prisoners had ever lived long enough to require housing.

Gaze fixed on the screen, he watched with rapt attention as she sat curled in an overstuffed chair by the living room windows, mug of something hot balanced on her knee, hair piled on top of her head, nose in a book she'd found on one of the shelves. Birds of New York, it was called. It seemed to fascinate and delight her.

She turned another page and nodded, a smile gracing her lush red lips.

Gabriel felt an unexpected flicker of warmth in his chest.

Bloody hell. He reached for the bottle of bourbon on his desk, poured a stiff drink.

He was obsessing again. It crawled through his blood, making him jittery. Making him weak. Whether it was another of her wicked spells or the failings of his own mind, Gabriel resented it. Resented *her.*

What secrets are you harboring, little moonflower?

"So this is why you were too busy to join us at Ravenswood?"

The voice startled him. Familiar. Cheery. Annoying as fuck.

"Aiden *bloody* Donovan." Gabriel pinched the bridge of his nose and sighed. "How did you get in here?"

"Door was open, mate. After I picked the lock, anyways. You really should see someone about better security—I hear the neighborhood has really gone to seed." He peered over Gabriel's shoulder at the monitor. "Wow. Didn't peg you as the voyeuristic type, princeling, but—"

Gabriel slammed the laptop shut. "Is there something I can do for you, Aiden? Or has my brother finally tired of your sunny disposition and endless witticisms and sent you to pester me instead?"

"Your bother adores both my disposition and my wit, and so do you." Undaunted by Gabriel's scowl, Aiden took the chair across from him and propped his feet up on the corner of the desk.

Gabriel tried to hold on to his irritation, but it quickly faded. While he wouldn't say he adored the man, Dorian's best mate had been part of their lives for centuries, long before they were all turned into vampires. Aiden was a brother to them all—in more ways than their actual brother Malcolm had been.

Guilt and sadness crept into his chest. Another shot of bourbon chased it away.

"Tell me more about your sudden infatuation with this witch," Aiden said. "Seems like a bad idea, mate. For her, I mean."

"Piss. Off."

"Hit a nerve, have I?"

"I thought you were staying in Ravenswood all week with your new little co-ed."

"Sasha is spending some much-needed quality time with her sister tonight. Which is lucky for you, because you need an intervention." Aiden glanced at the laptop again and laughed. "Infatuation is unbecoming for a royal vampire, Gabriel. Especially a broody, melodramatic one like yourself."

"Says the vampire infatuated with a teenager."

"She's nearly twenty."

"And you're that times a dozen."

"Aged like a fine bourbon. Bourbon? Yes, I'd love some, thank you." Aiden rose from the chair and retrieved a glass from the cabinet behind the desk, then poured himself a healthy glass from Gabriel's bottle.

"Remind me again why the fuck you've broken into my penthouse? Was it just to insult me and steal my alcohol?"

"We are here," Aiden said, holding up his glass in cheers, "to give you the report from Ravenswood and guilt you into being more involved in your brother's plans for the Council."

"*We?*" Gabriel turned toward the entrance, where Isabelle Armitage had just entered.

"Sorry I'm late," she said. "I got caught in midtown traffic."

"You're just in time, Isabelle." Aiden passed the witch his glass of bourbon, then poured himself another.

Gabriel sighed. Isabelle had more than proven her loyalty and would soon make her bond to the Redthorne family official, but after two-and-a-half centuries of learning things the hard way, Gabriel would need more than loyalty and a formalized bond to feel at ease around a witch.

"Dorian is the diplomat of the family," Gabriel said now, channeling as much of the king's diplomacy as he could muster. "Let *him* unite the bickering supernatural rabble. I'm useless at politicking."

"Agreed," Aiden said. "Your strengths lie in lurking and

skulking. Oh, and apparently spying on unsuspecting witches."

"She's hardly unsuspecting, Aiden. She—"

"Cole and his wolves found another nest of grays upstate," Isabelle said, heading off the looming argument. "He and Dorian believe there are still more nests in the area."

Cole was another old friend of Dorian's—wolf shifter, artist, and until just a few weeks ago, a total recluse. Thanks to the grays encroaching on his territory upstate, he'd come out of hiding and joined the fight.

Just in time, too.

"Did they execute them?" Gabriel asked.

"Some," she said, sipping her bourbon. "But a handful wore the amulets. They were able to overcome the attacks and escape. The wolves are still searching the woods."

Disgust churned in his gut at the mention of the amulets, the resurrection magic Jacinda had devised. It was illegal demonic spellcraft—a combination of advanced magics that prevented the gray's body from turning to ash by prolonging the moment of death, then reanimated the corpse with demonic energy.

He flipped open the laptop again. Jacinda had moved to the kitchen, where she'd just set a pot of something on the stovetop. A dark-gray sweatshirt hung nearly to her knees, and she'd pulled the hood up over her messy hair, a few curls spilling around her face. It made her look young and sweet and naive, a vision nearly impossible to reconcile with the truth.

Jacinda Colburn was neither sweet nor naive. She was a dark witch who'd tapped into the powers of hell and wrought the vilest, blackest magics. A witch who'd worked for his enemies and helped poison his brother. A witch who'd brought pain and death to the ones he loved.

No more than you, Redthorne...

"Whoever's controlling the grays," Gabriel said, his words sharper than he'd intended as he turned his attention back to his guests, "they won't be resurrecting them much longer. The witch is in my possession. I've got her phone and apartment wired, guards posted at the exits. I'm tracking her whereabouts at all times. She is no longer a threat."

"That doesn't mean they won't find another witch to continue the work," Isabelle said grimly. "Besides, the amulets are just prototypes. They were already working on more advanced spells when we raided Bloodbath. For all we know, they've succeeded."

Gabriel nodded. He'd feared the same.

"Has Jacinda shared anything with you about Duchanes' plans?" she asked. "About his associates?"

"I was going to ask you the same question," he said. "The wretched woman has stonewalled me at every turn."

"I questioned her when we first captured her, but she refused to cooperate." Isabelle shook her head, her brow tight with concern. "Jacinda Colburn is no ordinary witch, Gabriel. There's a darkness in her I can't quite place—one that goes well beyond her magical practices."

"Excellent!" Aiden said. "Another evil foe in our midst. Always love a challenge, you Redthornes."

"Not evil, no," Isabelle said. "Just... a darkness. She's shielding it well, but it's there, almost like an emotional current running just beneath the surface. It's as if—"

"Did you see that?" Gabriel, who'd only been half-listening to the witch's assessment, gestured toward the laptop. Jacinda brought a wooden spoon to her lips, tasting her concoction. "Is that some sort of... potion?"

"Indeed." Isabelle leaned forward and squinted at the screen. "Chicken noodle, from the looks of it."

"Soup? She's brewing *soup*?" Gabriel asked incredulously, as if the act of making soup were a worse offense than resurrecting grays.

"Goodness, Gabriel." Isabelle sat back in her chair and sighed into her drink. "You're a royal vampire prince whose family has just aligned itself with a powerful demonic crime syndicate. You might consider learning a bit of discernment."

"Wasting your time there, Izz." Aiden thumbed toward Gabriel as if he weren't even in the room. "Like a wrecking ball, this one. Smash first, discern later."

"Dorian should've let me kill her," Gabriel muttered, watching Jacinda dip the spoon for another taste. "One less witch tainting the city air."

"What did I tell you?" Aiden said to Isabelle. "Wrecking ball."

"You've made your feelings about my kind quite clear, Gabriel," Isabelle said coolly. "But everyone in this room knows you've never killed a witch and you're not about to start now."

He nearly laughed. The fact that Isabelle—an empathic witch with nearly forty winters behind her, a woman more shrewd than even his most ruthless Vegas pit bosses— believed such a thing...

Well. That only proved how deeply Gabriel's secrets ran.

He looked at his captive again, still stirring her soup. Still beautiful. Still maddening.

"Defiant little witch," he ground out. "Trapped in an apartment that doesn't belong to her, no allies, claimed as property by a royal vampire, yet she *still* won't admit she's been bested. I should kill her just for being so damned arrogant."

He wanted to, too. Snuff the flame right out of her eyes. Maybe then he'd stop thinking about what *else* would light her up. What *else* would make her tremble and gasp and call him Prince...

"Jacinda Colburn may be dark," Isabelle said, scattering his thoughts, "but she's as much a victim as a perpetrator. A pawn in a game she has no business playing."

"We're all pawns in *someone's* game, Isabelle. Some of us are just better at winning." Gabriel flashed a grin that would have most women melting into a puddle, but Isabelle was immune to his charms. The kind of woman who did not, as the saying goes, suffer fools.

Intending on finding a fresh bottle of bourbon from the cabinet behind him, Gabriel rose from his chair. But the movement had him swaying, stars dancing before his eyes.

For fuck's sake.

Three days on and he was still struggling to regain his full strength after the fight at Bloodbath. He'd lost count of how many demons he'd fed on, not to mention all the hospital blood bags he'd drained in the days since. Nothing had been enough to sustain him—a condition that was growing worse by the day. He was also increasingly sensitive to sunlight, and other than liquor, human food and drink—once an enjoyable indulgence—were quickly losing their appeal.

Unlike his secrets, the effects of the family curse were not so easily hidden.

"Give me your hands, Gabriel," Isabelle said flatly, standing to reach for him. There was no judgment in her tone, but he couldn't help but bristle.

Everything in him burned to resist the offer, but it was no use. He needed the magic of her spells just as his brothers did.

A vampire's fate was a cruel one—a cloak of immortality and superhuman strength stitched together with threads of weakness and depravity. Even if he weren't contending with the curse that amplified those weaknesses, without witchcraft, he and every other vampire would revert to their natural state.

A gray. The same feral creatures his brother and Cole were attempting to hunt to extinction.

He rested his arms on the desk and nodded for Isabelle to work her magic.

Hands hovering just above his skin, she closed her eyes

and muttered the spell. Heat and magic raced up both arms, tingling along the lines of the magical tattoos he'd received when he'd first been turned—remnants of another time, another witch he'd rather forget. The tattoos glowed brightly, then sank into his skin, darkening. He felt the effects immediately, a new strength coursing through him, a clarity of mind he hadn't felt in weeks.

A quick nod of thanks, and Gabriel turned his attention back to Aiden. "And you?"

Aiden didn't need further explanation. "No symptoms yet. We don't know if I'll be affected, though. Technically, we don't share the same bloodline."

"No, but we share the same sire. And you were our brother then, for all intents and purposes."

"For all the good it's done me." Aiden laughed, warm and genuine as always, despite the fact that Gabriel had all but ignored him for most of their natural lives and a good bit of their immortal ones.

Still. Gabriel *was* worried about him. He wouldn't wish this curse on anyone but his worst enemies. And since his own father had sired Renault Duchanes, Gabriel's current worst enemy was already cursed.

Missing, but cursed.

Gabriel rose and retrieved that bottle of bourbon, pouring himself another glass. "According to Malcolm, the… We have to… There's…" He trailed off, memories of his deceased brother rushing at him unbidden.

Malcolm, the traitor threatening Dorian, leading a

council of enemies to undermine their family and usurp the crown.

Malcolm, the bloodthirsty fiend murdering innocents in an alley to satiate his endless hunger.

Malcolm, the human teenager desperately trying to shield Gabriel from their father's blows on a rainy English morning, centuries past.

Malcolm, the ashes clinging to Dorian's skin after the battle at Bloodbath.

Malcolm, the mystery they would never solve until, perhaps, they were reunited in hell.

Gabriel cleared his throat. Swallowed half his drink. Tried again, his voice quiet with the pain of grief and betrayal he was still trying to bury. "The last time Malcolm ran into Duchanes, Duchanes insisted the curse was placed on our family, to be passed on to any vampires we sired. To me, that sounds like you're at risk. Do you agree, Isabelle?"

"It would depend on the precise wording and intention of the curse," Isabelle said, "which we'll likely never know. We have to assume the worst."

Aiden took another sip of his drink and shrugged. "I'll avoid any tropical vacations and let you know if I start feeling hungry. Well, more than usual. As for Duchanes, Malcolm said he was already showing symptoms. Worse even than Dorian."

"I'm less concerned with Duchanes' well-being and more concerned with the fact that he knows our family's weakness. He's still at large, Aiden. Likely regrouping. If word gets out about this curse, our enemies won't need to roast us with hellfire or form secret councils to overthrow us. They can kill us with rumors. A weak king is a dead king."

"A rumor is not the truth."

"No? What is the truth if not the thing most people believe? The thing being shouted by those with the loudest voices? Our enemies suffered a grave setback at Bloodbath, but they're not gone, Aiden. This is far from over."

"Dorian has aligned with Rogozin's organization. The royal vampires and the most powerful demonic faction in the city are united. He's inviting new blood onto a new council—younger vampires, demons from Rogozin's organization as well as those who are unaligned. Shifters and witches too. All will have a voice under your brother's rule. That's the pathway to lasting peace."

Gabriel sneered into his glass. "For all the peace my brother believes he's brokering, what good will it do if we're all dead in a month?"

"We'll find a way, Gabriel."

"There's only *one* way. Breaking this damnable curse before it breaks us." Gabriel's gaze shifted back to the laptop. Downstairs, Jacinda was sitting out on the balcony, drinking soup from an oversized mug and watching the sun sink behind the skyline. He glanced out his window, sharing the same view.

"Jacinda Colburn can help us," he said, though he wasn't sure which of them he was more eager to convince—Aiden, Isabelle, or himself. "Both in tracking down Duchanes and breaking the curse."

"Doesn't mean we can trust her," Aiden said.

Isabelle shook her head. "No, we can't. But Gabriel's right to try. I promised Dorian I'd continue researching the curse to the best of my abilities, but as I've told him, my experience with dark magic isn't as broad as that of a true dedicant. As grim as it may seem, Jacinda really is our best hope."

"She's already agreed to help," Gabriel said, "though she claims ignorance as to Duchanes' whereabouts and I haven't yet shared the details about the curse."

"Didn't she tell you to bugger off?" Aiden asked.

"I didn't say her help would be offered enthusiastically."

Aiden glanced at the laptop, where Jacinda—as if she knew she was being watched at that precise moment—turned and extended a middle finger toward the exterior camera.

Aiden found it highly amusing. "Or even *willingly*, from the looks of things."

"We have an understanding, the witch and I." Gabriel shut the laptop. "Or we will, once she accepts her predicament."

"And if she doesn't?" he asked.

Gabriel clenched his fist, the veins rising beneath his tattoos. Isabelle's magic was already fading. "Then I shall just have to be a bit more... *persuasive*."

CHAPTER SEVEN

All sorts of magic happened while Jaci slept.

In the week since she'd been captured and locked away, someone had delivered groceries, including more fresh produce and an assortment of fresh baked H&H bagels in every possible flavor, with every possible topping.

Someone had delivered an artful arrangement of flowers and plants for the balcony and window boxes, including some culinary herbs she could use in both cooking and spellcraft.

Someone had delivered the exact shampoo and conditioner she'd requested, along with a bunch of soaps, lotions, and nail polishes she hadn't.

And this morning, as she'd stumbled bleary-eyed to the living room after a restless night, she'd nearly crashed into a tower of boxes stacked just inside the door—all of her things from the basement at House Duchanes, mundane and magical alike.

House elves? Grocery fairies? Vampire henchmen? Jaci had no idea who'd delivered the goods—only that it wasn't the vampire prince.

As far as Jaci knew, Gabriel Redthorne hadn't bothered to grace her doorstep once since the day he'd unceremoniously abandoned her here.

Not that she was complaining. In all her years scrabbling to survive in New York, she'd never had so much peace and quiet, not to mention hot meals and a comfortable bed.

But...

What the hell was she supposed to *do* with herself? Gabriel had ordered her to track down Duchanes, but the vile bloodsucker did *not* want to be found—least of all by the witch who now worked for his enemy. And Gabriel hadn't said another word about that mysterious curse, either.

Typical man. Vampire, demon, human, they were all the same. Make a mess, drop a woman in the middle of it, and expect her to clean it up while they gallivant around like royalty, jerking off and taking all the credit for someone else's hard work.

Unfortunately for Jaci, Gabriel Redthorne *was* royalty. Supernatural royalty. And she needed to stay in his good graces and do what he asked, no matter how badly it chapped her ass.

Besides, he'd saved her a trip back to Duchanes' place. The fact that she'd never have to set foot in that house of horrors again filled her with an unreasonable amount of joy.

Followed by a slightly-more-reasonable amount of dread.

I hope we never *find that bastard…*

Shaking off old ghosts, she headed into the kitchen, desperately seeking caffeine. She'd just set her black vanilla tea to steep in the pot and dropped a sesame bagel into the toaster when the hairs on her arms stood on end, a crisp, wintery scent invading her senses.

"Just rolling out of bed, are we?"

"Shit!" She grabbed the closest weapon off the counter and spun around to face the invader.

Gabriel. Standing before her in all his late-afternoon glory, dressed in dark jeans and a fitted gray cashmere sweater, hair tousled, a few days' worth of stubble lining his jaw, looking hotter than anyone had a right to. "If you're planning to decapitate me with a butter knife, we're going to be here a while."

Huffing out a sigh, she set down the knife. "Damn it, Prince. You can't just sneak up on a girl like that."

"It's my building, witch. I can come and go as I please, sneaking or otherwise."

Fear gave way to annoyance, which quickly gave way to relief.

Relief? Yeah. She chalked it up to the fact that she hadn't interacted with anyone but her cousin all week and talking to a demon in the bathroom mirror wasn't the same thing as real, live company.

"Looks like you're settling in…" His mossy green gaze raked her from head to toe, taking in the sight of her flannel pajama pants and the oversized hoodie she'd basically been living in. "…comfortably."

Heat rushed to her cheeks. She wished she'd at least braided her hair, maybe put on a bra.

Flashing a too-wide smile, she said, "Oh, you bet. Should've put getting kidnapped and stashed in a stranger's apartment on my bucket list ages ago!"

"Consider yourself fortunate I've stashed you in an apartment rather than a dungeon. Most prisoners don't receive my courtesy."

"You think a cappuccino machine and a killer view means this isn't a prison? Maybe I should take my chances in that dungeon."

He took one step, then another, crowding into her space and bringing the chill with him. "Say the word, *witch*, and I'll gladly make the arrangements."

She held his gaze, searching his eyes for some hint of warmth. Humanity. Anything but that icy darkness.

The toaster popped, making her yelp.

Ridiculous.

Raising that stupidly sexy eyebrow, Gabriel took a step backward, and she pushed past him to the toaster and retrieved her bagel. As she slathered on the cream cheese, she couldn't help but wonder just how long it *would* take to decapitate him with a butter knife. Probably depended on the angle…

Good graces, she reminded herself.

"So, what brings you here today, Prince?" She set down her knife and lifted half the bagel to her lips. "Popping in for a spot of tea?"

Ignoring both questions, he asked, "Have you had any luck tracking Duchanes?"

"Oddly, he's not returning my calls. I think he's just not into me." She took a big bite, then an exaggerated frown, speaking through a full mouth. "Maybe I'm too clingy?"

The muscle on Gabriel's jaw ticked. "I assumed you had other means of tracking him. Magical means."

"Normally, yes. But I've only just received my supplies today, and whoever packed them made a mess of everything. I need time to look through it all, organize it, cleanse my tools, set up an altar, charge my crystals by the full moon, which isn't happening for another—"

"I don't need the play-by-play, Jacinda. Just find a way to get it done."

She shoved in another bite of bagel to stop herself from saying something rude. Something about gallivanting and jerking off.

"Tell me about the curse," she finally said instead. "Maybe we can get started on that while I figure out what to do about our missing vampire."

"It's old, dark, and deadly."

"Deadly to whom?"

He glared at her, waiting for the realization to sink in.

Oh. *Oh.*

"But… but you're immortal," she said. "How is a deadly curse against a vampire even possible?"

"That's for you to figure out." He reached for her face, swiping an errant glob of cream cheese from the corner of her mouth with his thumb. Then, licking it clean, "And break."

Jaci's appetite abandoned her. She turned away from him, forcing her heart rate to chill out and buying herself a minute to think.

The things that could kill a bloodsucker were few and specific. Decapitation, as he'd mentioned. A wooden stake through the heart, tearing out said heart, or—a favorite of demons everywhere—burning them with hellfire. She'd never heard of a vampire dying by curse—not a curse a witch could conjure on her own, anyway.

Which meant… *oh, fuck*. The curse wasn't just dark magic. It was demonic magic. It had to be.

An icy finger of dread slithered along her spine, colder than even the vampire's impatient glare. A curse of this nature combined the worst of both worlds—crafted by the darkest witch, bound by a demon with all the powers of hell. It was a rare combination—a dangerous mix that ultimately required the witch to sacrifice herself to hell in order to fully bind the spell.

As far as Jaci knew, no one had practiced demonic hexwork in centuries. Even her own dark work with the resurrection amulets paled in comparison.

"What's the curse, precisely?" She finally turned to face him again. "You're still standing here, so I assume it's not the sort of thing that kills you on a whim."

"A whim, no. This curse is more of the slow-torture variety." He took a step toward her, closing the distance between them again. His eyes carried a dark warning, one he didn't need to put into words.

There was only one reason he'd trust her with this.

Because he knew, as much as she'd tried to hide it, that Jaci needed him as much as he needed her. Maybe even more.

After all, Gabriel could buy himself another dark witch. But Jaci? She had nowhere else to run.

"Think of it as reverse evolution," he continued. "From vampire passing as a human, with all the luxuries and comforts that come with it, to a vampire suffering as a gray. Desperate. Hungry. Feral. And it's not just me who's at risk. It's our entire bloodline, including all future sired vampires."

Jaci blew out a breath and finally poured her tea, nearly forgotten in the wake of his visit. There was enough left in the pot for a second cup, so she made one for the vampire.

"And the witch?" She passed him the mug. "What do you know about her?"

Surprising the hell out of her, he took it, nodding his thanks. "Nothing. The curse is hundreds of years old, and most of what we know is hearsay."

"What about—"

"I've told you all I know, Jacinda." The warning flashed in his eyes once more, the steam from the mug only making him look more ominous. "Either you can help me, or you've got thirty seconds to devise another use for yourself. I'm not running a charity."

"You're not? And yet you're so kind and generous." With a roll of her eyes, Jaci gestured for him to follow her to the dining table, where she'd already started laying out her tools. She selected a silver athame from the pile, along with her favorite Tarot cards and a ritual bowl made of copper. None of the items had been properly consecrated in her new space yet, but she didn't know when the vampire would grace her with his presence again.

Or when he'd succumb to the curse.

They had to act now.

"Sit," she commanded. And for once, her vampire obeyed.

CHAPTER EIGHT

With a tight grip on her athame, Jaci sat in the chair beside Gabriel and reached for his hand.

Big mistake.

He jerked away so fast he knocked his mug from the table, sending it to the polished floor in an epic crash that would've pissed her off had the mug or the floor actually been hers.

Jaci sighed.

The vampire glowered.

"Newsflash, Prince," she said. "If you want me to figure out what kind of curse is messing with your blood, I'll need to use—you know—your *actual* blood."

"So you can devise some new way to curse me?" He laughed as if *she* were the crazy one, ignoring the shattered mug and river of tea at his feet. "Hard pass."

Jaci shrugged, trading her athame for the bird book she'd found the other night. "Let me know when you've come up with a better idea. Since you're so experienced in witchcraft and dark magic and ancient blood curses that can wipe your whole family off the map, I'm sure you'll think of something crafty. Get it? Crafty?"

Based on those brooding, angry eyes, she was pretty sure he didn't get it.

But he *did* give in.

Reluctantly, he extended a hand, his eyes never leaving hers, that intense stare making her shiver. It didn't help that he smelled so fucking good, and the tight fit of his sweater had her imagining what it would feel like to run her hands over the clean, firm lines of his shoulders and back…

Damn, girl. You really *need a better imagination. And maybe a vibrator…*

Ditching the bird book and her lusty thoughts, she took his hand in hers and turned it over, pushing up his sleeve to expose his wrist. His skin was cool to the touch, which didn't surprise her, but the rapid flutter of his pulse did. She watched it closely, that delicate vein throbbing below the surface, mirroring the beat of her own heart.

Instinctively she brushed her thumb across his skin, light as a feather.

Gabriel hissed as if she'd stung him.

"Sorry," she muttered. "Just… looking for the vein. If you'd hold still, I—"

"For fuck's sake, Jacinda." He grabbed the blade off the table and sliced his wrist. "Now tell me how it works."

She shoved the bowl underneath, catching the slow trickle of blood. "Depending on how powerful the witch was and how long ago she bound the curse, I'm hoping I can pick up the magical signature in your blood."

"And what will that do?"

"Think of magic like threads of energy, and spells or curses like tapestries woven from many different threads. The key to unraveling a curse lies in singling out each thread, then counteracting them with a different kind of magic—something that will either alter, minimize, or neutralize the curse."

"Why would we want to do anything other than eliminate it?"

Jaci smirked. "Afraid I'll turn you into a frog, Prince?"

His eyes widened. "Can you actually do that?"

"Not sure yet. Ask me again in fifteen minutes." She tried to match the vampire's deadly cool, but the look of terror in his eyes had her cracking up in a matter of seconds.

At her ridiculous outburst, a tiny smile flickered across Gabriel's mouth, making him look more human than she'd ever seen him.

Again, her heartbeat fluttered.

Again, he gave her the arched brow, no doubt sensing his effect on her.

Damn it.

Dropping her gaze, Jaci grabbed the Tarot cards and began shuffling, willing her cheeks not to blush.

"So you truly can't break it?" Gabriel asked softly, more disappointed than angry.

"I told you the other day, I'm no expert in curses. But I

do know that blood curses are generally permanent unless you know who cast them. In that case, destroying the caster would break the curse, but that's not an option for us." She gave him a reassuring smile, still not meeting his eyes. They saw too much, those eyes. Too deep. "The good news is, that doesn't mean we can't save you from the worst effects."

"But—"

"Quiet, Prince. I need to concentrate."

Like a scolded schoolboy, the vampire clamped his mouth shut and went completely still—so still she didn't think he was even breathing. Outside, the soundtrack of St. Mark's raged on—blaring horns, garbage trucks crashing over potholes, the warble and flutter of pigeons fighting over stale bread. But in the intimate space of the apartment, there was only the slow drip and splash of his blood into the bowl and the frenzied heartbeat thudding in her ears.

Taking a deep breath, Jaci fanned her cards out across the table, then ran her hand over the spread, selecting three that felt immediately hot to the touch.

She turned over each one, studying them intently.

The Devil reversed came first. On the card's face, a horned beast howled into the night, lost in the ecstasy of his animalistic passions. Two sensual angels clung to him, enraptured. At their feet, a cauldron of blood bubbled over an open flame, reminding her at once of the bowl holding Gabriel's blood. In the reversed position, the message was one of obsession, destruction, and enslavement rather than unbridled passion. It was all the confirmation she needed that his curse was demonic magic, binding him in ways that went far beyond the reverse evolution he feared.

Swallowing hard, she examined the next card—the Eight of Knives. It featured another horned beast, demonic in nature, this one chained to a wooden post and standing thigh-deep in a poisonous swamp. Behind him, ravens picked clean the bones of those who'd been chained long ago. The card always spoke to Jaci of imprisonment. Despite the irony of her situation, she knew at once the prison here was Gabriel's, not her own. Unless he found a way to break free, the curse would trap him, body and mind. Already he felt the walls closing in around him as the threat of torment and death drew near.

The last card—Three of Grails reversed—had her stumped. The image was of two women embracing a man before another huge cauldron of blood, all of them sharing in its life-giving delights. In its upright position, the card usually conjured up feelings of sisterhood and friendship, though Jaci rarely drew this one. The reversal made her feel like a dark shadow had crept over something once warm and beautiful, turning it rotten.

As hard as she tried, she just couldn't put together the story from these cards. The themes of imprisonment and darkness were clear, but there was something about the Grails card that left her uneasy.

"Well? Gabriel asked, his patience finally cracking. "What does my future hold, witch? Or am I to die in a swamp? Drowned in a cauldron of my own blood, perhaps?"

"We should both be so lucky."

"And *you* should—"

She hissed at him to shut up again, then plunged her fingertips into the bowl of blood, gesturing for him to do the same. Despite his apparent mockery of her methods, he did as she asked.

Their fingers brushed beneath the blood, warm and slippery, sending tiny shockwaves of magic and pleasure up her arm.

Jaci didn't have the courage to look at him. Couldn't bear to know whether he'd felt the same connection... or hadn't.

Instead, she closed her eyes, concentrated on the slick warmth of the blood, and uttered her spell.

> *Cast and bound the darkest hex*
> *By shadow we shall not be vexed*
> *What time and magic have concealed*
> *Flesh and blood shall now reveal*

Even before she finished chanting, his blood was already whispering its secrets. Flashes of color appeared behind her closed lids, like arcs of lightning in orange and blue and silver. She repeated the spell once more, and the flashes intensified, then scattered, revealing a complex weave of thousands of multi-colored threads, all of them bound together with a dark, heavy power, pulsating as if it were a living thing. She couldn't see it clearly, but she *felt* it, hiding in the spaces between the colored threads, the absence of all light, a darkness so profound it threatened to suck her in.

In her mind, she saw herself reaching for the threads, gently untangling them with her fingers. But even in the relatively safe space of her mind, the very act of touching the weave left her dizzy and disoriented, her whole body burning as if she'd tumbled into a thorn bush.

Whatever this curse was, it was beyond her magic. Beyond her understanding.

And if she didn't break the connection soon, it would taint her as surely as it had tainted him.

Panic shot through her limbs, and she pulled back in her mind, trying to release the threads. But the magic didn't want to release *her*. Something held her there, those invisible thorns digging into her flesh, burning, tearing, leeching the blood from her veins…

"No!" With a strangled cry, she finally wrenched free, jerking her hand from the bowl and breaking the connection. Her eyes flew open, shocked to see Gabriel slumped in his chair, his bloody hand clutched on his lap as though it burned, his chin resting against his chest.

"Prince?" she called, reaching out to touch his face. His flesh was hot and feverish. "Can you hear me?"

No response.

"Gabriel?"

Slowly, he lifted his head. Opened his eyes. Stared at her in a way that made her blood run cold.

His eyes were a soapy white, devoid of their familiar green. Devoid of their familiar *anything*.

The being sitting in front of her was no longer Gabriel.

"Show yourself, demon," she commanded, her heart threatening to gallop out of her ribcage. If this was the hell-beast who'd bound Gabriel's curse, she was pretty sure she and her vampire were both going to die today.

Gabriel's usual cocky smirk twisted into something much more sinister, and the voice that passed through those lips came straight from Jaci's worst nightmares.

"Been a minute, Lab Rat," the demoness said.

Suddenly, the rotten sisterhood card made perfect sense.

"Viansa," Jaci whispered. She couldn't get her voice to work. Couldn't even breathe.

The mouth reformed again, twisting into Viansa's cruel snarl. "This is just a preview. I can't *wait* for the real reunion. It'll be epic, and you're—"

The voice cut off suddenly, the vampire's features relaxing back into their usual grimness. The milky film faded from his eyes, the green irises reappearing seconds before he passed out again.

Jaci waited. Counted to a hundred. Waited again. When she reached out with her senses, she couldn't detect any more demonic energy. None but her own, at least.

Viansa was truly gone—for now.

Jaci blew out a breath. How the fuck had her sister even gotten here? She wasn't strong enough to fully manifest, but *something* must've connected her to this moment. This place. This… vampire?

Oh, fuck me…

Suddenly, the blood on her fingers began to burn and

itch. She glanced at the Tarot cards—Devil reversed, Eight of Knives, Three of Grails reversed.

Everything in her mind crystalized, clear and sharp and impossible to deny.

The demon who'd bound the dark witch's curse on the Redthorne line was one of the most ancient, powerful, terrible demons hell had ever known.

Her sister, Viansa.

She'd been wrong to think she could weaken or alter the curse. Next to Viansa, Jaci was a little girl brewing mud-puddle potions in the backyard.

And actually *destroying* the curse, now that she knew who'd bound it? Well, that was *definitely* not an option.

Not with her father's soul still on the line and no locator spell to speak of. Meech hadn't found him. Jaci's spells had so far been a bust. Viansa was the only one who knew where he was.

Obtaining that knowledge was close to impossible, but as long as *someone* knew where he was, she still had hope.

And she wouldn't risk that hope. Not for the dick-head vampire who'd kidnapped her and ordered her to fix his problems and smashed her mug without apologizing.

"Did you feel that?" Gabriel asked suddenly, making her jump.

"Hmm?" She lowered her eyes to the cards, pretending to be deep in thought.

"A buzzing. Something in the air, like…" He held out a hand, and from the corner of her eye, Jaci saw the slight tremor. "You said the words and I just… felt it. Are you sure it wasn't part of your spell?"

What the hell?

It was as if he'd been completely aware of the last several minutes.

Bullet dodged. Jaci *really* hadn't been looking forward to explaining his spontaneous demonic possession.

"Maybe you spilled a little too much blood, Prince," she said, dialing up the sarcasm. "Need some orange juice or something? A cookie?"

"What I need, witch, is for you to figure out this bloody curse before it drives me bloody insane and I take you along for the bloody ride." He seethed in the chair, hands clenched into fists, his anger masking the true fear she sensed beneath it.

For an entire second, she almost felt bad for the guy.

Then he kicked one of the shards of porcelain across the room and shoved his blood-stained hand through his hair, leaving a smear on his forehead that reminded her of their first conversation.

"Sorry." She headed into the kitchen to scrub her hands. "I can't help you. Not with this."

Gabriel was right on her heels, looming over her, sucking all the air out of the room. "So you couldn't get a read on my blood? I thought you were a skilled witch."

Jaci bit her lip, considering her next move. She wanted to tell him to fuck off—that her skills weren't the issue. That the trail on that old curse had gone as cold as his heart. That he should walk away and enjoy the last of his days, however long he had left.

But if Gabriel believed she couldn't help him, where the hell would that leave her?

Homeless. Hungry. Desperate.

Prey for whichever powerful vampire family decided she'd make a nice addition to their collection of slaves.

No. She wouldn't go back to that life. Not ever.

She turned off the water and dried her hands on the dishtowel, trying to decide how to backpedal. "I got a read, okay? It was just... kind of murky."

"What do you mean, kind of murky?"

Hell. Maybe the Eight of Grails *was* referring to Jaci's prison.

"I *mean*... I can't just bippety-boppety, hocus-pocus you back to normal, Prince," she snapped. "Your curse is ancient, dark, and highly complex—the kind of magic that isn't even practiced anymore because it's so damned dangerous. Figuring out what to do about—"

"Are you saying you can't?" he demanded. The veneer of his control began to crack, genuine worry seeping through.

"Not that I *can't*. Just... Just that it could take a few weeks. Months, even," she added quickly, buying herself a little more time. "And it's going to take intensive resources —a lot more than I have on hand. I'll need all new materials. Herbs, candles, crystals, spellbooks, unrestricted Internet access, an e-reader, a library card, digital library access—"

"*Jacinda*." He crossed his arms over his broad chest, the sweater pulling tight across his biceps. His eyes lasered in on her, another warning perched on his lips.

"Make a list?" she asked with a hopeful grin.

After a long, weighty glare, Gabriel finally nodded.

She opened her mouth to thank him, but he held up his hand, cutting her off. "Don't thank me, witch. I've got another job for you yet."

"On top of breaking a nearly-impossible-to-break curse and tracking down a nearly-impossible-to-find vampire?"

In response, he stalked to the front door and retrieved a small gift bag he'd left dangling from the doorknob. Pink tissue paper poked out from the top.

She knew better than to believe he'd actually gotten her something nice, but she couldn't help the little flutter in her chest.

"Dorian believes the key to forming lasting peace in our city is winning the hearts and minds of the supernatural communities," he said. "Convincing them we're all in this together."

"You don't believe it?"

"Diplomacy was never my strong suit."

"You don't say."

That small smile made a brief appearance again, then faded just as quickly. "In my experience, Jacinda, what keeps supernaturals—what keeps anyone, for that matter— from tearing out one another's throats is leverage."

Jaci laughed. "Wow. Have you ever thought of working

with children? Your cheery disposition is so damned inspiring."

"I don't work with children," he said gravely. "I eat them. Now, as I was saying—"

Jaci gasped, instinctively taking a step backward.

And Gabriel, prince of bastards, cocked an evil grin. "Consider it payback for threatening to turn me into a frog."

"You are such a jerk! I believed you!"

"That's what makes it so funny. So… Leverage. The easiest way to gain leverage is to inspire loose lips. The easiest way to inspire loose lips is by furnishing an environment that encourages debauchery, and paying very close attention to those that indulge."

"So that's what this whole club thing is about? You're in leverage extraction business now?"

"*We're* in the leverage extraction business." He handed over the bag, his grin turning cool once more. "Welcome aboard."

"Aboard? What, like… like a business partner?"

A dark chuckle escaped. "I don't have partners, witch. I have associates and servants. I'm allowing you to choose which label you'd like to apply."

She reached into the gift bag. "Has anyone ever told you no?"

"What do the stories say?" His voice was smoky, his eyes lidded, the smear of blood on his forehead making him look wild in a way that had Jaci imagining being chased. And caught. And bitten.

And loving every red-hot second of it…

But then she retrieved her so-called gift, and all the goodwill their teasing had fostered died in a blink.

She unfolded the black cocktail apron, holding it out by two fingers as if she'd just caught a rat by the tail. "Um. You said you were joking about the bartender thing."

"Circumstances have changed."

She shoved the apron back into the bag and tossed it onto the counter. "Fuck off, Prince. I'm not your barmaid."

He lifted a cashmere shoulder, as if her refusal meant nothing. "You said it yourself, Jacinda. You've got no leads on Duchanes. The curse work will take weeks or months—"

"Exactly! I've got enough to worry about without having to sling drinks for your rich friends."

"Sorry, did I give you the impression that you could live here indefinitely? Rent free? Making lists for every little whim and desire, with nary a cent to repay?"

Blood boiled inside, hellfire skittering beneath her skin.

"Fine. Evict me," she tested, knowing he wouldn't. He still needed her. She'd made damn sure of that, dangling him on the hook about that curse.

"That's not an option." He crowded into her space again, sliding a finger beneath her chin and forcing her to meet his gaze. His voice was deceptively soft, power simmering in every word. "Because you're my prisoner, Jacinda. My property. And while I may be forbidden from killing you, there's a *lot* of gray area between your current state of mild discomfort and your death."

Jaci shivered. She'd lived for years in those gray areas and certainly didn't need the reminder.

"Make your list," he said, releasing her and heading for the door. "Keep working on the curse. I'll let you know when it's time to start slinging those drinks."

CHAPTER NINE

After weeks of private contractor nightmares, zoning snafus, and more bribes and threats than Gabriel had ever dispensed, the renovations on the club formerly known as Bloodbath were nearly complete.

The main level was gorgeous, the epitome of luxury in a palette of deep blacks and rich creams, set up with a mix of cocktail tables and soft leather booths, two fully stocked bars, and a gleaming, multi-level dance floor made of polished black marble.

He'd kept the VIP rooms, redesigning them in the same exquisite colors, with large, tinted windows and a balcony that wrapped around the entire upper level and overlooked the main floor. The wine cellar reminded him of the Prohibition days, the original brickwork tunnels re-excavated and fitted with recessed lighting and new mahogany shelving. And after agreeing to a donation large enough to have an entire medical wing erected in his honor, he'd even managed to secure a regular supply of blood bags from the local hospital to keep his vampire clientele satisfied, especially since he'd be enforcing a strict no-humans-on-the-premises rule.

The whole place was a work of art. One that had even impressed his brothers.

But in all that time, despite all the resources he'd given her, all the bagels, all the witchcraft books, all the bloody special-order teas delivered direct from England, that damnable witch was no closer to locating Duchanes, unraveling the curse, or—worst of all—vanishing from his thoughts. All of them. Waking, sleeping, working, watching television… She'd moved into his head as readily as she'd moved into his building. Into his life.

If she were any other prisoner, she'd be dead by now. But when it came to Jacinda Colburn and her sassy mouth and her moonlight hair, Gabriel seemed to have a bottomless well of second chances.

Besides, it was like he'd told Dorian when they'd first taken her in Bloodbath after the battle.

She really *did* look good behind the bar.

Sitting on one of his new barstools, he watched her now, brewing up a row of new concoctions, still searching for the perfect signature drink.

She wore tight jeans that hugged every curve and an even tighter black T-shirt that dipped into a V over her breasts, a bar towel draped over one shoulder. Her hair was woven into a complicated series of braids that wrapped around her head like a crown and had him itching to unravel them, one silky lock at a time.

"Something I can do for you?" she asked, not looking up from her cutting board. A pile of cut citrus and fresh mint leaves sat on one side, a whole lemon on the other.

"I was thinking you might need a training manual," he said. "With popular drink recipes. Just in case you—"

"I don't need a manual, Prince. I'm an herbalist, a damn good listener, and a witch who's spent more time than most studying the desires of monsters." She scored a lemon rind into a perfect spiral and dropped it into a highball glass before her. Milky liquid fizzed and frothed up to the rim, then turned clear. "I know what *every* man needs—"

"Somehow I doubt—"

"—to drink. Here." She pushed the concoction across the bar and grinned. "I made this one *especially* for you. I'm calling it Heart of Thorns."

Gabriel let out a dry laugh. "Poisonous, no doubt."

"Well, you know what they say." She leaned across the bar on her elbows, giving him a cherry-red smirk and a view that made him want to dive over the bar and bury his face in the V of that shirt. In a low, sexy-as-sin voice, she said, "Fuck around and find out, Prince."

He shifted on the barstool, trying to relieve the pressure of his suddenly tight pants on his suddenly hard cock.

A challenged flashed in those beautiful blue eyes.

He shot her his best death-glare, but he wasn't about to let the witch—or her mouthwatering curves—scare him off.

Grip firm on the icy glass, he lowered his gaze again. If

he was going to die at her hand, he'd be leaving this world with a damn good view of her tits.

"Cheers, then." He brought the glass to his lips and tipped it back, hoping for the best, expecting the worst.

Icy liquid slid down his throat, carrying the cool flavors of mint and licorice with just a hint of citrus. There were other flavors too—crisp and complex. He was still trying to identify them when the explosion hit.

Without warning, fire seemed to crackle in his mouth.

His head spun, then righted, a pleasant warmth spreading down his throat and across his chest.

The witch's brew was no ordinary cocktail. It was a fucking *experience*. A damned good one at that. And it hadn't killed him—not yet, anyways.

Gabriel took another sip, this one even better than the first. His whole body tingled with a pleasant buzz. Before he could stop himself, he was smiling.

"Told you," Jacinda said, her laughter like a symphony.

Beautiful. Sassy. Brilliant with the bottle. For fuck's sake, if he'd had a bartender like Jacinda in Vegas, he could've tripled his already impressive profits.

"It's… decent," he said evenly, forcing a casual shrug. "I'm sure the *hellspawn* will love it."

Her face paled, and something dark flickered behind her eyes, but she kept that smart little grin in place. "Too strong for you? I figured a big bad vampire prince could handle the heat, but if you need me to water it down—"

"I said it's decent." He curled his hand protectively around the glass and took another sip, trying to ignore the fissure of guilt in his gut. Her laughter had been here and gone in a flash, and now he missed it. Missed the heat in her eyes when she teased him.

Now, that heat turned to fire.

"Take it or leave it, Prince," she snapped. "You say we're not partners? Fine. But I'm not some little apprentice either. I'll work for you—sure. I'm your prisoner, so it's not like I can say no, and believe it or not—I actually *do* regret my role in hurting Dorian and—"

"*And* in aiding and abetting demons in a planned takeover of the city? Resurrecting grays and turning them loose on innocent humans? Come now, little moonflower. Don't be modest."

"—and," she said, yanking the towel from her shoulder, "I'm willing to do what I can to make amends and earn my keep."

"Then we're in agreement. You'll continue working for—"

"You haven't heard my terms."

She wiped her hands on the towel, then tossed it onto the bar as if she'd worked a hundred jobs in a hundred places just like this one. Maybe she had, and for a moment, Gabriel wondered what her life was like before she'd gotten mixed up with House Duchanes. Did she have a family? Parents? A mage and witch back home in Buffalo or Cleveland or Los Angeles, wondering what had become of their vivacious young daughter? Some poor sap of a boyfriend waiting for her to return to his bed? To give him a soft, warm place to stick his shriveled excuse for a cock?

Jealousy simmered in his blood.

He finished the drink. Let the warmth of it calm him.

"Well?" she prodded.

Gabriel sighed. He couldn't believe he was even entertaining this. "Terms, right. Let's have it, then."

"You don't have to like me. You don't even have to be particularly nice. But you *will* treat me with respect. No more reminding me of all my mistakes, no more reminding me I'm your property. I get it, okay? And another thing— I'm keeping all my tips, which will be substantial, believe me."

He had no doubt about that.

"Those are your terms, then?" he pushed the empty glass back to her, nodding for another one. "Respect and tips?"

"Yes. Oh!" She grinned, the teasing spark returning to her eyes. "And I drink free. Whenever and whatever I want —on the clock and off. It's all part of the gig."

"How do you figure?"

"You want leverage from these people? They need to trust me. So if they're drinking, I'm drinking. When in Rome, right?"

"This isn't Rome."

"You're right. It's New York City. Way more cutthroat." She whipped up two more of Hearts of Thorns, one for each of them, holding her glass up in cheers.

Clinking his glass to hers, Gabriel held her gaze for an eternity, wishing he had a guardian angel on his shoulder, a clear voice of reason in the chaos.

Because right now, only the devil whispered in his ear.

Bloody hell, he needed this witch behind his bar like he needed a stake through the fucking chest. But something compelled him to keep her close. Something that went far deeper than his need to punish her, deeper than his quest to find Duchanes and his need for leverage and his desperation to unravel the curse. Punishment could be meted out swiftly. Leverage could be bought, as could dark witches who unraveled curses—he'd learned that the hard way in his early days as a vampire, in his early desperation to break another sort of curse.

So why hadn't he ended this charade yet?

You don't need her, you damned idiot, said the devil in his ear. *You* want *her. So fucking claim her…*

He waited for the angel's reply. It never came.

"Obsidian opens next weekend." Gabriel sipped his drink, then slid a credit card across the bar, his gaze wandering down the V of that tight T-shirt once more. "Order yourself some suitable things to wear."

CHAPTER TEN

Gabriel wanted everything to be perfect.

And as he walked through the main level and took in the sight of his new club, he realized everything *was* perfect…

Except for the bloody witch.

An hour before Obsidian was set to open, she sauntered through the front doors as if she quite literally owned the place, hair swept into an elegant twist, a glamorous red smile painted to perfection. All heads turned to her at once —his security staff, the other bartenders, the cocktail servers, the VIP attendants.

And of course, Gabriel himself. He couldn't help it—the pull of her commanding presence was an electromagnetic force that tugged on his entire body.

He gaped at her. His heart thudded. His mouth went as dry as the Nevada desert he'd left behind.

Fuck, little moonflower. What are you doing to me?

Not only had she ignored his demands to call for an escort before leaving the apartment, but when it came to wardrobe choices, apparently he and his witch had *wildly* different ideas about the definition of "suitable."

Spiked silver heels gave her five inches of new height and all the confidence to match. Her black leather pants looked as if they'd been painted on, and her top was little more than a few studded leather straps strategically positioned to cover all but the most sensitive areas. The elegant slope of her neck and the bare curves of her shoulders shone with some sort of silver powder, her skin luminescent in the dim light.

He was about to ask her who the fuck gave her permission to wrap two seatbelts around her chest and call it a shirt when her low whistle of appreciation cut him off.

"Wow, Prince. You clean up well." That gorgeous red smile stretched wide as she took in his appearance—bespoke black suit, a dress shirt and silk tie the color of pale butter, silver cufflinks.

Fifteen minutes earlier, Gabriel had thought it the height of elegance. But now, next to the witch's way-too-sexy leather ensemble, he felt old and stodgy.

And thanks to the sudden bulge of his cock, the fitted suit pants were quickly becoming a fucking nuisance.

He turned away from her and took several deep, slow breaths, trying very hard *not* to imagine tying her to his bed with those studded straps…

"Something wrong, Prince?" she asked.

"You aren't supposed to leave your apartment without an escort," he barked out over his shoulder.

That was it. All the words he could force from his useless mouth.

Undeterred—or perhaps just accustomed to his foul moods by now—the witch walked around to the other side, where she could look into his eyes once again.

Her own gaze sparkled with mischief. "And yet I made it *all* the way here on my own, an entire half-block away, in heels mind you, without getting into any trouble at all. I probably deserve a raise."

Annoyance simmered in his gut, but as much as he tried to stoke it into a proper rage, he just couldn't. She was too fucking beautiful, and her bubbly, upbeat demeanor was warming him in all the wrong ways.

"Listen, Prince." She stretched up and reached for his tie, loosening and re-knotting it, then smoothing her hand down the front of his chest. He was grateful for the low lighting; the gesture only made his below-the-belt situation worse. "This place is going to be hugely popular," she continued, "which means you're about to get *real* busy. If you think you'll have time to babysit me twenty-four seven, by all means, continue your incessant stalking. But—"

"Stalking?" Gabriel scoffed. "I'm merely… looking after my investment."

"Investment, right." Jacinda laughed, the music of it drawing out his smile and melting another layer of ice from around his heart. "Well, I suppose that's a step up from property."

He leaned in close, whispering into her hair. "And two from prisoner."

She smelled like lavender tonight, a hint of spring flowers floating just above the dark-earth scent he'd come to know.

To crave.

"Hey, I'll take the wins where I can get 'em." Still grinning, she glanced around at the main level, letting out a soft sigh of wonder. It was the first time she'd seen the space with all the finishing touches in place, and now, Gabriel tried to view it through her eyes.

It was dark, yet inviting, with hidden recessed lighting that made the entire space look as if it were cast in moonlight. Massive obsidian mirrors hung on muted black walls, offset by panels of rich, wine-colored velvet. The club managed to look edgy and elegant at the same time, giving off a sleek, mysterious vibe that lacked pretension while still suggesting an air of exclusivity.

It was exactly as Gabriel had envisioned.

For some inexplicable reason, her approval meant a lot to him.

"So, you ready for this?" Jacinda turned back to him, sharing another bright smile. "The big reveal!"

In that moment, she seemed so purely happy, Gabriel was overcome with the ridiculous notion that Obsidian hadn't just been his own dream, but hers as well. A thing they'd created together. A thing they would now celebrate, sharing in each other's joy.

He closed his eyes, quickly dismissing the sentimental

thoughts. For fuck's sake, he hadn't even started drinking yet. What spell was she casting on him now?

"I'm ready," he said, meeting her eyes once more. "Are you?"

She glanced over at the bar, where all the liquor and ingredients she'd requested awaited her magic touch. "The question is, Prince... Are they ready for *me*?"

Another laugh, another shimmer in her eyes, a loose curl falling free and skating across her shoulder.

"Jacinda." He reached for that evocative curl, gently brushing it behind her shoulder, her skin like warm silk.

She shivered at his touch.

He stared at her mouth.

He wanted to tell her she looked good. Stunning, actually. That every supernatural beast who walked through those doors tonight would love her, would love the drinks she concocted, would return again and again just to watch her work her magic behind the bar.

He wanted to tell her the truth—that for the first time since he'd dragged her into his vicious world, he was bloody glad she was here.

But he'd already been too open, too vulnerable. Too fucking close. And the ghosts of his past, however ancient, still whispered in his ear, their icy claws still scraping against his heart.

So in the end, Gabriel fell back on the words he knew would douse the heat between them, would shut that door and bolt it tight before she kicked it open for good.

"Don't disappoint me tonight, witch."

CHAPTER ELEVEN

"The vampires certainly love her," Gabriel grumbled. "As do the Rogozin hellspawn."

From the center of the leather alcove where the Redthorne royals currently held court, Dorian raised his glass of scotch and smiled. "Congratulations, brother. Seems you were finally right about something."

"Right about what?" he asked. "You're the one who invited the bloody demons."

Dorian pointed at the bar, where the vampires *and* the demons lined up a dozen bodies deep, all of them waiting for one of Jacinda's magic brews. "Not six weeks past, you and I sat at that very bar after the Bloodbath massacre. And you told me the witch would be working for you, looking damn good while doing it, and winning customer service awards in no time."

"Three for three," Dorian's woman Charlotte said, her hazel eyes glittering. Since their recent engagement, the pair had only become more disgustingly sappy. *Everything* seemed to make them smile now.

It ought to have turned his stomach, but deep down, Gabriel couldn't have been happier for his brother.

Not that he'd ever show it.

"This calls for a toast." Colin, who'd finally pulled himself away from his new medical practice long enough to share a few drinks tonight, raised a glass of warm blood, his dimples flashing. "To our little brother. Not only was he finally right about something, but he's managed to survive for hours in an actual suit, trapped in a room full of drunk supernaturals, and he hasn't committed a single murder yet."

At this, Gabriel cracked a smile. "The night is still young, Dr. Redthorne."

"To wonders never ceasing," Dorian said with a broad grin. Then, with a note of true pride in his voice, "To Gabriel. To Obsidian. To fresh starts. Congratulations, brother."

"Here, here," Colin said, and all of them clinked glasses —Gabriel, his brothers and Aiden, Charlotte and her sister Sasha, Cole. Even Isabelle had turned up, everyone gathered to celebrate tonight's grand opening, to show the supernatural world that in the wake of Augustus Redthorne's death and the end of his terrible reign, the Redthorne royal family really *was* eager to welcome a new era of peace.

Dorian with his newly formed council and strategic alliances.

Gabriel with his club where all were welcome… until they weren't.

On the surface, it seemed the evening had been a smashing success, both for the larger community as well as Gabriel's family. Everywhere he looked, his patrons were enjoying themselves immensely, drinking too much and dancing just enough, laughing, forging new friendships and one-night affairs.

Here at the Redthorne's table of honor, genuine affection and happiness flowed among his brothers as freely as the booze.

It was almost too good to be true. Too good to trust.

The empty place at the far end of the table, set with an untouched glass of blood and a white rose, was an ever-present reminder of just how fragile everything really was.

In the weeks since Malcolm's betrayal and death, none of them had ventured to talk about it, but Gabriel knew their fallen brother was never far from anyone's thoughts. Gabriel dreamed about him still, and sometimes, when Colin laughed a certain way, or Dorian gestured with his left hand instead of his right, or Gabriel caught his own gaze in the mirror at an odd angle, it felt as if Malcolm had returned to him, just for the briefest moment.

A hello? A goodbye? A warning? A figment of his imagination?

Perhaps a bit of everything.

Shaking off the morbid thoughts, Gabriel turned away from the empty space and looked around the club. In addition to Jacinda, he'd hired dozens of other servers. Most of them had transferred here from his former properties in Vegas, still owing him one favor or another. All of them had been chosen for their professionalism and discretion.

Yet his witch—who was neither professional nor discreet—had proved to be the most popular by far. With so many patrons waiting for her attention, it was as if the other bartenders and staff didn't even exist.

Not that Gabriel could blame them.

Every time she leaned over the bar to hear another request, the straps of her top shifted, revealing another inch of creamy skin, another unexplored curve he wanted to map with his hands and mouth.

"Problem, Gabriel?" Dorian asked, grinning as if he knew something Gabriel did not.

"I'm not paying that devious little witch to flirt with the seedy supernatural underbelly of this city."

"As a bonafide member of that seedy underbelly, I resemble that remark." Cole, who'd surprised them all by washing the wolf stink from his hair for tonight's celebration and donning a suit that wasn't made of flannel, grinned. "Tell you what, Little Red. I'll flirt with her for free if it'll help get your princely panties out of a bunch."

"Try it and you'll be *choking* on my princely panties." Gabriel tore his gaze from the bar and hissed into his bourbon. "She's got them all under some sort of spell, no doubt."

"Seems your patrons aren't the only ones the witch has entranced," Dorian said.

In the long silence that followed, Gabriel looked up to

find all of them watching, some smirking, some outright laughing, all of them one more comment away from getting banned from Obsidian for life.

"Brilliant observation, King Shitehead." Gabriel grabbed an ice cube from the champaign bucket and chucked it at his eldest brother's smug face. "You do recall she's the same witch who tried to murder you? Am I the only one who remembers?"

"And forcing her behind the bar is your idea of vengeance, then?" Dorian laughed. "I'm honored, brother. Truly. Remind me not to die in battle, lest you put the enemy troops to work mending your clothes and shining your floors."

"That'll teach 'em to mess with you Redthornes," Cole said, and they all cracked up.

"Forgive me, Gabriel." Aiden rubbed his stubbled jaw as if he were deep in thought. "I'm a bit behind in royal politicking, not being a prince myself, but is it typical to provide one's prisoners with a furnished apartment, a clothing allowance, and a paying job?"

"And tips," Gabriel admitted, gritting his teeth. "What? It's only fair. Bartending is grueling work."

And she was damn near running herself ragged, too. Dashing back and forth from her customers to the register, mixing drinks, cutting fresh garnishes, smiling at even the worst of clients.

Fending off their filthy advances, no doubt.

Charlotte tried to hide her laughter with another sip of her wine. Failed miserably.

"I have a plan, you know." Gabriel downed the last of his bourbon and set his glass on the table, harder than he'd meant to. Bloody hell, after fifty years apart, nary a word spoken among them, he'd forgotten what an exhausting lot his brothers could be. "Right now, Jacinda is our only link to Duchanes and our best shot at defeating this bloody curse. Or have you conveniently forgotten about that too?"

"And she's on board with helping you?" Charlotte asked skeptically. "Honestly?

"Not only that," he said with a smirk, "I think she's actually starting to like me." He thought back to the way she'd fixed his tie tonight, the soft touch of her hand on his chest.

Charlotte's laughter exploded in earnest. "That is some *serious* Stockholm Syndrome shit right there."

"I think I liked you better before you became a bloodsucker."

Still laughing, Charlotte said, "And I *never* liked you, so I'm actually okay with that."

Sasha piped in next. "Don't take this the wrong way, Gabe, but if kidnapping is your idea of building trust and getting someone to like you, you probably need therapy. My interpersonal psychology professor says—"

"Don't call me Gabe. Bloody hell, girl. Are you even old enough to be in here?"

Sasha shrugged and picked up her caramel appletini. "I've got connections."

"Perhaps I should kick them out as well."

Sasha laughed and stuck out her tongue, and Gabriel

couldn't help but smile. Even in her most annoying moments, Sasha's exuberance had a way of making everyone laugh. That, along with the fact that Aiden was damn near in love with the girl, was the only reason Gabriel had allowed her to break the no-humans rule.

"It's been well over a month," Colin said. "Chernikov's demons are all but gone. No trouble from Duchanes. Perhaps he's given up."

"No word from Duchanes is not the equivalent of no trouble." Gabriel looked out across the sea of supernatural faces crowded into the club—vampires and demons from every powerful family in New York, witches and mages, shifters he'd never even seen before. "*Someone* must know something. Must have heard a rumor, a whisper. Vampires like Renault Duchanes don't simply ride off into the sunset, never to be heard from again."

"Perhaps he met an untimely death at the end of a pointy object?" Charlotte offered.

"You know damn well luck don't work that way, Charles," Cole said, and Gabriel nodded. As much as the thought of Duchanes impaling himself on a stake filled him with a special kind of joy… No. He'd know it if the bastard were dead. He'd feel it.

"It's opening night, brother," Dorian said, clamping a hand over Gabriel's shoulder. "Enjoy yourself. Whatever secrets are locked up inside the hearts and minds of these reprobates, they'll still be lurking there tomorrow."

"Now, about this witch," Aiden whispered to Sasha, as

if none of the rest could hear. "I do believe he's got a bit of a crush."

Sasha giggled, looking younger than even nineteen. "Ya think?"

"All right, brothers." Gabriel rose from the table, eager to leave his meddling family behind. "Enough gossip."

"Bored of us already?" Colin asked.

"Not so much bored as longing for the days when we skipped the chit-chat and jumped right to beating the bloody hell out of one another." He laughed, a bit of the knot unbunching from his so-called princely panties. "Enjoy your evening, brothers. I need to mingle, lest our unsavory guests forget who's actually hosting this night of debauchery."

"You're going to charm the secrets out of them, aren't you?" Charlotte asked with a sly smile.

"I'm starting to understand why my brother keeps you around," he teased, leaning in to kiss his future sister-in-law's cheek. "When you're not busy sticking your nose where it doesn't belong, you're actually pretty damned brilliant."

CHAPTER TWELVE

The booze, the music, and the blood supply were holding strong.

Gabriel's patience, however, was not.

In the hours since he'd left his brothers, he'd been propositioned by no less than a dozen female vampires, groped by several of the males, jostled, spilled upon, crashed into, and—thanks to a trio of drunk, overeager alpha wolves trying to impress their fated mates with their terribly uncoordinated dance moves—suffered no less than three broken toes.

Thank the bloody devil for vampire healing.

Despite the abuse he'd suffered at the hands—and feet—of his own patrons, Gabriel was no closer to learning anything about Duchanes as he was the day he'd interrogated Jacinda.

Either the bloody supernaturals didn't understand his less-than-direct questions, or they were all playing hardball.

Now, standing on the balcony that overlooked the main level, he watched his brothers at a distance, laughing and sharing stories. He wished he could join them—forget about politics for one more night. He couldn't recall a time when they'd all seemed so genuinely happy.

Certainly not while their father had been alive.

A wave of revulsion rose in his chest, but he swallowed it down. Augustus Redthorne was a dark cloud whose passing had brought long-sought relief, finally given them permission to breathe again.

But the previous king's passing had also come with complications—one of them being Renault Duchanes, the bastard Augustus had allegedly sired… and then promptly scorned.

Leaning over the balcony railing, Gabriel scanned the crowd, wondering who among them might be harboring his family's enemy. Who among them might be willing, for the right price, to betray that enemy's trust.

And what *was* that right price? Money? Allegiance?

Jacinda. The name whispered through his mind. Not for the first time, he wondered how badly Duchanes wanted his witch returned. If he wanted her returned at all.

Fuck. Everything was always so bloody complicated in this city. In Vegas, Gabriel had built an empire that catered to every man's sins simply so he could cash in on them later, every indulgence a down payment on some future favor owed. The strategy had served him well, but he was beginning to think he couldn't replicate it in New York.

Never before had that fact been so clear. Here among the

supernatural elite, leverage was less about sin and more about subtlety. The fine art of pressure and persuasion.

Politics.

With Augustus dead and gone, the game belonged to his brother now, and he would've loved nothing more than to leave Dorian to it.

But Dorian couldn't do it alone. Not if he wanted to survive.

Shame burned in his gut, that old, sharp-edged companion. Fifty years ago, he'd walked away from his brother during the darkest days of his life. At the time, he thought it was his only option.

Gabriel wouldn't make that mistake again.

He would find Renault Duchanes and tear the heart from his chest. He would break this dark curse. He would protect his family in all the ways their father never had.

"There you are, Prince!" The exasperated call broke into his thoughts, and Gabriel turned to see Jacinda speeding toward him along the narrow balcony, her face flushed. "Shit! I've been looking *everywhere* for you."

Panting slightly, she propped a hip against the balcony, her bare stomach glistening, the lean muscles of her abdomen rising and falling with every rapid breath.

Alarm spiked in his chest, and he reached out to cradle her elbow. "Is everything all right?"

"Yeah, we're just… We're out of mint." She sucked in another breath and glanced up at him, her blue eyes wide, cheeks pink. "Just wondered if you'd stashed it somewhere I hadn't checked? I really thought we'd ordered enough."

"Mint?"

She laughed. "You know, leafy green stuff? Goes in drinks? Tastes... minty?"

"Bloody *hell*, woman. If we're out, we're out. Use peppermint schnapps."

She looked at him as though he'd just suggested the blood of live puppies.

"I thought something happened," he tried to explain. Too gruff. Too cold.

"Um. Something *did* happen." She spoke slowly, as if he were a dense child. "We ran out of mint. I can't make my Heart of Thorns without it."

"Then make something else, for fuck's sake!"

"Seriously?" Her eyes narrowed. "You're mad at me because I want fresh mint?"

Gabriel pressed his lips together, trying not to taste the scent of her blood. Her skin. Even now, knowing she was perfectly safe, he still couldn't shake off the bad mojo.

Seeing her running toward him like that, nearly breathless...

No, it wasn't anger that had him on edge. It was fear.

For a split second, he'd thought she'd been threatened or hurt, and it had fucking scared him. Not because he'd lose his so-called leverage or his connection to Duchanes and the curse.

But because he didn't want her to come to harm at Obsidian.

He didn't want anything bad to happen to her, period.

A new wave of anger washed through him, this time at

himself. He'd taken the witch against her will. He'd been holding her captive for over a month, barely sparing a single kindness. Everything he did for her—the clothes, the apartment, the supplies—was all in his own best interest.

So why the fuck was he suddenly so concerned about her well-being?

"You're the head bartender, Jacinda," he snapped. "Figure it out."

Hurt rippled in her gaze, but then it vanished, replaced with her usual fire. "Message received, dickhead. Guess I'll just give 'em boring-ass rum and cokes instead."

"I don't care what you give them. Don't ever raise the alarm for something so ridiculously mundane again." He released her elbow and stomped off, back down the spiral staircase to the main level and straight out into the misty Manhattan night.

He returned fifteen minutes later with a grocery bag full of her precious mint—packets of clipped leaves, jars of dried ones, bottles of extract, three potted plants she could tend to her heart's content, and—just to be extra rotten— three packs of spearmint gum and a bottle of mouthwash.

Finding her behind the bar once more, Gabriel elbowed his way through the throng of eager patrons and passed over the bag.

She eyed him skeptically, then finally peeked inside, a smile lighting up her face. "Are you serious right now?"

"I smell like toothpaste right now," he grumbled.

"Thank you, this is perfect!" She beamed at him again, the earlier hurt and anger replaced with something much sweeter. Much more dangerous. "If you weren't such a dickhead, Prince, I might actually kiss you for this."

"Fortunately for both of us, I *am* such a dickhead."

Jacinda's smile didn't falter. She held his gaze, her eyes bright and beautiful in the dim space. A few more of her curls had fallen loose, skimming her silver-dusted shoulders. All around them, vampires and demons and mages chattered on, laughing, shouting. Music floated on the air, the heavy base thrumming through his bones. But for a moment, everything faded to a din, leaving Gabriel and Jacinda suspended in time and space, connected by that strange, electromagnetic current.

Maybe it was magic.

Maybe it was imagination.

Maybe it was all a fucking game.

Her glossy red smile finally faded. She bit her lower lip. Gabriel stared at her mouth, wondering what she tasted like. What her tongue felt like. Whether their kiss would be soft or ravenous. Whether his lips on hers would unleash a sigh or a moan.

Whether she'd call him dickhead or Prince or Gabriel…

Heat pulsed through his cock. Again, he tried to convince himself that his need—his obsession—was strategic. Duchanes. The curse. A bartender. Something safe. Logical.

But Gabriel wasn't a liar. Not even to himself.

He closed his eyes. The sounds rushed back at once, raucous laughter and a brand-new song, too loud, too fast.

Against the witch's dark powers, Gabriel had only one defense—one he was beginning to rely on far too heavily.

Without another word, he turned and walked away.

An hour passed. One more. Gabriel needed to see her again.

He wanted to ask about the mint. That's all it was. Just wanted to make sure Jacinda had everything she needed—that the patrons were satisfied, that he didn't need to do another grocery run.

But his witch wasn't behind the bar where he'd left her. The woman serving drinks now was one of his former Vegas bartenders, Maritza.

The bad mojo from earlier crept back up along his spine, squeezing his throat.

He searched the main level, the VIP rooms, the wine cellar. He paced the balcony, scanning the crowds for a glimpse of her silver-blond hair. He even checked the restrooms, startling a threesome of witches who'd been particularly… engrossed.

Jacinda was nowhere to be found.

He returned to the other bartender, shouting across the bar to be heard. "Have you seen Jacinda?"

"She's not back yet."

"Back from where?"

Maritza shrugged. "Said she had an errand to run. It's no big—I've got her covered."

Gabriel nodded, but the vampire behind the bar was wrong. It bloody well *was* a "big."

The traitorous little witch had skipped out on him.

Biting back a string of curses, he headed outside, picking up her scent at once.

And just beneath it, another scent, smoky and repulsive, laced with adrenaline and lust.

Fucking demons.

"Problem, princeling?" Aiden appeared at his side, Cole trailing out the doors after him. "Saw you storming out here like your cock was on fire."

Gabriel took another deep breath. Fresh fear spiked in his chest.

His fangs burst through the gums, adrenaline giving him new strength.

"Colin was right," he said. "I really *can't* be expected to go this long without committing a murder." Then, turning to the pair with a fanged grin, "You boys up for a bit of bloodshed and mayhem?"

CHAPTER THIRTEEN

Jaci lifted the spoon to the old man's mouth, tipping apple-sauce between his cracked lips. Despite his best attempts at swallowing, most of it ended up on his chin and shirt.

Vacant blue eyes glanced down at the wet stains, then back up at her. She wondered if the stains bothered him. If *anything* bothered him.

Forcing a smile, Jaci blotted away the applesauce. "Don't worry, Dad. You're still the best-looking guy on the wing. All the nurses have crushes on you."

The ghost of a grin touch his lips, but that's all it was. A ghost. Her own memory and wishful thinking projecting it onto his placid face, the mark of a guilty subconscious trying to protect her from the truth.

From what she'd done to him.

Behind his bed, the oxygen machine whirred, the heart monitor marking the passage of time with its steady beeps.

The soundtrack of his existence.

Jaci fisted the collection of tubes and wires, the lifelines that had kept him alive these past seven years, kept his body functioning even when his mind could not.

In the darkest recesses of her heart, she wondered if she should pull the plug. If she should let her father go. If she should've let him go seven years ago, when he'd died in her arms in an alley in Little Italy mere minutes after they'd escaped hell.

In our city, witch, death is a rare kindness. That you'd seek to overturn it is nothing less than madness…

Gabriel's old words echoed, harsh and cruel. Bracingly accurate.

But the truth of those words hadn't stopped her from bringing her father back that night. And they wouldn't stop her from letting him linger now. *Nothing* would. How could she let him die when she knew what awaited him on the other side? What his soul was already enduring at the hands of her so-called family?

Zachary Colburn may have been soulless, but if she let his body die too, there would be no place for that soul to return to when she rescued him, no beacon for it to follow home. It would remain in hell, eternally bound, eternally tortured. It's what Viansa and their demon mother had intended—a fate they believed they'd already sealed.

After all, that was the deal her father made.

Let Jacinda go. Take me instead.

They'd assumed Jaci wouldn't last long in this city on her own. Assumed her father's death would drive her mad, drive her to take her own life. Failing that, her own stupidity and uselessness would surely usher in a swift demise, sending her straight back to the hell she'd finally escaped.

That she'd actually survived was a constant thorn in Viansa's side—one Jaci knew her sister would remedy the moment she physically manifested on earth.

But Viansa didn't know that Zachary's body was still alive. Only Meech knew.

And Jaci had every intention of keeping it that way.

Other than that one time with Gabriel, Viansa hadn't made another appearance, and Meech hadn't heard anything more about her manifesting efforts. But Jaci knew it was only a matter of time before her sister sunk her claws into the earthly realm and dragged herself out of hell.

Vengeance was a powerful motivator.

She released the wires and went back to the applesauce, bringing another spoonful to her father's mouth.

This time, he managed to swallow it.

"I'm sorry it's taken me so long to come visit," she said. "Life has been a little crazy."

The hospital was only a twenty-minute walk from her apartment and the club, but with Gabriel's guards constantly up her ass, she hadn't wanted to risk sneaking off. It was only tonight, with Gabriel and his security staff focused on the Obsidian crowds, that she saw her opportunity.

So, after scrubbing the makeup from her face, she'd wrapped herself up in a hat and jacket borrowed from one of the other bartenders and slipped out through one of the newly excavated tunnels in the wine cellar. A few twists and turns, a quick climb up a ladder, and she was back out on street level, just a few doors down from Obsidian's main entrance.

"I have a semi-regular job now—can you believe it?" Jaci laughed. "Well, that's not entirely true. Gabriel Redthorne is anything *but* a regular boss. He's a vampire—a royal. Not the best company to keep, but for all his grumbling, the prince is a *much* better bloodsucker than Renault Duchanes. I'm choosing to see it as an upgrade."

The steady beeps of the heart monitor spiked.

"Dad? You okay?" She took his hand, gave it a squeeze. There was nothing new in his eyes, no flicker of recognition. But he'd understood her. She was sure of it.

What she didn't understand was why the mention of Gabriel Redthorne had kicked up his heart rate.

A minute later, it dropped again, settling back into its regular rhythm.

She let out a sigh of relief and closed her eyes, holding tight to his hand. It felt small and frail, a cruel contrast to the big, strong hands she once clung to as they'd roamed the realms of hell, hiding from the demons who'd imprisoned them there. The hands that had cradled her head, offering her comfort after another of Viansa's cruel experiments.

The hands that had clutched her face as he died in an alley, his eyes full of terror.

Terror for *her*.

"Oh, Dad." She opened her eyes, attempting another

smile through her tears. It was a soft smile, full of a little girl's hope, but a smile nevertheless. "I *will* figure this out. And when I do, we're going somewhere warm and sunny, just like we talked about." She tossed the applesauce cup into the trash and cleaned up the last few blobs from his shirt. "I just need you to hang in there a little longer for me. Okay? Just long enough for me to find you, get you out of there, and bind Viansa's power."

Her elbow bumped the bedside tray, knocking her purse to the floor. When she crouched down to grab it, she noticed two Tarot cards had slipped out, both facing up.

The Eight of Knives again, the demon bound to a post in the poisonous swamp.

And the Eight of Grails, featuring a death-like figure wearing a crown and a black shroud, carrying a cup of blood, his wrists bound with chains. A dark castle loomed in the distance. The shrouded figure had left it behind. He was escaping.

The minute she touched the cards, the message slammed into her, a blinding flash of insight that left her reeling.

She'd had it all wrong before.

Ever since Meech had told her about Viansa's plans to manifest, Jaci assumed she'd have to save her dad's soul first, *then* bind Viansa's power.

But maybe that wasn't the case at all.

What if she could find a way to bind her sister, and use that as leverage to force Viansa to reveal the location of the soul? Viansa wanted nothing so badly as to escape hell—a chance to come topside and take over. It's one of the reasons she'd always resented Jaci so much—Viansa was an original demon, ancient, eternally bound to hell. Jaci was half witch, bound only as long as her mother had wanted her there.

Being trapped in hell without a chance of manifesting in this realm would be torture enough for Viansa.

Being trapped there without any power at all? *That* would be like a death sentence. One that could easily make her desperate enough to release Jaci's dad.

She tucked the cards back into her purse, a new plan formulating. With Meech's help and her own dark magic, she was pretty sure she could make this work. She just needed—as always—the right spells.

A soft knock on the door, and a kind nurse with short salt-and-pepper hair and bright pink scrubs stepped into the room. "Zach? Time for a blood draw, hon. You about finished with your snack?"

Jaci returned the woman's kind smile. "Perfect timing. We're all set."

She gathered up her things and leaned down to kiss her father's forehead. "I'll be back as soon as I can, Dad. I love you."

"It's good that you talk to him," the nurse said softly, looking at Zach with compassionate eyes. "Visiting him. Lots of folks get old, maybe can't communicate so well, and all the people they used to love just abandon them here."

Flames of anger burned through her chest at the thought. "I'll *never* abandon him."

"I know, sweetie. I can always tell." She touched Jaci's arm, her smile turning sympathetic. "Dr. Daniels would like to see you in her office, if you've got a second before you head out?"

Across the oak expanse of her desk, Dr. Amelia Daniels leveled Jaci with a stern gaze.

"He's had a difficult week, Miss Colburn. Each day he becomes a little less responsive to treatments. His organs are still functioning, but he's showing less interest in exercise and movement. He's losing muscle mass faster than we can help him rebuild it."

Jaci nodded, unable to speak through the tightness in her throat.

"We'll continue to care for him," the doctor continued, "to make sure his needs are met, but at some point, it's just a matter of keeping him comfortable. I don't want to give you false hope that this is a recovery situation."

Recovery situation. Jaci nearly laughed. What would Dr. Daniels say if she knew the truth? That her father's soul was trapped in hell? That the only path to her father's recovery lay in fighting her way through a fiery wasteland and betraying the mother and sister who'd much rather see her burn than help the mage lying in that bed?

But none of this was the woman's fault. She was only trying to help.

Jaci cleared her throat and forced a smile. "I understand.

And I appreciate it. Deep down, I think my father does too."

Dr. Daniels smiled, but it didn't last long.

Jaci knew what was coming next.

"I'm sorry to bring this up, Miss Colburn. I don't mean to be indelicate, but…" She sighed, but didn't lower her eyes, which Jaci appreciated. Bad news always went down better with eye contact. "The paperwork from your father's insurance company keeps getting sent back to us. They're going back and forth with the state, still trying to verify his eligibility."

"I don't know what the issue is," she said, knowing full damn well what the issue was—every single document she'd ever given them was a forgery. Sometimes it worked, sometimes it didn't, and lately, her old tricks weren't cutting it. "I've been calling and faxing them, trying to sort it out… Here, I brought a payment at least. Five hundred, just to start."

She fished the envelope of tips from her purse and handed it over. Five hundred dollars was a stellar haul, especially for her first night on the job.

But it wasn't enough. It would never be enough.

Dr. Daniels did her the courtesy of setting aside the envelope without counting it.

"I'll keep trying with the insurance company," the woman said kindly. "If that doesn't work out, we can try other avenues. Social services, grants, something."

Jaci nodded, grateful for the kindness, and quickly said her goodbyes.

Her father deserved better than this—better than a daughter who couldn't fully care for him.

At least he was in a nice place, she told herself. Not the fanciest, but the staff was kind, they fed him three meals a day, kept him comfortable, did what they could to help. She wasn't sure how much longer she could keep up the insurance ruse, but with tonight's payment she hoped she'd bought a little more grace. A little more time.

Back out on the street, an icy drizzle had glazed the pavement, turning it into a blurry mirror reflecting the buildings above. Jaci tilted her face up toward the dark sky, letting the rain mist over her cheeks. The nights were getting colder now, the holidays fast approaching. Soon the city would be draped in glittering white lights—a beautiful snowglobe fairy tale she wanted to love, but never could.

At a time when friends and families gathered in celebration, lights and Christmas music and big turkey dinners and pumpkin spice everything only reminder Jaci how alone she truly was.

"Bad night for a little girl to be out walking alone."

Jaci startled and spun on her heel, suddenly face-to-face with three demons.

"Hello, little witch-demon," the middle one sneered.

"Witch-demon?" Jaci barked out a laugh, hoping it hid the terror. "Sorry, boys. Sounds like you got the wrong girl."

No one topside knew who she really was. *What* she really was. Her magic protected her, keeping her demon side invisible, even to her own kind.

So what the fuck did this asshole know?

And who had he learned it from?

"Oh, we got the right girl all right." Caveman took a step toward her, the other two following. She tried to get a read on their marks—the brands on their necks that would reveal their demonic alliance—but she couldn't see past their heavy leather jackets. They were American, though, which meant they probably weren't Rogozin's.

And if they weren't loyal to Alexei Rogozin, they sure as hell weren't loyal to the Redthornes.

Fuck.

There was no way she could outrun them. Not in her spiked heels in the rain. Her athame would do her little good. By the time she called up her hellfire, the three of them would've roasted her with their own.

Slowly backing away, she held up her hands, trying to stay calm. "Look, I don't know who you think I am, but I'm telling you, you've got the wrong—"

A dry, wheezing snarl cut off her words, paralyzing her with new fear.

Only one creature made that bone-rattling sound.

Grays.

She darted a quick glance over her shoulder. Three of them emerged from the alley, their pale flesh naked and bruised, eyes vacant, bones protruding from open wounds. All three were leashed on thick chains, their movements controlled by two vampires she recognized as Renault's favorite thugs.

Double fuck.

Nowhere to run. Nowhere to hide. Thanks to the weather and the late hour, the street was deserted.

Besides, screaming for help would only get some innocent human killed.

She turned back toward the demons just in time to catch Caveman's backhand across the mouth. She dodged his next blow, but one of the other assholes grabbed her from behind, wrapping an arm around her throat and pressing a knife against her ribs.

"That's enough, witch-demon," he growled into her ear, his rotten breath nearly making her gag.

"If you kill me," she said, "the Redthornes will hunt you down like dogs."

She had no idea if that were true. Gabriel didn't care about her personally, but he might do it on principle. She was *his* witch now, just as she'd been Renault's witch before. Her murder would be taken as a direct offense against the royal family—one they wouldn't let go unpunished.

Right?

"In fact," she said now, pushing a whole lot of false bravado into her voice, "Gabriel's probably already out looking for me."

One of the vampires laughed, the sound of it raising the hairs on the back of her neck. Tristan, his name was. Shaved head, dark eyes, hands the size of baseball mitts. He used to like cornering her at Renault's place while Renault was busy with his blood slaves, whispering into her ear all the things he'd do to her if he ever found her alone.

"We're betting on it, sweetling," he said now.

"I always love a betting man myself," a voice echoed from the shadows. Dark. Dangerous. Cold. "They make for good sport."

The owner of that voice stepped into the light, his vivid green eyes slicing right through her.

Gabriel.

He'd come for her after all. Along with Aiden Donovan, who looked a hell of a lot more intimidating than he had in the club, and Cole Diamante, who'd arrived in his wolf form and was already growling at her would-be attackers.

Jaci nearly wept with relief.

But right now?

Ass-kicking took precedence over tears.

In the momentary confusion that followed, Jaci wrenched herself free of the demon's grip and dropped into a crouch. Reaching between her legs, she grabbed his ankles and pulled hard, lunging backward and dropping his ass to the pavement like dead weight.

Gabriel grinned, a sight that made her happier than it probably should have, considering how much trouble she was in.

"Nice work, witch," he said, that whiskey voice giving her chills. "We've got it from here."

CHAPTER FOURTEEN

Gabriel pounced on the felled demon. While the fucking cunt was still conscious, he grabbed his arm—the one that'd been wrapped around Jacinda's throat—and ripped it clean off. But he didn't like the asymmetry of it all, so he tore the other one off too.

The demon's tortured screams were a damned symphony. Gabriel let him sing for a few more seconds, then grabbed his head and bashed his skull into the ground. In that moment, he didn't care if the demon's essence found another human vessel to occupy. Let him come at Jacinda again—Gabriel would rip off the new arms just as swiftly as he'd ripped off the old.

While Cole went after the vampires and grays, Aiden took down the second demon, tearing out his throat.

No singing for that one, then.

A burst of hellfire exploded behind him, and Gabriel

whipped around to see Jacinda grappling with the last demon, the front of her coat singed black.

In a blur, Gabriel barreled into them, shoving Jacinda out of the way and slamming the demon face-first into a brick wall. He punched a hole clear through his back, wrapped a fist around his spine, and yanked it right out.

He would've loved to piss on the corpse too—really send that message home. But there was no time.

"Cole!" he shouted, and Aiden nodded, both of them charging into the fray. He and Aiden took down the bloodsuckers, leaving the grays to Cole. The wolf had already sliced-and-diced one of them, its heart destroyed, but the vile beast hadn't turned to ash.

Fuck.

"Cut the amulets!" Gabriel shouted, frantically searching for the tell-tale pouches they wore, the dark magic that allowed them to rise from the dead.

"I don't see any." Aiden charged at one of them— another heart torn loose, another killing blow.

But it didn't kill the beast.

Gabriel, Aiden, and Cole were much more powerful than three uncoordinated grays, but no matter how badly they wounded them, the grays just wouldn't stay down. Skulls bashed in, hands severed, hearts torn free, guts spilling from broken flesh, and still the monsters fought.

"We can't just leave them here," Aiden said. He managed to grab their chains and hold them at bay, but the beasts refused to die. "What the fuck do we do?"

Cole lunged at one of them, biting into its femoral artery. Blood sprayed from the wound. Yet even with the wolf's jaws clamped around its thigh, the creature didn't fall.

"Nice work, boys. I've got it from here."

Gabriel turned toward the sound, the unmistakable voice of his witch.

She stood before them, three bloody hearts clutched in her hands. The look in her eyes was as feral as the grays'.

"For fuck's sake, witch. Get back before you—"

"*Move.*" Without waiting for a reply, she raised the hearts over her head, blood falling on her face like rain. Magic crackled around her, a thousand tiny sparks of lightning that flashed and sizzled.

"Now!" she shouted.

Stunned by the power in her command, Gabriel and the others obeyed, dropping the chains and darting away from the writhing, clawing tangle of grays. The witch stepped forward, chanting her spell.

> *Hearts of darkness, beasts of hell*
> *This breath shall be your last*
> *Death has come to break the spell*
> *Unbind the magic that was cast*

With every word, the magic surged around her, wrapping her in a storm of pure, pulsating energy. After her third recitation of the spell, she pitched the hearts at the grays' feet.

The bloody mess landed with a plop, then exploded in a dark flame.

The grays and every bit of ruined flesh around them turned to ash.

Jacinda's magic vanished. On a deep exhale, she fell to her knees.

No one spoke. No one moved. No one even drew breath.

Two barely-civilized vampires and a wolf, who'd just spent the last ten minutes basically bathing in blood and gore, and the witch had managed to immobilize them all with shock, awe, and—if Gabriel were being honest—a good dose of straight-up terror.

"Well." Aiden finally broke the silence, scooping up a handful of gray ash and letting it sift through his fingers. The creatures were well and truly gone. "Not one to judge, of course. But Gabriel... She's a bit spooky, mate."

Cole, who'd just shifted back into his human form, let out a low whistle. "If I still had my pants, pretty sure I woulda just pissed 'em."

Gabriel passed his phone to Aiden. "Call Enzo. Tell him to send a cleanup crew. And do a quick sweep—make sure there weren't any witnesses. Cole, find something to cover yourself, for fuck's sake."

"Who the bloody hell is Enzo?"

Ignoring Aiden's question, Gabriel headed over and crouched down next to Jacinda, gingerly helping her back to her feet.

"Are you hurt?" he asked, scouring every inch of her

with his eyes. Whatever those demons had done to terrorize her, they hadn't drawn blood—even with the mess of demons and grays, Gabriel would've scented it.

But there were worse things than drawing blood, especially when it came to demons, and he had no idea how long they'd been batting her around before he and the others arrived.

Jacinda looked up at him. Blinked. Swayed on her feet.

Gabriel gripped her shoulders, steadying her. The coat she wore was a black, ruined mess. "Did that bastard burn you? You smell like hellfire."

The word seemed to shake her out of the trance, and she glanced down at the coat. A gasp escaped, but she shook her head. "That wasn't—no. It missed me."

"Jacinda, what—"

"Holy shit." She pulled out of his grasp, heading back toward the demon carnage. "Are those… arms?"

"They never should've touched you," he said plainly. Blood leaked down his face, sliding into his mouth.

Jacinda stared at him, her face a nearly identical reflection.

It reminded him of that time in Bloodbath, the interrogation after the massacre.

Once again, he felt Death's whisper on his skin. Too close.

"How did you do that?" he demanded. "And how were those grays able to resurrect without the amulets?"

She turned in a slow circle, still taking in the scene. It seemed the shock of it was finally catching up to her.

"Just… magic," she said softly.

"And you're all right? The demons—"

"They were just trying to scare me. You heard them—they were trying to lure you out."

"So they didn't—"

"I'm fine. Just tired." She found a clean spot on her sleeve and used it to wipe the blood from her face.

Relief rushed from him in a deep sigh he quickly couched as irritation. "Why did you leave Obsidian in the first place? You were expressly forbidden—"

"I had something important to take care of."

He glanced up at the building behind her—the only place open at this hour.

The hospital.

All that relief evaporated. "Are you ill?"

Could witches even get sick? And if so, couldn't they just whip up a miracle cure? She was a self-proclaimed herbalist, for fuck's sake. Now she was sneaking out to go to the hospital?

Gabriel clenched his jaw, sucking in a breath of cool air, waiting for an explanation that never came.

"Tell me what's going on, Jacinda."

"It's not a big deal. I told Maritza I needed to run out—it's not like I wasn't planning on skipping town."

His hands shook with rage. He wanted to shout at her. Wanted to remind her about the consequences of disobeying him, of pushing him. But every time he opened his mouth to try, an image flashed before his eyes—that sodding demon, his arm wrapped around her neck. The fear in her eyes.

Jacinda swayed on her feet again, damn near breaking an ankle with those spiked heels.

Gabriel bent down and scooped her into his arms, lifting her against his chest. He expected her to put up a fight, but she merely sighed, her body going limp with exhaustion.

Inexplicably, he drew her closer, pressing his nose to her temple and taking a deep breath.

Lavender and damp earth. Flowers and secrets. Magic and darkness.

A shiver rolled through his body.

"Despite my brother's alliances," he said softly, doing his best to hide her effect on him, "House Redthorne still has many enemies. You are now a target of those enemies. I can't protect you if I don't know where you are."

"Protect me?" She glanced up at him, her blue eyes full of confusion. Full of vulnerability. Full of gratitude he hadn't earned and did *not* want to accept.

A wall of ice slammed down around his heart, cutting him off.

"I told you," he said coolly. "I always look after my investments."

He had no idea what flashed through her eyes next. He refused to look. He kept his focus on the street, walking in the direction toward home, trusting Aiden and Cole to meet up with Enzo's guys and take care of the demon mess.

But Jacinda's body stiffened, heating in his arms. If she

had any strength left, Gabriel knew she'd be clawing his eyes out to get away.

"Fear not, Prince," she snapped. "Your *investment* is safe and sound. So instead of protecting me from your enemies, why don't you take all that Ragey McRagerson bullshit and channel it into something productive. Knitting, perhaps? Interpretive dance? Yoga for Dickheads? I hear it's all the rage. Pun intended."

Gabriel sighed. When it came to the vampire and his witch, why did it always feel like one step forward, thirty-seven steps back?

Because you're a monstrous asshole who should've been put out of his misery centuries ago...

He dismissed the voice of reason. Reason had no place in this city. No place with this witch.

"In light of this evening's events," he said firmly, "I'm adding an addendum to our arrangement." He brushed his lips against her temple once more, whispering his final warning. "Disobey me again, little moonflower, and you won't have to worry about the bloody demons. I'll send you to hell myself."

CHAPTER FIFTEEN

Hell was a complicated clusterfuck of a place.

Born and raised in its fires, forced to fight through its deadly realms for the first eighteen years of her life, Jaci knew it all too well. And while lots of people liked to toss it around as a curse or a threat, when it came down to it, sending someone there wasn't all that easy.

Lucky for her.

Unlucky for her, that fact didn't stop Gabriel from making her life a hell on earth.

Fucking vampire.

After "her little stunt" on opening night, as he'd taken to calling it, the dickhead had her working back-to-back shifts at Obsidian for the past ten days, keeping her in his sights at all times. Even when the club wasn't open for business, she was still expected to show up. The one time she'd tried to blow him off, he'd shown up at her apartment, scooped her into his arms, and carried her there, dressed in nothing but a short bathrobe and slippers, a towel wrapped around her head.

Every day since, she'd arrived as expected, trying to keep their interactions to a minimum. By day, she was helping with inventory and supplies, polishing bottles, rearranging bottles, polishing them again. By night she was slinging her addictive concoctions, flirting shamelessly, always keeping one ear to the ground for the scoop on Renault Duchanes—an endeavor that had so far proven useless. It was as if the asshole had literally dropped off the face of the earth.

The only time she could find any peace was in the bathroom, and even then, if she took just a little too long, Gabriel would barge in and bang on the stall door, demanding to know if she was okay.

To make everything shit-suckingly worse, he still expected her to work on breaking his curse, and she was still searching for the spell to bind Viansa. The two challenges were intimately connected—that much was certain. Viansa had bound the Redthorne curse, which meant the solution to both problems likely existed in the same magic —a variation on the same spell, perhaps.

Jaci had performed bindings before—Renault was constantly cursing witches and demons he'd thought wronged him in some way, using Jaci to carry out his revenge. She knew the basics of the spells, but when it came to Viansa, she also knew the basics weren't going to cut it.

That meant dragging her grimoire, research books, and Tarot cards to the bar every day, and squeezing in time between Gabriel's ridiculous bouts of busywork to make her notes and theories.

She was working on another one of those theories today, books spread out on one of the cocktail tables, grimoire open in her lap. Every few minutes, she'd find a reference to some arcane spell, some curse, and make a few notes in her grimoire. But after an hour of skimming through an old tome on demonic possession clearly written by a drunk priest in the fifteenth century, Jaci was done with third-hand accounts. She needed a different sort of guidance.

Setting aside the library books, she pulled out her Tarot deck, shuffling as she concentrated on the problem.

Viansa's power. The blood curse. The key to binding her. The missing ingredient. The magic. All of it.

She fanned out the cards across the table, selected three that spoke to her, and turned them face up.

A silver-haired girl sitting in a snow-covered cemetery stared up at her from the Three of Knives. She clutched a dagger in one hand, a blood-drenched white rose lying in the snow before her. The look on the girl's face was one of sadness and vengeance, like a scorned lover who'd just carved out a man's heart.

The Death card appeared next, a white corpse lying in repose, black serpent coiled around her body, a crown of dead roses circling her head. Something about her wasn't entirely lifeless, though—it was almost as if she were resting, preparing to rise once more.

Fighting off an inexplicable shiver, Jaci turned her attention to the final card—the Ten of Knives. A raven-haired woman lay on white silk bedding embroidered with black roses, a dagger shoved through her chest, blood spilling from the wound as the life leaked from her eyes.

Betrayal.

Jaci studied the cards, trying to piece together the messages.

Roses and snow. Daggers and blood. Death and betrayal. What was she missing here? She felt as if the answers were right within her grasp, but hidden with veils and cobwebs. Every time she swiped one clear, another appeared in her mind.

Roses and snow. Daggers and blood. Death and betrayal.

If she could just see past that damned veil…

"Jacinda. What are you doing, woman?"

The icy tone broke Jaci out of her trance, her gaze snapping up to find Gabriel looming over her, brooding as always.

The sight was nothing new. The tie, however, was. White silk, embroidered with black roses.

She shot up from the chair so fast, she knocked the cards from the table.

"Bloody hell." Gabriel crouched down to pick them up. "We open the doors in ten minutes. You need to put this stuff away and get behind the bar."

"But… ten minutes?"

How was that possible? It wasn't even noon when she'd shuffled those cards. She glanced around now, noticing how dark everything had gotten. Music she hadn't heard earlier drifted to her ears. Two other bartenders were already setting up behind the bar, chatting with one of the cocktail servers.

Gabriel rose to his feet, handing over her cards. She plastered on a smile, trying to ignore the sight of his tie, trying to calm the wild thing hammering in her chest. When she reached for the cards, their fingers brushed, the contact making her flinch.

The vampire took a step closer and grinned. "Don't tell me my dark little witch is afraid of Death."

She glanced down at the cards, Death's white corpse staring up at her. The words whispered through her mind, a dry wind scraped across ancient ice.

Vita mutatur, non tollitur.

Life is changed, not taken away.

"Jacinda."

She met the vampire's eyes again, green and mysterious. His brows pinched together with something that looked like genuine concern, and he reached for her face, tucking a lock of loose hair behind her ear, the touch making her shiver.

Making her want.

She pulled back, tucking away her cards. "I'm not afraid of anything, Prince."

Gabriel only nodded, his eyes as veiled as the answers she so desperately sought.

CHAPTER SIXTEEN

Vita mutatur, non tollitur.

Hours later, the whispers still haunted her. Still eluded her.

Life is changed, not taken away. The dead shall rise. The dead shall return.

Pouring three glasses of cabernet for one of her cocktail servers, Jaci thought again of the cards—Three of Knives, Death, Ten of Knives.

Blood and vengeance. A severed heart.

Death. Resurrection.

Blood on the sheets. Betrayal.

She slid the wine glasses across the bar, then turned to toss the empty bottle into the recycling bin.

The dead shall rise. The dead shall return.

Vita mutatur, non tollitur.

Blood on the roses. Blood on the sheets. Blood on the snow. Blood on the grave.

Blood... Was that it? No. It couldn't be that simple.

Sure, the Redthorne blood was connected to Viansa's power—that's how the demon was able to momentarily slip into Gabriel's body. His blood and Jaci's spell had essentially summoned her, and Jaci was already thinking about how to work that knowledge into her spell. If she could summon Viansa here again, and somehow trap her in a different vessel long enough to do the binding, she wouldn't have to travel to hell to hunt the bitch down. She could trap her here, force her to reveal the location of her dad's soul, and send Meech to retrieve him.

But there was more to it than blood—there had to be. Blood could draw the demon here, but it wasn't strong enough to hold her on its own, and it certainly wasn't strong enough to totally bind her powers.

Jaci closed her eyes, conjuring the images of the cards in her mind, chasing them down the dark hallways of her memory.

Blood and vengeance. A severed heart. Death. Resurrection. Blood on the sheets. Betrayal.

The dead shall rise. The dead shall return.

Vita mutatur, non tollitur.

Blood on the sheets.

Betrayal.

A severed heart.

The dead...

Holy shit.

Jaci's eyes flew open.

That was it. The key to her binding spell. The missing piece.

Everyone always said the eyes were the window to the soul, and that was true. But the heart? The heart was the house. It held the very essence of the vampire—of any being. It controlled the flow of his blood as well as the path of his life. Every beat was like a note in a symphony, a complex pattern that recorded the patterns of his life, the silence of his death. It was the purest, most powerful thing about him.

The thing that truly could bind the powers of an ancient demon who'd cursed him.

Normally, removing a vampire's heart was one of the most efficient ways of icing him. But when the blood-suckers died, they turned to ash—their bodies, their bones, their blood, their heart. All of it.

Which is where Jaci's resurrection magic came in.

Vita mutatur, non tollitur. Life is changed, not taken away.

Just like she'd done with the grays, she could postpone the moment of Gabriel's death, allowing her to tear out his heart without turning it to ash. It wouldn't even kill him.

She closed her eyes once more, an image of his face floating before her. That strong, stubbled jaw, always clenched, always tight. Those ice-cold eyes, always leering at her.

The quirk of a smile when she'd caught him off guard with a joke.

The mint he'd brought her. The gum.

Damn it.

Guilt knifed through her chest, hot and sharp, but she quickly smothered it. What did she have to feel guilty about? After those early skirmishes, she'd tried to be kind to him. Tried to be…well, if not his friend, at least his associate.

And all he'd ever done was complain. Criticize. Demand. Expect.

Jaci opened her eyes and blew out a heavy sigh. She was just about to reach for a new bottle of wine when a sense of dread skittered up her spine, a dark presence lurking behind her.

Spinning on her heel, she came face to face with a ghost. One she hadn't seen in over six weeks.

She'd assumed—hoped—he'd been killed in the Bloodbath massacre.

But once again, fate was not so kind.

"Hello, butterfly," the ghost said, his Russian accent as thick as his neck. Kostya wore the mark of Rogozin now, but Jaci knew him from his Chernikov days. Days when he'd sworn fealty to the old guard, trading favors with Renault.

Collecting payment from her.

Her body burned with old wounds. With all the scars you couldn't see.

Another monster stepped up beside him. Jaci knew his face, knew his eyes, knew the cruel bite of his laughter, but not his name. Never his name.

He has no name, butterfly, Kostya's old words echoed. *We call him He Who Likes to Watch…*

Fear paralyzed her, even as her heart damn near exploded in her chest. Her eyes darted around frantically, but no one was paying them any mind. The bar was too crowded, the music too loud, the other servers too busy.

Kostya stepped behind the bar. Reached for her face.

"Don't," she whispered, trembling so hard a lock of her hair vibrated before her eyes.

"Now, now. That is no way to greet old friends." He leaned in close, nuzzling into her hair, his wet tongue darting out to lick her ear. A hand snaked down between her thighs, rubbing. Squeezing. Pinching. "You have missed me, butterfly."

Jaci swallowed down bile.

Behind him, He Who Likes to Watch watched. And laughed. And the sound of it—like rusty nails and broken glass and everything brutal and terrible that made her long for the tortures of hell instead—finally shattered her paralysis.

She reached behind her, grabbing the first bottle she could get her hands on.

Then she brought it down hard on the demon's head.

"I said *don't*." She clutched the jagged end, holding it toward his face.

Behind him, the watcher watched. Laughed.

Blood and gin leaked into Kostya's eyes, but it didn't hide his raw fury. Ignoring the wound, he reached out and grabbed her throat, his other hand snatching at her weapon, slicing her arm as he wrenched it away.

He tightened his grip on her throat, cutting off her air.

Spots danced before her eyes. She saw the wrath burning inside his.

Saw the blood leaking into his mouth.

Saw his arm cock back, the jagged edges of the bottle aimed at her face…

And then, in a move so fast she nearly missed it, Kostya went down hard.

Jaci sucked in a sharp breath and leaped backward as Gabriel descended, a blur of fists and fangs and blood.

It was nearly soundless.

It was nearly beautiful.

Seconds later, the vampire rose to his feet.

Kostya did not.

And He Who Likes to Watch had apparently found something he *didn't* like to watch because that asshole was long gone.

"You… you killed him," Jaci breathed. She stared at Kostya's limp, ravaged body, at the black stain pooling on the floor. Wondered what'd happened to the demon's essence. There were no humans in the bar, which meant he'd have to find another victim elsewhere.

Likely, he'd be back. Maybe not tonight, but eventually.

You have missed me, butterfly…

"He shouldn't have put his filthy hellspawn hands on you." Gabriel's voice shook with rage, his mouth glistening with demon blood. He pulled out his phone and sent a text

—probably ordering someone to come clean up the mess. Then, leaning in close, "Come with me. Now."

Clutching her wounded arm to her chest, Jaci followed him out through the crowd and up to the VIP level. At the farthest end was his office. He led her inside, closed the door behind them.

For a few beats, he remained at the door, his forehead pressed against it, his breath ragged.

Jaci sat on his desk and sucked in a few deep breaths, still trying to calm the fuck down. To soothe the burn of those old wounds. To forget the murderous look in Kostya's eyes.

"That should not have happened." Gabriel finally turned away from the door. The look in his eyes was inexplicably pained. "I thought my enemies knew better than to provoke me in my own establishment."

Jaci shook her head. "That particular enemy wasn't trying to provoke you. He… he was one of Renault's old pals."

"But not yours?"

Jaci closed her eyes, her teeth grinding together to keep the bile from rising again. Everything in her itched. Everything in her burned.

Somehow, she kept the tears at bay.

When the wave of revulsion passed, she opened her eyes.

Gabriel stood before her. Close. Too close. He watched her intently, and in that intense gaze she tried to count all the different shades of green, forest and spring grass and moss and olive, all of it flecked with gold that sparkled in the dim light.

"Let me see," he said softly.

Jaci lowered her arm toward him.

With the gentlest touch, he ran his fingers along the inside, parallel to the wound from the glass, his touch so soft it nearly made her weep.

His nostrils flared, his eyes filling with more emotion than she'd ever seen there. Anger. Worry.

Desire.

Gabriel released her arm. "I've got a first aid kit somewhere. I'll—"

"It's fine. Just a scratch, really."

Ignoring her protests, he found the kit in a cabinet behind them, then shrugged out of his suit jacket and rolled up his sleeves.

"Does it hurt?" he asked.

Jaci glanced down at the wound. She'd barely felt it when it happened, but now it was starting to sting. "I'll live."

Gabriel snickered. "I should certainly hope so. Your shift isn't over yet."

She snapped her gaze to his, ready to unleash hell, but his sexy smirk stopped her.

"Come now, little moonflower," he teased. "I'm not *that* much of a bastard, am I?"

A matching smirk rose on her lips. "This is a trick question. It has to be."

"One you're required to answer."

Her smirk stretched into a smile. "In that case, no. You're not *that* much of a bastard. Only like, twenty percent bastard. The rest is all dickhead."

His velvet laugh, warm and genuine and unexpected, soothed the raw ache of Kostya's attack.

When the laughter finally faded, Gabriel took her arm once more, but he didn't move to clean it. Didn't move to patch it up. Didn't move at all, actually.

He stared at the wound, seemingly mesmerized by the slow trail of blood sliding along her pale skin. His breathing grew heavy, his fingers hot where they touched her.

"Gabriel?" she whispered.

He finally glanced up at her, the sight making her gasp.

Red flooded his irises, chasing away a thousand shades of green.

Jaci had seen vampires feed before. Renault had thought nothing of using her as his personal juice box whenever he got bored of his blood slaves. But something about the change on Gabriel's face—in his eyes—it shook something loose inside her, a longing so deep and endless, she thought it might consume her.

Wordlessly, she lifted her arm to his mouth. Blood ran from wrist to elbow, as dark as her thoughts. As dark as her heart.

The vampire's nostrils flared again as he took in the scent. A low, desperate moan rumbled inside his chest, primal and sexy. Possessive.

Blood dripped onto his tie, reminding her of the Ten of Knives card. Black roses on white silk. Ruby-red blood.

Betrayal, betrayal, betrayal.

Gabriel's, some secret plan he was keeping from her?

Her own, yet to be committed?

Vita mutatur, non tollitur....

Jaci closed her eyes, that white-hot guilt coming back to bite her. An hour ago, she'd been so convinced she'd figured it all out—how to bind Viansa, how to save her father, all of it. But now, looking at the vampire prince with his red eyes and his sexy mouth, the echo of his laughter still lingering, the warmth of his touch... Jaci wasn't so sure.

Could she really do it? Could she trap him in a state of perpetual un-death and carve out his heart?

Life is changed, not taken away...

Gabriel's lips were close to her skin, warm and soft and full, and suddenly she wanted nothing more than to *feel* them. To feel his tongue lapping up the blood, to watch those red vampire eyes, to experience the euphoria of a vampire bite she actually wanted rather than one that was forced on her.

Blood and vengeance. A severed heart.

Death. Resurrection.

Blood on the sheets. Betrayal.

Blood and ice.

Magic and fire.

Jaci's heart pounded furiously. There was no way to hide her desire; she knew the vampire could sense it. Smell it.

Gabriel's breath was ragged, almost pained, as if he

were trying to hold back the force of a tsunami with nothing but his bare hands.

"It's okay," she whispered, her voice trembling. Fear? Desire? Hope? Shame? All of them collided in her heart, spinning and swirling, leaving her dizzy.

Touch me, she whispered in her mind. *Taste me.*

As if he could read her thoughts, Gabriel opened his mouth, a glint of fang shining in the dim light.

She pressed her flesh against his lips.

His tongue slid against her skin, and then…

"*Don't* do that again." He backed away from her so fast, she nearly toppled off the desk.

"I… I didn't…" Frustration tangled her words. "I was only—"

A sudden rush of cold air erased her words, and then she was on her feet again, immobilized against the wall by his muscled body, her wrists trapped above her head in one impossibly large hand.

She sucked in a breath, trying to reorient herself after the unexpected blur. "Gabriel. I thought—"

"No, you didn't think." Gabriel slid a hand around her hip, clutching her tight. His tone dripped with menace. "Because if you *had* thought—for even a single minute— you would've talked yourself out of whatever game you're playing here."

Fresh blood trickled down her arm.

The sight of it made him shudder.

"It's not a game," she said. "I was trying to—"

"Be clear about something, as I'm only going to say this

one more time." He leaned in close, lips tickling her jaw as he brought his mouth to her ear. His dick was hard, pressing against her lower belly, hot and eager despite the coldness in his touch. In his voice. "I *own* you, witch. If I want something from you, I'll bloody well take it."

CHAPTER SEVENTEEN

Hours before the club's opening, tucked away in a leather alcove in the darkest corner of Obsidian, Gabriel eyed up the demon who sat across from him.

The useless fuck hadn't even bothered to put on a suit for the meeting. No skin off Gabriel's back, but the demon might've thought better of donning a blue-and-white tracksuit if he'd known he was about to be buried in it.

He glared at Gabriel, strumming his fingers impatiently on the table, his eyes completely black. An intimidation tactic, pure and simple.

Gabriel let him enjoy it. It would be his last.

"Thank you for meeting with me, Michael," Gabriel finally said.

The demon clenched his fist, still trying to call up some of that so-called intimidation. "It's Mikhail, *comrade*."

"Apologies, *comrade*. You see, it's only in the last hour that I learned you even *had* a name."

Gabriel had Enzo and Cole to thank for that. After the attack on Jacinda last night, they'd done a little digging. Found out all sorts of things about Kostya and his shadow here, He Who Likes to Watch. Gabriel didn't know how often they'd crossed paths with the witch before, or in what context—Enzo and Cole weren't able to find anything on her involvement. But judging from the pungent scent of fear in her blood when he'd caught them harassing her, it wasn't too hard to connect the dots.

Just the *idea* of this fuckstain watching anything about her…

Gabriel closed his eyes.

The scent of Jacinda's fear had sent him into a rage last night. If Kostya hadn't been there, he was pretty damn sure he would've torn out the throat of any unlucky bastard in his path.

But her *blood*?

That had sent him into a fucking tailspin. One taste of it on his tongue, and he'd about lost his damn mind. A fierce, feral possessiveness took over, chasing away all logic. All human-ity. It was a fucking miracle he didn't devour her right there.

And this demon, this hellspawn filth had stood by and laughed while Kostya put his hands on her? While Kostya groped and threatened her?

Gabriel reined it in. Took a deep breath. Forced a wide, amiable grin.

"I have many names," the demon finally said. "But you may call me—"

"So, listen, Mike. I've got a proposition for you."

"About the witch, yes?" Yellow teeth shone from a sharklike grin. "Can we be frank, Gabriel?"

"Mr. Redthorne."

The grin faltered, just for a moment. "Mr. Redthorne. Look, witch is... How can I put this? Prime piece of ass on silver platter. Yes?"

Gabriel said nothing. Agreed to nothing. *Did* nothing but imagined the bitter taste of the demon's blood sliding down his throat.

"If Kostya knew you were already..." The grin was back in full force, and Mikhail made a circle with one hand, shoving a finger inside it with the other, laughing at his own cleverness. "...marking your territory, he would not have touched her. She is your property now, this I understand. So." He lifted his glass of vodka and nodded. "As saying goes, let bygones be bygones?"

Now it was Gabriel's turn to grin, his fangs sliding out, ready to feast. "Absolutely. Good talk, Mike."

Then, before the demon could flash his ugly, yellow-teethed sneer one more time, Gabriel launched across the table, grabbed his throat, and sank his fangs into the fucker's artery, draining him.

From the table behind them, hidden by a velvet divider, Isabelle worked her magic, quickly trapping the demon's essence and banishing it to oblivion, ensuring it wouldn't repossess a new vessel.

The monster hadn't even realized he'd been sitting on a

devil's trap, a sigil carved beneath the chair for the express purpose of preventing his otherworldly escape.

Done and done.

Gabriel got to his feet, leaving the demon carcass for the cleanup crew.

Fucking hell, that was satisfying.

"What happened to letting bygones be bygones?" Isabelle came out from around the divide, attempting a scolding glare. But behind her steely gaze, Gabriel noticed a glimmer of approval.

"I got half of it right, didn't I? The gone part?" Gabriel grabbed a cloth napkin from the table and wiped the blood from his mouth, then smiled at the witch. "Bloody hell, I feel so much better. Don't you?"

Isabelle sighed and held out her hands. "Let's be sure you stay that way."

Gabriel was so pleased with his accomplishment, he didn't even resist Isabelle's magic infusion.

Standing beside Dorian on the balcony later that night, Gabriel looked out across the sea of bodies, eyes peeled for any sign of demonic trouble.

Dorian sipped his scotch, then shook his head, his shoulders heavy with some new weight. "Two dead Rogozin demons in as many nights, Gabriel? Kostya and Mikhail were on track to becoming some of Alexei's top dogs."

"Then Alexei needs to send his dogs back to obedience school." Gabriel scoffed. "Be serious, brother. Kostya and Mikhail? They weren't top of anything. Rogozin bought their loyalties from the bargain bin of Chernikov's leftovers."

"Rogozin's organization has assimilated several dozen of Chernikov's former associates, and many of them are proving quite reliable."

"Foolish me. And here I thought our new demon allies were actually on our side." Gabriel swallowed the last of his bourbon—his fifth in an hour. Sixth? He'd lost count. It did nothing to eradicate the filthy taste of demon blood from his mouth, but he didn't want to eradicate that. He needed it. Needed the foulness of it to linger as long as possible, chasing away all thoughts of the witch. Her scent. Her blood.

His fucking *need*, growing darker and more terrifying by the day.

"Wasn't Rogozin supposed to eliminate Chernikov's organization?" he asked. "Why the fuck are there still so many of them skittering about this city like cockroaches?"

"Rogozin took down the *organization*, yes," Dorian said. "And its leader. But a lot of those demons were little more than freelancers, eager to prove themselves to whoever holds the most power."

"Never trust a man whose loyalties can be so easily swayed. Especially a man of questionable origins. And trust me—it doesn't get more questionable than demons." Gabriel tossed back his glass again, the emptiness of it pissing him off. He reached for Dorian's scotch instead, finishing it in one slug.

Dorian sighed. "Regardless of their origins, brother, those demons are now Rogozin-sworn, which means they *are* our allies. You can't go round killing them all, or—"

"For fuck's sake, Dorian. If those demons had hurt Charlotte, you would've torn their balls off."

"No." Dorian clamped a hand over Gabriel's shoulder, the look in his eyes dark and menacing. "I would've torn their balls off, set them on fire, *and* fed them to their former owners while all their friends watched. Do you know why?"

"Yes. Because Charlotte—"

"Because *Charlotte* isn't some pet I've leashed for entertainment, to be cast off whenever she begins to bore me. She's my life, Gabriel, and I bloody *love* her. If any demon so much as considered… oh." The look in his eyes changed from menacing to confused, then irritated, then completely amused. "For fuck's sake. Seriously?"

"Seriously what?"

"You're in love with the witch?"

"Piss off." Gabriel shook off his brother's grip, the implication setting his blood to boil. "This has nothing to do with love. I don't even like the woman."

"Yet you assassinated two demons who—"

"Rogozin's mutts attacked a woman in *my* club, putting *my* patrons in danger, damaging *my* property, and injuring *my* staff. I retaliated with a message that such offenses won't be tolerated."

Dorian scrutinized him for a long beat, his accusatory gaze practically burning the flesh from Gabriel's face.

"And the witch?" Dorian asked.

"Jacinda Colburn is neither a pet nor a lover."

Dorian laughed. "Then what is she?"

Gabriel looked out across the main floor again, past the vampires and shifters and demons, past the sleek marble and velvet decor, his eyes immediately finding Jacinda behind the bar, smiling at a mage couple as she mixed up their drinks. For all her darkness, she lit up the room like no one else could, a bright spot in a sea of gray and black. His patrons loved her. His staff adored her. And everything she touched, somehow, turned to magic.

He watched her a moment longer, admiring how effortless she made it look. Bartending, entertaining, looking runway-model gorgeous. She wore a champagne-colored dress tonight, strapless satin overlaid with black lace, and sheer black stockings that showed off her toned legs. Jeweled clips held her hair off her shoulders, creating a tumble of curls down her back. And always, that red lipstick, dark and seductive, driving him fucking insane.

He wanted that lipstick smeared all over his sheets. All over his cock…

"Right," Dorian said.

Gabriel forced himself to meet his brother's eyes. "She's a *person*, Dorian. And she's on our side. For fuck's sake, brother. You're the one who forbade me from killing her."

"I don't need your justifications, Gabriel. But understand something. These violent impulses of yours, while appreciated in certain situations…" Dorian shook his head, frustration mounting between them, as always. "Rogozin and his demons, however unpleasant, are our allies now. Those alliances don't come with a no-conflict guarantee. Our arrangement simply means that when conflicts *do* arise, we seek diplomatic solutions rather than trial by combat. For fuck's sake, brother. Our position is precarious enough."

"I was *quite* diplomatic in the ripping out of their throats, I assure you." Gabriel gripped the balcony railing, the taste of demon blood souring in his throat. "After what they did to her, they're lucky I gave them such a quick demise."

He scanned the club once more, his eyes finding Jacinda's across the dark space. She smiled briefly, then returned her attention to Charlotte, who'd just entered the club.

"Careful." Dorian fisted the back of Gabriel's hair and gave him a quick shake, but there was no teasing in his tone.

It was a warning, plain and simple, and it wasn't about his fondness for assassinating demons.

It was a warning Gabriel should've heeded the very first night they'd captured the witch and he'd decided, for some *stupid* reason, to keep her. Put her to work—on Duchanes, on the curse, behind the bar, anything to keep her in his sights.

But Dorian's warning had come far too late. And every night that passed, every hour, Gabriel was falling deeper under her dark enchantment.

"Another?" He held up both empty glasses and grinned, some of the tension between them dissipating. Drinking was the only language they both spoke fluently, the common ground that had spared them more arguments than not.

"No, thank you," Dorian said. "I've got a date with my fiancée."

He'd said the f-word as if he were tasting the finest scotch and turned his attention down toward the bar, where the fiancée in question was currently sharing a secret with Jacinda that had both women glaring up at Gabriel and laughing.

"Hell, she's beautiful," Dorian said, practically salivating at the sight of his woman.

"Hell, you're repulsive," Gabriel said, but there was no ire in his insult.

"Quite." Dorian smacked Gabriel's cheek, shot him one last warning glare, and then he was off.

Gabriel watched him head down the spiral stairs, slowly making his way toward the bar.

Guilt roiled in his gut. Dorian was right, of course.

At this point, it was obvious Jacinda had hit a roadblock with the curse. She needed more information—information that none of them had. If Malcolm was to be believed—and that was a big if—the only vampire alive who knew anything more about the dreaded curse was Renault fucking Duchanes.

Gabriel shook his head, cursing under his breath. The best solution for all of them was to track down Duchanes and break their curse. The sooner he could accomplish both, the sooner Jacinda would be out of his life.

That idea unleashed a burn of a different sort.

But Gabriel refused to let it smolder into a flame.

He was the vampire with the coldest heart, the cruelest smile. The vampire whose touch turned women to ice.

He held his breath. Felt the quick thud of his heart.

In all the centuries of his immortality, no one had ever penetrated it.

Fire had no business there. One red-hot little witch wasn't about to change that.

CHAPTER EIGHTEEN

"Sapphire and tonic, please."

The smooth, sultry voice pulled Jaci from her thoughts about dark spells and bloody vampire hearts, and she turned to find a gorgeous female vampire smiling at her across the bar.

Charley, Dorian's fiancée. Jaci remembered seeing her at the Ravenswood fundraiser the night Dorian had invited her to roam the gardens—felt like a hundred years ago now, though it had only been a few months. Charley had been human then, but she was definitely a card-carrying member of the fanged and the furious now.

Dorian's work, no doubt.

Jaci grabbed the bottle of gin and a Copa glass. "If you're here to tear my heart out, please make it quick—I'm dying for an excuse to get out of these heels. Also, I totally get it, and I forgive you in advance."

Charley's dazzling smile widened, her eyes shining with

warmth and amusement. "Tempting, but... Not tonight, hon. I just got my nails done." She fluttered her fingers along the bar.

Jaci couldn't help but notice the massive red diamond glittering on her ring finger. "Congratulations, I think?"

Charley beamed. "Thank you."

Fairly certain the woman wasn't going to leap on her jugular, Jaci turned her attention to making the drink, then handed it over, waving off Charley's credit card.

Charley tipped the glass in cheers, then sipped, her eyebrows lifting. "Wow. That's fucking *good*."

Jaci laughed, some of the tension easing. "My boss is pretty demanding."

A nod. Another sip. Another smile.

Finally, Charley set down her drink and sighed, the warmth in her eyes cooling a bit.

"Look, Jacinda," she said. "I'm not here to pretend that what you did was okay. I just—"

"I didn't know."

Charley cocked her head. "About?"

"I didn't know the poison was for Dorian," she blurted. "I mean, that's not to justify anything. It was super fucked-up either way. But Renault didn't give me any details—just the assignment, and I did it without question. Which... yeah. The end result was still the same —Dorian nearly died, you got dragged into it, and..." She blew out a breath, regretting opening her big, fat mouth in the first place. "For what it's worth, I'm sorry. If I could go back..."

Charley offered a soft smile. "But we can't, that's the kick in the ass."

Jaci poured herself a shot of gin, then touched it to Charley's glass. "To leaving the past in the past."

"Here, here."

The women drank, and Jaci darted off to help another customer. When she returned, Charley was still there.

"Listen, Jacinda—"

"Jaci. I mean, you can call me Jacinda if you want to, but Jaci works too."

"Jaci." Charley ran a manicured finger around the rim of her glass, the picture of elegance. "I came here to say... I'm not justifying what you did—not by a long shot. But let's just say I know what it's like to be stuck in a shitty situation with no way out when your only options are a shit sandwich or a shit sandwich on fire."

Jaci couldn't help but laugh. "Yeah, that's exactly how it feels sometimes."

She liked the woman, and she suspected the woman liked her too, even though they should probably be on the floor already, clawing each other's eyes out.

"But," Charley said, and Jaci sighed.

"There's always a but."

"*But* if you betray Gabriel's trust, if you come after Dorian or anyone in my family again in *any* way—shitty situation or not—I won't hesitate to sacrifice a manicure to tear your heart out. And no, I won't make it quick. And yes, you will remember me in hell, and when I finally make it there myself, I'll track you down and do it all over again."

SARAH PIPER

"Understood." Jaci believed her, but the sudden flare of emotion that burned down her spine wasn't defensiveness or fear.

It was jealousy, plain and simple. Not for Charley's confidence, her poise, her complete badassery—though all were admirable traits.

But because Jaci had no fucking idea what it felt like to be so completely devoted to anyone, much less to an entire family.

And she wanted to.

"Oh, one more thing, woman to woman?" Charley leaned over the bar, eyes glittering with a conspiratorial gleam. "Don't let Gabriel fool you. He's not as much of an asshole as he wants everyone to believe."

Jaci cracked up at that. "Sorry, Charley. Gabriel Redthorne? He's the biggest asshole I've ever met."

"Oh, he's definitely the biggest asshole, bar none. Just not as big as he lets on."

"We'll have to agree to disagree on that."

"Disagree all you want, but…" Charley shrugged and finished her drink, then leaned in close again, dropping her voice. "He *did* take down two Rogozin demons just for messing with you, which seriously pissed off his brother."

"Two?" She knew about Kostya—she'd had a front-row seat to that one. But *two*? "Which demons?"

"Russians. Former Chernikov goons—talk about the world's biggest assholes." Charley shuddered in a way that suggested she was intimately familiar with the bastards. "One of the guys didn't even have a name. Something about eyes? Watching? All I know is Gabriel wanted to send a message that you, blondie, are not to be fucked with."

Jaci poured herself another shot and downed it quick, doing her best to hide her shock.

He killed He Who Likes to Watch? For me?

"*There's* my little prowler." Dorian approached the bar, sweeping Charley into his arms and smothering her with kisses.

With a breathless laugh, Charley winked at Jaci, tucked a twenty under the glass, then left with her man.

Jaci was so entranced by their adorableness, she didn't even realize she had another customer until she heard the impatient clearing of a throat.

She turned to find Gabriel eyeing her up across the bar.

"Bourbon," he said flatly. "If you can spare a moment from your daydreaming to do your job."

"Since you asked *so* nicely." Jaci reached for the bottle, the brand she knew he loved, and poured a glass for each of them. She held his gaze, refusing to let him get under her skin.

Yes, he was an asshole.

So much so that if asshole were a disease, he would be terminal.

But he'd killed two demons for her. Demons who'd tortured and brutalized her. Demons who'd done things to her that still haunted her nightmares, all with Renault's blessing.

A surge of gratitude rose in her chest, making her eyes

water. She downed her drink, then worked up the courage to say the words trapped inside.

"Thank you, Gabriel Redthorne."

He let out a soft sigh, a hundred thoughts flashing through his eyes, none of them readable. "For what?"

"Charley told me what you did to that other demon. He Who Likes to Watch."

Gabriel's fist tightened on his glass, but he said nothing.

Jaci squeezed his arm.

He glared at her fingers as if her touch burned him. "*Don't.*"

She pulled back, surprised at how badly his rejection stung. "Don't what?"

"Do *not* get emotional over this."

"I'm... wait. Emotional? What?"

"I'm not your white knight, Jacinda. I didn't eliminate those demons for you." He held out his empty glass, gesturing for her to refill it.

She did as he asked, swallowing the knot in her throat. When she spoke again, her voice was high and tight. "Then why? Why provoke Rogozin?"

"It was no different from the night of your little stunt at the hospital. Anyone who touches or damages my property will be dealt with swiftly. Let one infraction slide, and we'll have the whole lot of vile, hellspawn beasts showing up whenever they please, pawing my servers, acting as if they own the place. Bloody hell, it's bad enough I have to let them in the door at all. There's only *one* place on earth demons belong, and it *isn't* Obsidian. In fact, it isn't even on earth at all."

Jaci clenched her fists at her side, her body vibrating, her face hot.

Charley was wrong. Gabriel Redthorne was every bit the asshole he fashioned himself, and every time Jaci came close to forgetting it, he swept right back in with a firm reminder.

To think she'd wasted even a *minute* of her life feeling guilty about the idea of sacrificing his heart to save her father's soul… What a fucking joke.

Gabriel tapped on the bar and held up his glass, empty once again, gesturing for her to pour another.

But she was done serving him. Done dealing with his bullshit. Done with all of it.

"Any man who equivocates getting emotional with a genuine thank you clearly hasn't gotten enough of either in his life." Jaci shoved the bottle of bourbon at him and stormed off, feeling the icy touch of his glare on her backside with every step.

CHAPTER NINETEEN

Gabriel found the witch in the wine cellar, precariously balanced on a step ladder as she reached toward the top shelf for a bottle of his rarest Bordeaux. She hadn't heard him approach, and as he tried to cobble together some sort of apology in his mind, he took a moment to pause and enjoy the view.

Another thing he should probably apologize for, but wouldn't.

She stretched up on her toes before the floor-to-ceiling mahogany shelving, fingers wrapping around that bottle, the hem of her dress inching up to reveal another intriguing secret:

Her stockings didn't go all the way up.

Gabriel swallowed hard, his throat working as he imagined running his tongue along the garters, snapping them with his teeth…

Jacinda's sharp, sudden gasp shook him out of the

fantasy. Gabriel glanced up, saw the ladder wobble. Saw the bottle slip from her hand as she lost her footing and fell.

He blurred into the room. Caught the witch and the bottle both.

It happened so fast, she didn't even have time to blink. One moment she was falling, the next she was cradled in his arms, her mouth rounding into a glistening pink *oh* of surprise that stirred his cock to rapt attention.

Wordlessly he set her back on her feet, one hand still holding the wine, the other gripping her hip. Her dress was slightly askew, and beneath the fabric, her skin radiated warmth. Gabriel didn't want to release her.

Jacinda blinked away the shock, her mouth twisting into a scowl as she glared at his hand, still firmly attached to her body.

"Seriously?" she snapped.

He set the wine on the shelf behind her. "Not nearly as serious as it would've been had I not caught you."

"Quit saving me, Prince." She jerked away from him, smoothing her dress back into place, losing one of her hair clips in the process. A fall of curls tumbled over her bare shoulder.

Gabriel resisted the urge to bury his face in those locks and breathe her in.

"Quit needing to be saved, witch." He shrugged as if he couldn't care less—as if the loss of contact didn't bother him. But already his hands itched to touch her again. To feel her softness. Her heat.

Jacinda's cheeks darkened, nostrils flaring. Seeing her

flustered only made Gabriel want her more, but his little witch looked about five seconds from nuclear meltdown—an explosion he wasn't sure he'd survive.

"Every time you help me," she snapped, "I'm obligated to thank you. But—"

"There's no need for—"

"—clearly *that's* the wrong thing to do, lest I offend his royal lordship's delicate sensibilities with all my messy, complicated emotions."

"Jacinda, I—"

She held up a hand, cutting him off. "Here's the plan, vampire."

"Oh, you have a plan now?" Gabriel's laughter rang with mockery. "Let's have it, then. The witch's master plan. Brilliant, no doubt. Should I find a paper and pen? Wouldn't want to miss any of the critical details."

Jacinda rested a hand on her hip, right over the spot he'd so recently touched. Anger radiated in hot waves from her skin. Even her blood smelled like scorched earth.

Like hellfire.

When she spoke again, her words came through gritted teeth. "From now on, we're going to make things super easy for everyone involved."

"How's that, witch?"

She pointed to the ceiling, where one story above, Obsidian's inebriated guests fondled one another on the dance floor. "I'm going to tend that bar and suss out intel on our boy Renault, just as you've ordered me to—wait, scratch that. Just as you've *blackmailed* me to do. And you're—"

"Blackmailed? I hardly think that's—"

"And *you're* going to keep right on doing what you do best."

"Saving you from a bloody head injury? A demon attack? A brutal mauling by the very grays you—"

"Brooding in the shadows," she said. "Criticizing the rest of the staff. Fighting with random demons. And flirting with anyone in a tight skirt until you convince some poor, naive girl to crawl into your bed after last call and warm your cold, dead heart."

Her insults echoed across the cellar, full of venom.

"Jealous, witch?" Gabriel's lips curved into a smile, and in a flash he grabbed her hand and pressed it to his chest. His heart answered the call of her touch, pounding like the bass of Obsidian's music. "In two-and-a-half centuries, *nothing* has warmed this heart. But you're more than welcome to try."

Her own heart thundered in return, that dark, sexy blush spreading from her cheeks to her throat.

Without breaking their intense gaze, the witch stretched up on her toes. Her lips were close enough to bite.

Gabriel thought she might kiss him. Hoped for it, despite everything.

His heart raged beneath her hand, still pressed firmly to his chest.

Jacinda let out a soft hum. And then, with a twisted

smirk, her deadly whisper fell against his lips, cloves and cinnamon, sugar and fire. "I would rather warm my *grave*."

Upstairs, the din of red-hot revelry faded, the DJ switching to a slower track. Quieter. Silence descended, and for several long beats, neither of them said another word. Neither took another breath. The air crackled between them like a flame biting into that first piece of firewood, licking, teasing, desperate to ignite.

"Stay out of my way, vampire," the witch finally said. "And no more saving me." She snatched her hand out from beneath his grasp, grabbed the wine from the shelf, and stalked past him, knocking into his shoulder as she did.

But Gabriel was faster. Gabriel would *always* be faster.

His hand shot out and grabbed her wrist. With a swift, single jerk he yanked her right back into his orbit.

Bodies collided.

The bottle of rare Bordeaux crashed to the floor.

Gabriel wrapped an arm around her and fisted her hair. Took one step, then another, backing her toward the wooden rack. Glass crunched under his boots, and the pungent scent of the ruined wine filled the air. Her shoulders hit the mahogany. A hundred bottles clattered.

"What... what the hell are you doing?" she gasped.

He slid his other hand up around her throat. Fucking *reveled* in the fevered pulse thrumming against his palm. "The opposite of saving you."

CHAPTER TWENTY

Fangs descended like hot iron, a rush of raw hunger flooding his body. The demon he'd drained earlier had done little to sustain him, and now his primal need surged, mixing with other, baser needs until everything in him ached to sink deep inside her—his cock. His bite. His tongue.

Jacinda shoved against his chest, but Gabriel wouldn't budge.

"I told you, Prince," she hissed. "I'm no one's butterfly."

A dark chuckle rumbled through his chest. "Not even mine?"

"Especially not yours." Hatred filled her voice, her eyes glittering with malice.

It only turned him on more.

"Despite what you think," he said softly, "I've never harmed a butterfly. But demons?" His gaze swept down to her mouth, then back to her eyes, where he nearly drowned. "I've bled and burned them. Vampires? Staked and incinerated them. Shifters? Starved them, poisoned them with molten silver, broken the wild beast that raged inside until there was nothing left of it but memory and shame."

Her eyes widened, but the witch offered no reply.

"I've carved my name into the flesh of my enemies," he continued. "Watched them bleed, rubbed salt into the wounds, and waited for them to heal—all so I could do it again. I've tortured without mercy, murdered without regret, sent more monsters to hell than there are bottles in this cellar and trust me when I tell you that *nothing* pleases me more than the sound of a fallen immortal begging for death."

Gabriel shared all of this, his dark résumé, his private shame, his quiet threats, as if he'd ever carry them out against her. As if his soul was so far beyond repair it would allow him to mar so much as an *inch* of her smooth, perfect skin.

No, he didn't want to mar her. Only to frighten her off. To force her to say the words that would stop this inevitable train wreck, because he sure as fuck couldn't do it.

Yet there she remained. Silent. Pulsating beneath his grip. Clove and cinnamon on her breath, eyeliner smudged beneath those bewitching blue eyes, glossy mouth parted in a bated breath held only for him.

He buried his face in the curls draped over her shoulder, nosed the soft skin behind her ear. Her raw-earth scent was intoxicating. Dizzying.

In his firm hold, Jacinda's body heated, her heartbeat a frantic thing that seemed to know instinctively what the rest of her did not.

The witch was in *serious* trouble.

In a low growl, he issued his command.

One he needed her to obey... for both their sakes.

"Tell me to stop, Jacinda Colburn."

He released her throat, his hand already sliding down her rib cage, down to her hip, then lower still, down past the hem of her dress where satin and lace gave way to those sheer black stockings. He gripped her thigh, held tight. Squeezed when all he really wanted to do was bite.

"I've a black soul and an even blacker heart," he whispered, his warning as dark and deadly as the broken-glass wine. "The things I could do to you..." He nearly shuddered at his own depraved thoughts. "Tell me to stop."

Still, the witch said nothing.

"Say it," he ordered again, hitching her leg up around his hip and reaching beneath her dress. His fingers crept past the top edge of her stocking, trailing along the garters and brushing the bare skin at the back of her thigh, all the way up to the silky mound of her arse, barely contained by a lace thong. Goosebumps pebbled in the wake of his touch. His cock ached.

A gasp escaped Jacinda's lips, but the word he so desperately needed to hear did not.

Dipping between her thighs, he traced the thong's path with one finger, barely brushing the scrap of lace over her clit. Heat radiated from her core, and when he pressed against that inviting warmth, she shivered.

"*Say it,*" he ground out, his control slipping, his mind spinning with lust and fury in equal measure.

And oh, he *was* furious. Furious that she'd tempted him. Furious that she'd haunted his fantasies. Furious that of all the witches he'd encountered and despised and feared in this long immortal dance, this one—this prisoner, this enemy, this conspirator had thoroughly entranced him.

Jacinda closed her eyes. Bit her plump lower lip. Drew a deep, shuddering breath.

And then, finally, firmly, she spoke.

"*No*, dickhead."

Gabriel stilled. His fangs receded.

Frustration and disappointment battled in his chest. Relief followed. Acceptance came in dead last, but there it was.

Disaster fucking averted.

"Good girl." He exhaled into her hair and unhanded that silky-smooth thigh, but her leg tightened around his hip, drawing him closer.

A fresh blaze ignited in her eyes, and she fisted his shirt with both hands.

"I meant *no*, dickhead. I *won't* tell you to stop."

CHAPTER TWENTY-ONE

Fucking hell.

Gabriel's hand found its way back to her thigh, fingers digging into the soft flesh as he ground against her center, his rock-hard cock unable to ignore the call of her wet heat. "You know better than to disobey me, witch."

Jacinda shrugged. "Ask nicely next time. I'm not good with demands."

"I'll *destroy* you." Gabriel's grip on her thigh tightened. His heartbeat clamored as if it was trying to warn them both. "Tell me to bloody well stop before—"

"I don't *want* you to stop, Prince."

The fiery admission shattered the last of his resistance. He felt it crack and fall, a thousand shards crunching beneath his boot like the bottle.

"Then what is it you want from me, little moonflower?" he breathed, bringing his lips to the dark hollow of her throat, his own breath ragged as he moved up to her jaw, her chin. Then, hovering just before her mouth, "A kiss?"

Jacinda's eyes widened with raw, honest fear—the first he'd ever found there—and she snapped her mouth shut and turned away, giving him her cheek.

Curious...

"Hmm. Not a kiss, then." He stashed the thought away for later examination and reached for the black ribbon that secured the front of her dress. It was laced up tightly, rounding the tops of her breasts in a way that damn near made him forget his name. "A touch, perhaps?"

His fingertips brushed the soft skin behind the ribbon, and Jacinda turned her face toward his again and sighed, her warm cloves-and-cinnamon breath ghosting over his lips.

"Oh, yes," he said softly. "I think we're getting warmer." He untied the ribbon and pulled open the corset, revealing the marvel of her breasts—soft, no bra, fucking perfect.

Gabriel groaned at the sight.

At the barest caress of his thumbs, her dark pink nipples rose, beautiful and tempting, begging to be sucked. Savored. He wanted them in his mouth, hardening with every swirl of his tongue. Wondered if he could make her come like that, kissing and biting, tongue and teeth and hot, heavy breath alone. But he forced himself to hold back, palming her breasts instead, his fangs descending again, throbbing with the need to bite that tender pink flesh. To taste her.

All of her.

"Tell me to stop," he warned once more, voice trembling with the effort of his restraint. Fucking monumental, that restraint. He'd never had to use it before. When it came to Gabriel and his women, they either said yes, and he bedded them, or no, and he didn't. In a centuries-long life fraught with more shades of gray than a storm, that was the only clear line he'd ever drawn. Black and white. Yes or no, stay or go.

But this? This sorcery, this devilry, this dark pleasure had swept him away like a wild, restless sea, no light to guide him home but the stars in her eyes and the moonlight shimmering in her silvery hair.

Even with his fangs bared, Jacinda shook her head—another order disobeyed, another frantic refusal to head off this epic fucking disaster.

So instead, Gabriel embraced it, welcoming the crash and its inevitable ruin.

He lowered his mouth to a dusky rose peak, brushing his lips across her flesh. Her bare skin was hot to the touch, just like everything else about her, making his mouth water. He sucked one nipple, then the other, savoring her creamy skin as much as he savored the soft, decadent moans his tongue was unleashing. Every teasing, tantalizing lick made her shudder and gasp, all for him.

Jacinda's hands slid into his hair, and her grip tightened, her back arching, pressing her flesh harder against his eager mouth.

"One time," she breathed. "Just once. Yes?"

Gabriel kissed his way up her chest to her throat, blazing a hot path to her ear.

"One time, what?" he asked, though he'd be a fool not to see where this was headed. Where *they* were headed. They'd been on the collision course ever since he'd taken her prisoner and she'd threatened to grind his bones into dust, her stubborn fire turning him on beyond all reason.

"Don't play games," she said hotly, still panting as his fangs grazed her earlobe. "God, you're infuriating!"

"And you're… Hmm, let's assess, shall we?" He slid his fingers between her thighs again, grazing the damp fabric of her panties, letting her desire speak for itself. "The sooner you tell me what you want, witch, the sooner I can make you come."

Another breathy moan. Another tug on his hair.

"One and done," she said. "A quickie. Take me to bed for a polite little roll in the sheets, then we never mention it again and I… Oh, *fuck…*"

His fingers were past the panties now, gliding over hot, silky skin as his own desire roiled, his cock more than eager to replace his touch.

But annoyance buzzed through his chest like an angry hornet.

Why the fuck had her words bothered him so much? One and done, whispered on a breathy moan? Never mention it again? It was practically Gabriel's mating call.

But something about Jacinda was spreading through his veins like the very poison she'd mastered in her craft, and he no longer cared if it killed him. Whether his death came as a slow, plodding torture or in a brutal flash of violence, it mattered not—so long as he could first take his time claiming this infernal witch in all the dark, wicked ways he wanted her.

Death whispered against the back of his neck. Taunted him.

He thought of his brother Malcolm. Blood and ash. Thought of his father, the fallen king. Thought of his nightmares, his memories, his victims, his ghosts.

A growl vibrated through his chest, and he spun her around and pushed her face-forward against the wine rack, flipping up the bottom of her dress and shoving aside the thong. He slid two fingers inside, damn near moaning at the feel of her, wet and willing, the molten fire of her body an inferno that promised a deeply satisfying end to his eternal suffering.

"If I ever invite you into my bed," he whispered, "the things I'll do to you there will not be quick. They'll not be polite. And you can call it a one-and-done deal all you'd like, but I promise you, witch. The only word you'll be uttering when I'm through with you is *more*."

He thrust in deeper, making her whimper. A slow tremor began in her thighs, and she gripped the shelving for balance as Gabriel stroked and teased, wine bottles clinking above and below.

"Damn, you're... That's just... *Wow*," she breathed, and he grinned, knowing he was weaving his own sort of spell. With every teasing thrust, every deep slide, he enticed her closer to the edge, ready to shatter at his command.

He slid his other hand around the front, grazing her clit.

Jacinda gasped. "Oh, God. I'm… I'm going to—"

"No, you're not." He licked the shell of her ear and stilled his fingers, the warning in his tone as dark and deadly as the broken-glass wine. "I *own* this body now, little moonflower. I own the breath in your lungs, the beat of your heart, the quake in your thighs. Every cry of pleasure, every desperate moan, every gasp of exquisite torment belongs to me, and you'll come only when I bloody well *command* you to come. Is that understood?"

Shivering in his hands, panting, Jacinda turned her head to glare at him over her shoulder.

The witch did *not* understand—that much was clear. Her eyes blazed with that familiar blue fury, her brow furrowed, her mouth parting to tell him *exactly* what she thought of his so-called commands.

Gabriel could hardly wait for the fight.

He feathered across her clit once more, and again, the witch lost all her words.

She turned away from him on a soft sigh, her body surrendering even as her mind railed against it.

Gabriel stifled a laugh.

"I see," he said, slowly working her again. She melted into his touch, riding him, taking him in deeper, wanting more, desperately chasing that elusive release. He knew when she was close again—her blood sang with it, the telltale tremor rolling through her thighs in earnest, her breath ragged, her soft little moans growing louder.

Gabriel slowed his thrusts, dragging out her pleasure as well as his own.

"The dark witch likes to play games?" he murmured, drawing circles on her clit, harder and faster as he slid deeper inside. "So does the vampire. Guess who's going to win?"

"You're... such an asshole," she panted, still writhing at his touch, arching her hips back to draw him in deeper.

"This is true," he admitted. "But one who makes you wet nevertheless."

"I knew this was a terrible idea."

That annoying hornet buzzed through his chest once more.

"Yes, you're having a right terrible time of it, aren't you?" He quickened the pace of his circling, his thrusting, pushing her closer to the breaking point.

Jacinda gripped the shelves so tightly her fingertips paled. "Go... go fuck yourself, Prince."

"Fuck *myself*? That's not where I saw this going at all." Though it was almost physically painful to let her go, Gabriel was tired of her games. Her insults. He disentangled himself and took a step backward.

Bloody *hell* how he wanted to slide his fingers into his mouth, to taste her.

The scent alone was driving him mad.

Fuck.

Fuck.

She turned around to face him again, the fire in her eyes

nearly as hot as the fire coursing through her blood. Through *his* blood.

He waited for her to speak. To break. To beg him for another touch.

This time, he wouldn't deny her. Wouldn't tease.

One word and he'd be on his knees in the broken glass, his tongue buried so deep in that pussy he wouldn't even hear her begging for more. He'd give it to her anyway. More. More. *More.* Again and again and again until she came so hard, so many times, she'd need to be carried out of that cellar. Straight out of Obsidian and into his penthouse, where he'd tie her down and fuck her into the next life.

His cock bulged again.

Jacinda only gaped, incredulous. Feisty. Ready to spar, as always. Her whole body practically hummed with it.

But the witch folded her arms across her bare chest, refusing to give him the satisfaction of a response.

"Sorry," he said in a tone that assured her he wasn't. "Was there something else you needed? Help reaching the wine, perhaps? Damaged merchandise comes out of your tips, and that Bordeaux was a rare vintage."

Despite the untamed desire surging in her eyes, the witch still wouldn't bend.

Gabriel grabbed a dishtowel from a stack on a nearby shelf and wiped his fingers. A dick move—one that made his gut clench with revulsion at his own boundless capacity for assholery—but if he walked out of that cellar still wearing her on his skin, he wouldn't be able to function.

Wouldn't even make it up the stairs before he marched right back down again, ripped off that thong, shoved her against the racks, and buried himself deep inside.

Hurt flickered in her eyes, but the fire burned it away fast. "Seriously? You're just… leaving?"

"Unless you need me for something?" he repeated. Then, met only with raging silence, "Perhaps next time you'll reconsider the prudence of playing games with a professional gambler. Oh, and Jacinda?" he tossed the towel into the puddle of wine at her feet. "Clean that up, or instead of mixing drinks you'll be chasing rats."

CHAPTER TWENTY-TWO

Hours later, pacing her apartment like a caged animal, Jaci was still pent up and overheated. Lust and anger simmered in her blood in equal parts, her whole body on fire from Gabriel's filthy touch.

Bruises marked her thigh where he'd gripped her, a stark reminder of his strength. His ferocity. His wildness.

She despised what he'd done to her. Despised even more that she wanted him to do it again. Even after an ice-cold shower and a few stiff drinks, she still couldn't erase the memory of his hands searing her skin. His mouth on her breasts. His fangs grazing her sensitive flesh as he drove his fingers maddeningly inside her again and again…

"Fucking asshole vampire!"

Hellfire tickled her palms, aching to burst free. Gabriel was lucky he'd left her alone tonight. If that motherfucker had come anywhere near her right now, she would've roasted him on sight.

Yeah. Sure you would've, girl.

Defeat tasted bitter on her tongue.

Curling her palms into fists, she willed the hell magic to abate and flopped onto the bed in resignation.

One and done? A polite roll in the sheets? Why had she said those things? Why had she spoken to him at all? The instant he'd put his hands on her, she should've just told him to stop. He'd given her the option, but nope. She just *had* to keep pushing those buttons.

And he just *had* to keep enticing her with that hot, filthy, mind-erasing mouth.

The only word you'll be uttering when I'm through with you is more…

Jaci rolled over onto her stomach.

Punched the pillow.

Fisted the blankets.

Reminded herself of all the horrible things he'd confessed.

Reminded herself she was supposed to be figuring out how to steal the beating heart from his chest.

Reminded herself he'd kidnapped her. Forced her to work for him. Ordered her around like his personal servant.

And still, her pussy ached for him.

Flipping over onto her back again, she glared up at the ceiling, catching sight of the tiny red light that told her the all-seeing eye was still filming her every move.

Of *course* it was. Even if she'd *wanted* to take care of herself tonight, she couldn't. Not without that cocky vampire watching her.

Watching her…

Wait. Now *there* was a thought to ignite a fresh fire in her belly.

And in his…

With a wicked grin—and most certainly a gleam in her eyes to match—she got herself situated on top of the blankets. Closed her eyes. Let out a deep, satisfying sigh.

And unleashed her beautiful revenge.

CHAPTER TWENTY-THREE

Why the fuck had Gabriel spent so many centuries despising witchcraft? A beautiful woman with a devious mind was infinitely more powerful than the darkest of hexes. Even stripped of her grimoires, *this* one—this wicked little temptress—had corrupted him like no magic could.

He sat at the desk in his study, laptop open, utterly transfixed at the images splashed across the screen.

The witch he detested more with each passing second now lie on the bed, unwrapping her bathrobe as if she were opening a gift, all for him.

With trembling hands, Gabriel sipped his bourbon. The sharp scent of the alcohol reminded him of the spilled wine in the cellar where he'd left her standing in the broken glass. Where he'd left her aching. Left her wound up and flushed and flustered beyond all hope of deliverance.

Yet as he'd turned his back and walked up the cellar stairs, Gabriel was the one who burned inside, blazing with guilt and desire both. The next time he saw Jacinda, she was flirting with some demon at the bar—one of Chernikov's leftovers who'd surrendered to Rogozin.

The sight had stirred in him another kind of fire. A murderous kind.

A dozen times he thought to apologize in earnest—for leaving her in such a state, for the wretched things he said, for punishing her with coldness and cruelty all for the grievous sin of saying thank you—and a dozen times he talked himself out of it.

In the end, he'd only been punishing himself. Forcing himself to watch her work the bar for the remainder of the evening as every demon in the place eye-fucked her, flirted with her, touched her as if she belonged to them instead.

Fuck his brother's diplomatic efforts. If one more demon laid so much as a passing *glance* on his witch, Gabriel was officially barring any hellspawn from the premises and obliterating any who dared to enter.

He took another sip of bourbon, desperately trying to steady himself.

Fucking pointless.

On the screen before him, he watched as Jacinda slid her arms from the robe. She wore nothing beneath it. Nothing but soft, beautiful bare skin. No corset, no stockings, no thong.

The sheer, unobstructed sight of her nakedness made Gabriel's balls ache.

One hand wrapped around his glass, he slid his other to

his waistband, unbuckling his belt, unzipping. Deftly freeing his cock. Fisting it.

Fuck, it was a pale imitation to the heat of her touch. Another exercise in futility that only served to further enrage him.

With delicate fingers, Jacinda traced the contours of one breast, then the other, nipples rising at her gentle touch, bringing him right back to those heated moments in the wine cellar. The taste of her skin filled his mouth. The memory of sucking those pert nipples made his fangs burn.

She palmed her breast, just like he'd done, teasing and tugging. Her other hand trailed down to her belly, drawing slow, lazy patterns, and though he couldn't hear her, he imagined a breathy moan tickling his ear.

Moonlight spilled across the bedroom, painting her skin in all the places he wanted to touch her. To kiss her. The witch's own touch followed, drawing invisible lines he longed to retrace with his tongue.

Fingers tight around his glass, fist tight around his cock, Gabriel watched, panting like a starved beast as she slid her fingers down to the juncture of her thighs.

The sound of his own heartbeat thudded in his ears, teeth clenched tight as she dipped a finger inside, then drew back, lightly rubbing her clit. Her lips parted again, settling loose another imagined sigh that quickly cascaded into a moan, blood darkening her cheeks and chest just like it had in the cellar. And just like in the cellar, Gabriel knew when she was getting close. Her body was so responsive to every touch, and here she revealed its secrets and tells, one thrust, one dip, one soft circle at a time.

Jacinda's hips undulated, her body writhing as she gave herself the very pleasure he'd denied her.

His cock fucking *throbbed* for her, but he wouldn't give in.

The witch *wanted* him to touch himself, just as she was doing. Wanted him to break, knowing it was all because of her little games. Her little power play.

Gabriel was mere seconds away from giving her the victory.

Bloody hell, the woman called herself a witch, but what she was doing to him right now went beyond spellcraft. She was a damned demoness. A dark enchantress sent from the bowels of hell to ruin him. To burn him.

To grind his bones to dust, just as she'd threatened.

Gabriel's knuckles turned white around the glass. He slammed back another swig of bourbon, but the burn of the alcohol did nothing to soothe the flames of desire.

The mere sight of Jacinda touching herself onscreen was enough to drive him to the fucking brink.

But the fact that she was doing it for him, *because* of him, knowing he'd be watching her, knowing he'd be hard and desperate and fucking *powerless* to stop her as she made herself come…

Her body arched suddenly off the bed, every muscle drawn tight, lips glistening, eyes closed, fingers working faster and faster and then…

Fuck…

The glass shattered in his hand.

Gabriel got to his feet. Shook the broken glass and bourbon from his fingers.

Whipped the leather belt from his pants.

And headed upstairs.

Time to teach my witch a lesson she won't find in any spellbook…

CHAPTER TWENTY-FOUR

The force of the orgasm was still coursing through Jaci's body when the bedroom door slammed open, biting into the plaster wall behind it.

She sat up at once. Gabriel stood in the doorway, his body limned in light, pants undone, a leather belt clutched in his fist.

"Tell me to stop," he demanded.

Despite the fact that she'd just given herself the best orgasm of her life, all thanks to fantasies about the vampire now glaring down at her, her whole body turned to molten jelly at his words.

Pride and sanity told her to do it—tell him to stop. Tell him to go fuck himself, just like she'd told him in the cellar.

To stick with her fucking plan.

But then his eyes roved her naked body, burning her skin as if he'd branded her, his fist tightening around the belt, his breath as wild and ragged as hers, and all that pride evaporated.

Fuck sanity. Fuck vengeance. Fuck plans. Fuck their silly little games. Fuck *all* of it but his cock slamming into her pussy, his filthy mouth whispering all the ways he was going to absolutely ruin her.

"*No,*" she shot right back, and the vampire advanced on her at once, looming over the edge of her bed like a monster come to drag her to the depths of depravity.

His eyes blazed, heat burning away the ice. With one hand he unbuttoned his shirt and shrugged it off, revealing the thick, corded muscles of his arms, the ridges of his abs, the v-shaped muscles that arrowed down beneath his hips.

Jaci had never wanted to lick anything as badly as she did at that moment.

Gabriel knelt on the bed, leaning close.

His scent washed over her, making her dizzy with desire.

"I mean it this time, Prince," she said, hands pressed flat against his pecs, rock-hard beneath her touch. "If you mess with me tonight, I'm going back to the demons at the bar and you can go right to hell."

"The only place I'm going tonight, witch, is right between your thighs." In a flash he grabbed her hands, pinning them behind her back and binding her wrists with the belt.

One hard tug, then another, and she was well and truly captured.

He got to his feet and cupped her face, holding her gaze for a beat.

Then he hauled her to the edge of the bed, dropped to his knees on the floor, and wrapped her thighs around his neck.

Seven hells.

Jaci had never particularly liked men. Never had time for their bullshit. She'd learned to take care of her own needs long ago, and after all this time on her own, she actually believed she'd gotten quite good at it.

Fifteen seconds beneath the vampire's mouth dashed those silly thoughts.

Gabriel Redthorne was a fucking *menace*.

Just as she'd feared.

Just as she'd hoped.

The monster had been unleashed from his cage, and now he was all over her, everywhere at once, sexy stubble scratching her thighs, fingers digging into her flesh, his hair brushing against her bare skin, his hot mouth searing as he licked and sucked and devoured and licked again.

Without the full use of her arms, Jaci's muscles trembled with the effort of keeping her body upright, but she didn't dare lie back. Didn't dare miss the sight of his dark head between her thighs, his misty-forest gaze glinting in the moonlight. Alternating with teasing flicks across her clit and deep, hot thrusts inside her, every stroke of his tongue left her gasping and hot, her body tight and tingling, her nerve endings electrified.

She felt it building up inside, flames licking across the

deepest places, scorching a hot path up through her belly and into her chest and then…

"Gabriel!" she cried out, thighs clamping around his face as the orgasm took hold and he pushed her beyond the brink, licking, sucking, plunging inside her as she let herself be utterly consumed.

Moments later, still perched on the edge of the bed with her wrists bound, Jaci could hardly breathe.

Gabriel rose to his feet. The look in the vampire's eyes was feral, his mouth shining with the evidence of what he'd done to her. She felt the heat of his glare on her body again, on all the places where his passionate kisses had marked her.

He was hungry for her. Starving.

And in that moment she knew, without hesitation, that whatever order fell from his lips next, she'd obey.

He leaned in close again, a deadly whisper brushing across her mouth. "On your knees, witch."

CHAPTER TWENTY-FIVE

His witch knelt before him, wrists bound behind her back, eyes wide, that ripe red mouth a seductive invitation Gabriel wouldn't refuse even if someone had a stake pressed to his heart.

He was drunk on the taste of her. High from the way she'd cried out his name as he'd coaxed so much pleasure from her body. Dizzy just from looking at her.

And if he didn't fuck her soon, he was quite certain he'd burn to ash.

One and done, dickhead, he reminded himself. *One and fucking done.*

"Open your mouth, little moonflower." Caressing her jaw, he pressed his thumb to her lower lip, and she obeyed, parting easily for him.

Gabriel fisted his cock and grinned. "Hmm. For all the sass, it seems my witch *likes* being told what to do in the bedroom."

The desire flooding her eyes was all the confirmation she offered.

"Good girl," he whispered, threading his other hand into her hair, fingers tightening in the warm silk. She opened her mouth wider, her velvet tongue darting out to taste him, just as he'd done to her.

In a single thrust, he slid inside that hot, wet haven, forcing himself not to groan at the sight of her lips wrapped around his cock.

Then she moved her tongue. A slow, erotic tease, her teeth scraping the top of him, hot breath caressing him. Her soft moan sent ripples of intense pleasure down his rock-hard length.

Fucking hell…

His knees nearly buckled, and he tightened his grip on her hair, pulling back, then thrusting inside again, deeper this time, making her gag.

"Relax," he growled, and again she obeyed him, relaxing her throat and taking him all the way in. Tears glazed her eyes, but when he tried to pull back to let her breathe, she groaned her refusal and sucked him harder, that devious little tongue doing its damndest to completely destroy him.

Thirty more seconds of it and he'd…

No. Not yet. Not like this.

If this was to be their one-and-done deal, Gabriel was going to make it fucking last.

He pulled out of her soft, seductive mouth, leaving her gasping. Then, in a move so fast she didn't even have time to draw another breath, he hauled her up, unbound her wrists, and tossed her onto the bed.

"Spread your legs for me, witch."

She responded without hesitation, and Gabriel took a moment to admire the sight of her, naked and glistening. Even after he'd made her come with his mouth, she was already ready for more. Desperate for it.

"You knew I'd be watching you tonight," he said, stepping out of his pants and boxers. "On the cameras."

A silent nod, a fresh blush creeping across her chest. Her gaze raked over his body, head-to-toe and back again, leaving a trail of fire in its wake. The scent of her blood was almost as strong as the scent of her desire, both threatening to overpower him.

He could still taste her on his tongue, and now he wanted more.

When Gabriel spoke again, his voice was rough.

"Touch yourself, Jacinda. Show me *exactly* how you wanted to drive me wild."

She arched her back and slid a hand between her thighs, fingers grazing her clit, then dipping inside, pulling back to skim across her clit once more. With every stroke, her skin grew darker, the twin scents of blood and lust invading his senses. Unraveling him.

"Were you thinking of me before?" he whispered, taking a step closer to the bed. "Wondering what my mouth would feel like?"

"Yes," she breathed.

"Are you thinking of me now? Remembering how hard you came on my tongue?"

"*Fuck*. I... yes."

"Yes *what*, little moonflower?"

"Yes, I'm thinking of you now. I'm *always* thinking of—"

She cut off abruptly, but the confession was out, hanging on the air between them, driving him wild.

"Stop," he commanded.

Her fingers stilled, and Gabriel climbed on top of her, grabbing her wrists and pinning them over her head. The belt lay discarded beside her, so he snatched it up and bound her once more, looping the ends around a spindle in the headboard, pulling it tight.

Cupping her face, he met her desirous gaze and whispered against her mouth, "Tell me to stop."

A vehement shake of that silver-blonde head, and he was on her once more, mouth descending on her throat, slowly kissing his way down the length of her body, gripping her thighs and pushing them apart, desperate for another taste.

He buried his face in that red-hot pussy, licking and teasing, taking his fill. Jacinda writhed and bucked beneath him, but this time, he wouldn't let her come so easily. This time, it was all for him.

His tongue swirled around her superheated flesh, sucking, kissing, demanding. He brought her to the very edge, then stopped, kissing his way back up her thighs, her stomach, her breasts.

Hovering over her once more, he lowered his mouth

toward hers, ready to claim her in a kiss that would leave her breathless.

"Stop. Stop!" She jerked her head to the side, avoiding his kiss.

Gabriel went still. Cold.

"Afraid to taste yourself on my tongue, little moon-flower?" he whispered. "Or are you finally coming to your senses and calling off this madness?"

"I'm… neither. It's just…" Jacinda let out a trembling sigh. Beneath the press of his body, her nipples stiffened, her flesh hot and silky.

"Tell me," he demanded, doing his best to school his irritation, undoubtedly failing.

Jacinda turned to face him. Narrowed her eyes. "You don't even remember me, do you?"

Gabriel's brow furrowed. What game was she playing now? What did his recollections of her have to do with the fact that she wouldn't kiss him?

"From your brother's party," she prompted. "At Ravenswood?"

"Should I?" he teased.

Hurt flickered in her eyes, but she was as talented as Gabriel at donning a mask, and in the span of a single heartbeat, her smirk was back in place.

With a casual shrug, she said, "Heard you fooled around with one of Renault's blood slaves. Human girl. Billie?"

"Right." He brought a hand to her breast, drawing a light circle around her nipple. "You'll have to be more specific than that."

"Red hair, tight dress. Gorgeous."

"Hmm. Still doesn't ring a bell."

Her smirk faded. "Seriously?"

"I don't know what to tell you, witch. Guess your little friend didn't make much of an impression."

"She's not my friend."

"Nor mine, apparently."

"I hate you," she breathed, and the surge of fire in her eyes told him she'd meant it.

Good. Gabriel hated her too. Hated the way she made him feel—unhinged, untethered. Hated the fact that he'd been dreaming about this moment ever since that first fucking time he'd seen her in the gardens that night, bent over some exotic plant in his brother's collection, looking more at home in the dirt than he'd ever felt anywhere in his pathetic immortal life.

Remember her?

Fucking hell, he'd watched her from the shadows for an hour, silently following her from one path to another. And in that hour, she'd lodged herself so thoroughly in his head that later that night, when another woman offered her artery, then dropped to her knees and took his cock in her mouth, the only reason he didn't stop her was that he'd hoped it would get the witch out of his fucking head.

Hadn't worked, though.

In Gabriel's mind, it was *Jacinda's* soft gasp as he bit into the vein pulsing on the other woman's neck. *Jacinda's* silky locks he'd fisted, fucking her hot little mouth. *Jacinda's* blue eyes gazing up at him as he spilled down her throat…

Gabriel wrapped his hand around her throat, drawing his mouth close once again. In a low growl, he said, "I don't need you smitten, little moonflower. Just willing."

She clenched her teeth, frustration warring with desire in her eyes, as if the latter stood a chance.

Gabriel shifted between her thighs, teasing her entrance with his cock. "Stop or don't stop?"

"I... oh, *fuck*," she whispered. "No kissing. Not on the mouth."

"Fine."

"I mean it."

"As do I." He flashed a wicked grin. "From now on, your smart little mouth is reserved solely for my cock."

Lust heated her gaze, and she lifted her head, pressing the gentlest kiss to his earlobe. The gesture felt uncomfortably intimate. "Swear it, Prince."

"Bloody hell, woman. I swear it."

"Then my answer is don't stop." She lowered her head and looked into his eyes once more. "A hundred *million* don't stops if you'll *please* just fuck me and—"

Gabriel clamped a hand over her mouth and plunged inside her.

No more talking. No more swearing. Only thrusting and grinding and fucking and holy *hell*, minutes later he was halfway to Death's door, ready to call it a day on two hundred fifty-odd years.

Fucking her mouth had been ecstasy. But this?

Bloody hell, she felt so good. Perfect. With his hand still clamped over her mouth, Gabriel stopped and rested his head on her chest, ear pressed to her heart, its wild rhythm nearly hypnotizing him.

Jacinda sighed, her warm breath stirring his hair, and for a moment they lay together, unmoving, unhurried. Gabriel felt as if they'd stopped time.

Maybe the little witch had done just that.

But all too soon her hips were writhing again, thighs tightening around him, and Gabriel began a series of slow, torturous thrusts, pushing in deep and dragging out, inch by devastating inch, every movement making him more hungry for her. More needy.

Without warning she bit the fleshy part of his hand between thumb and index finger, hard enough to draw blood, then licked his thumb, sucking it between her lips. The blood stained her mouth a dark cherry, a sight that sent a shock of urgent heat to his balls.

More. Harder. *Deeper.*

He slid his hand down to her throat, wrapping her in a bloody grip, absolutely *owning* her as he fucked her in the moonlight. It painted them both in washes of silver and blue, eerie and incandescent. Gabriel felt like a ghost. A nightmare. A wicked thing sent from some foul, unnamed hell to destroy her, just as he'd warned.

Everywhere his mouth touched her flesh, he marked her, sucking and biting, claiming.

Then, when he knew she couldn't hold out another moment, when he knew he wouldn't be far behind, he tightened his grip on her throat and made his final command.

"Come for me, little moonflower."

He rocked against her clit, hitting her slow and deep, her thighs quaking as he continued to dominate her, and then he felt it—fucking *hell*, he felt it—the blood rushing through her veins, her heart slamming against her ribs, the white-hot burst of desire exploding inside her. He released his hand and she cried out for him, her body pulsating around his cock, thighs gripping his hips, everything about her drawing him down into that dark, beautiful spiral.

A tremor rolled through his body, and when he came, he roared with the force of it. He held her face in his hands, and in the depths of her mesmerizing blue eyes, Gabriel saw the stars.

He rolled onto his hip and looked at his witch, studying her curves in the moonlight. The dark smear of his blood still glistened on her chest, the taste of her still lingered in his mouth. A dark, possessive hunger unfurled inside him.

He slung an arm across her body, pulling her close.

"*Mine.*"

The word came unbidden, as much a declaration to her as it was a warning to himself. He'd just come harder than he'd ever come in his fucking life, yet already he wanted her again. Craved her—the feel of her skin. The taste of her desire. The kiss she'd thus far denied him.

All of it.

Which meant he absolutely couldn't have her again.

One and done. That's how it had to be.

Because if he didn't walk away now, that craving would turn into a full-blown addiction. And *that*... Well, Gabriel preferred not to think about where that might lead.

He rolled over and straddled her again, but instead of plunging back inside her like he desperately wanted to do, he loosened the belt and released her.

"Okay?" he asked, gently massaging her hands.

Jacinda nodded, still dazed from their encounter.

Gabriel knew the feeling.

Forcing himself to finally back away, he left her alone in the bed and retrieved his shirt from the floor, shoving his arms through the sleeves.

But he couldn't tear his gaze from hers.

Jacinda sat up on the end of the bed, toned legs dangling over the side. From her tantalizing perch, she watched him fasten each button as though she'd never seen such a modern marvel as a men's dress shirt.

Heaviness hung in the air between them. Desires still unmet, fetishes unexplored, territories unmapped.

Lips—regrettably—unkissed.

When she spoke, her tone was light and teasing. "You're a lot of things, Prince, but I never thought I'd be calling you a liar."

"Excuse me?"

"Tonight, in the wine cellar. You said if we ever hooked up, it wouldn't be quick." She glanced at her wrist as though she wore a watch and flashed a devilish grin, the playful light in her eyes unlocking something inside him that needed to go *right* back into its fucking cage.

Half dressed, Gabriel climbed onto the bed and crawled over her naked body, forcing her to lie back again, her eyes alight with some new challenge, some new fire.

And there again, just as it was the night he'd found her outside the hospital and carried her home, the tiniest flicker of vulnerability.

He lowered his mouth to hers, hovering just above her lips, everything in him demanding that he break his vow and steal the kiss she'd refused him.

He wondered how long she'd truly resist.

Again, she turned her face away, avoiding a collision of mouths and tongues, breath and teeth.

It only made him want it more.

He'd licked and tasted her most intimate curves, fucked her, owned her.

But he still hadn't kissed her.

"What I said in the wine cellar, witch," he whispered, "applies only if I've invited you into my bed. This was neither my bed nor an invitation."

"No?" She reached for the buttons he'd just finished securing, already working them loose again. The gentle scrape of her fingernails against his throat made him ache with need. "What would you call it, Prince?"

Scorching.

Mind-blowing.

A fucking fantasy to revisit in the shower every night for the rest of his cursed immortal life...

His cock stirred between her thighs, the evidence of desire—his and hers both—still hot and wet between them.

"Why did you refuse my kiss?" The words were out before he could stop them, and before he could take them back, Jacinda's eyes filled with sadness.

"Not just yours. *Everyone's*. Kissing just isn't something I... I've never... It's the one thing I won't do with someone unless I..." She trailed off, embarrassment staining her cheeks.

Love them, she'd wanted to say. He could almost taste the words. Could almost feel the weight of them in his heart.

"Never?" he asked, smiling softly, despite himself.

"Look, I know it's stupid, okay? But no, I've never kissed anyone. Let the mockery commence."

He traced the outline of her cupid's bow lips with his thumb, his smile fading. In that moment, he almost wished he and Jacinda didn't hate each other. "It's not stupid, Jacinda. It's—"

"Stay with me," she whispered urgently, loosening another button on his shirt. "Just a little longer. One more time, then we'll call it a night."

Her hips arched toward him, enticing him with her heat. Her scent. He stared at her soft mouth, marveling at the fact that no one had tasted it.

Never kissed anyone... Let the mockery commence...

When he finally met her gaze again, the crack of vulnerability in her eyes widened into a fissure, and he knew if he stayed any longer, he'd fall right into it.

One and done, you knob. Remember?

Before she could ensnare him with another of her deadly spells, Gabriel batted her hand away from the buttons and rose from the bed, taking his belt with him. For some inexplicable reason, he didn't bother with the pants.

It was his building, after all. If anyone had a damned thing to say about it, he'd tear their bloody hearts out.

"Goodnight, Jacinda." It was all he could spare before he turned away and stalked off, leaving her to bathe in the eerie winter moonlight alone.

He was out of her bedroom and nearly to the front door when he heard the siren call of her voice again. If she was bothered by his abrupt dismissal, she didn't reveal it. Instead, she laughed—at him, near him, fucking *surrounding* him—and called out, "Does this mean you're not interested in what the Chernikov demon told me about Renault Duchanes?"

CHAPTER TWENTY-SIX

Tea. That's what the situation called for. It gave Jaci something to focus on, something to keep her hands occupied when all she really wanted to do was grab that infuriating vampire, shove him against the wall, and climb him like a fucking tree.

At the same time, she also wanted to hex him and punch him in the nuts.

The contradiction was inconvenient, to say the least.

Frustration bubbled up inside, making her tremble. She did her best to steady herself, pouring two steaming mugs of vanilla mint tea, the leaves harvested from the plants he'd bought for her on Obsidian's opening night.

She'd kept one for her apartment. Every time she saw it or caught a whiff of its bright, invigorating scent, she thought of Gabriel and smiled, even when she was pissed at him.

She wondered if he even remembered.

"I hope you like mint." She carried the mugs to the dining table, where he sat waiting patiently. Silently. Maddeningly.

"It's fine, Jacinda." He reached for his tea just as she handed it over, the brush of his fingers sending a little zap of pleasure across Jaci's skin. She drew back, hating that little zap. Hating the vampire who'd caused it.

It was good she was dressed now. In layers. With a hood and zipper that went all the way up to her chin. Layers meant fewer chances of spontaneous loss of wardrobe resulting in hot kisses on bare skin and smooth, velvet-soft strokes of his—

Nope. Not going there again.

One and done, just like she'd wanted.

"Tell me about the demon, Jacinda," Gabriel said now, his icy veneer firmly back in place.

Seven hells. How was it even possible that not half an hour ago, she was having the most intense, incredible, life-altering sex with the guy? Had she imagined it?

She closed her eyes. Let out a slow breath. A dull ache pulsed between her thighs, flooding her with heat and memories and desperation...

Are you thinking of me now? Remembering how hard you came on my tongue?

"Jacinda?"

"Yes!" she breathed. "I mean..." She opened her eyes. Cleared her throat. Took the chair across from him and buried her face in her mug, cursing herself for letting him so thoroughly invade her mind.

Cursing herself for wanting him to so thoroughly invade the rest of her.

Again.

"I've been working the guy for days," she finally said, forcing herself to focus on the demon from the bar. "He thinks he's got me wrapped around his finger."

"Does he?"

The sharp note in Gabriel's voice made her look up.

Those piercing green eyes narrowed, his broad shoulders tensing. He'd put on his pants but hadn't finished buttoning his shirt, and now it gaped open, giving her another glimpse of his smooth, hard pecs, all the dips and shadows her mouth still longed to explore.

Jaci turned back to her tea, taking a deep, clarifying breath of mint. Dodging his question, she said, "We need the intel, Prince. Leverage. Isn't that what you wanted?"

Gabriel sighed. From the corner of her eye, she caught him folding his arms across his chest. "And what leverage have you managed to gain?"

"For one thing, the grays. It's not the amulets we need to worry about now."

"I gathered as much when we fought them at the hospital."

"The original resurrection magic was mine—that's why I was able to stop them with another spell that night. But the delivery…" She wrapped her hands tighter around the mug, a chill racing across her skin that had nothing to do with the vampire. "Renault had another witch working on injectables—something that couldn't be stripped off in a fight."

"*Working* on?"

"The night of the Bloodbath massacre, Renault sent me there to meet with her—wanted me to drop off some more magical supplies for the spell. But then you guys attacked and I never got the chance. Renault disappeared, the other witches were questioned and released… As far as I knew, they never finished the formula. But—"

"But the grays at the hospital disproved your theory."

Jaci nodded and took another sip of tea, grateful for its warmth. "Then this demon starts hanging around at the bar, one of Chernikov's old minions. He's not dumb enough to criticize you outright, but I got the sense right away he wasn't too happy about the new alliance. So naturally, I drop a few hints about what a terrible boss you are—"

"Excuse me?"

"—all to get in his good graces, mind you."

Gabriel scoffed. Jaci took great pleasure in it.

"So this demon and I start to get chummy—"

"Chummy?"

"—and one night, he lets it slip that in his opinion, Renault is still a major player. That he heard the vampire's sitting on something big, waiting for the right time. A few more drinks, a few more flirty smiles and innuendos, and he tells me Renault has some new magical friends."

"Witches?" Gabriel asked.

Jaci shook her head. "Mages. A group calling themselves the Keepers of the Dark Flame, claiming to have direct access to immense demonic powers that make the work I was doing look like a dip in the magical kiddie pool."

"Keepers of the Dark Flame? Have you ever heard of them?"

"No, and frankly, the whole 'direct access' thing sounds like bullshit to me. Even for those of us who practice the dark arts, it's not a simple matter of texting your buddies in hell and ordering up a hit. But it *is* the kind of thing that sounds scary as fuck and gives power-hungry guys like Renault a hard-on."

"So you believe he's bought into this scheme?"

"Absolutely. The demon said these mages were working on advanced resurrection magic not just for the grays, but for other supernaturals too. Shifters, namely."

"Bloody hell." Gabriel rose from the table, pacing the living room and undoubtedly picturing the same thing as Jaci—feral, undead wolves, panthers, and bears, all of them running wild through the streets of New York at Renault's command. "If Duchanes is working on this, something tells me he's not far. He wouldn't leave an operation like this to chance."

"I agree."

"So how do we find these mages?"

Abandoning her tea, Jaci joined him at the doors that led out to the balcony. The moon was low in the sky, casting them both in calming silver-blue light. "I tricked him into telling me where their little club likes to meet."

He turned toward her, that muscle ticking in his jaw again.

Damn, he's sexy...

"Do I even want to know how you did that?" he asked. The sharp edge had returned to his voice, but his eyes held a spark of mischief, a keen appreciation for scheming she knew they shared.

"It wasn't easy. As much as I tried to paint the picture of my *complete* dissatisfaction with my current predicament, the demon knows I'm Redthorne property, so—"

"Not Redthorne property. *My* property." His eyes blazed bright in the moonlight. "There's no sharing involved."

Jaci swallowed hard. *Good to know...*

"Either way, I knew I couldn't offer myself up as bait. No demon would risk double-crossing you. Not after what happened to Kostya and Mikhail."

Gabriel's eyes turned cold again, his body tensing, fists clenched at his sides. "Only the *dimmest* bulb in the hellspawn bunch would—"

"I know." She placed a hand against his chest, fingertips brushing the bare skin exposed by the half-open shirt. Beneath her palm, his heart thudded, hard and fast. "I told him I had a friend looking for work. *Not* the kind requiring an apron and a nose for wine."

"Dark magic," Gabriel confirmed, and she nodded.

"They meet every other Saturday at Shimmer. It's an exclusive witch and mage club out on Montauk. Ocean view, killer food and drinks, ritual rooms, the whole nine."

"You've been?"

Jaci almost laughed. "Sure, Prince. I turn down invitations to fancy parties and exclusive clubs on the regular."

Her father had been there, though. Back before he fell for her mother's demonic tricks and landed in hell. He worked there as a young mage, a private server for the ritual rooms. Later, when he grew more fully into his own power, he was a member. He'd told Jaci about it so many times, she almost felt like she *had* been there.

"Excellent work, Jacinda." Gabriel reached for his phone. "I'll get my best guys on it, and—"

She grabbed his arm, stopping him from hitting the call button. "No. No guys."

"But—"

"My so-called friend is a witch. A woman. Assuming the demon is as slippery and loose-lipped as I imagine, he'll leak word to someone, and eventually, it'll get back to Renault and these so-called Keepers of the Dark Flame that a witch is going to show up and crash their party, looking for work. It has to be me."

"But the demon knows what you look like. Knows you're my—"

"That's what glamor magic is for, my sweet prince."

"Let me guess. Another of your specialties?"

"A girl has to be prepared for anything."

"Something tells me you always are."

"Remember that, Prince." Jaci grinned.

After a long pause, Gabriel finally sighed and slipped the phone back into his pocket. "Fine. But you're not going in alone."

"Oh, really? You've got some magical friends up your sleeve? You think Isabelle is up for some nefarious spy games? Of course, she reports to your brother, and I'm not sure Dorian would be on board with this, so…"

Gabriel continued to glare at her, those eyes flashing with mischief once more.

And then it arrived, slow but sure—the infamous smirk.

"Wait… you?" Jaci laughed. "A brooding vampire sneaking into a mage club? A *royal* vampire, besides? Are you insane? Everyone will recognize you and our cover will be blown to bits."

"That, my sweet witch," he whispered, the look in his eyes so devastating it made her want to peel off every stupid layer of clothing and fling herself repeatedly in the direction of his dick, "is what glamour magic is for."

Her heart slammed against her ribs, but it wasn't just his overwhelmingly sexy presence that made her so jittery. This was a crazy plan—one that could very well get them both killed, and a whole lot of other people hurt in the process.

And that wasn't the only thing.

There, pulsing beneath the wild beat of her heart, was another truth. Inconvenient, but no longer so easy to ignore.

Despite everything he'd done to her—the kidnapping, the forced labor, the moodiness… Despite everything she'd planned to do to him—the machinations, the lies, the stolen heart…

Maybe Jaci wasn't in such a hurry to see Gabriel eviscerated after all.

"I'm not letting you walk in there unprotected, Jacinda," he said firmly. "We're either going together or not at all."

After a long, heavy sigh, she finally thrust her hand between them, holding his dark gaze. "Partners?"

He glanced down at her hand, eyebrows lifting in surprise, and Jaci waited for the sneer. The indignant huff. The reminder that his *highness* Gabriel Redthorne had associates and servants and a wide array of bootlicking, butt-kissing minions at his beck and call, but not partners.

Especially not ones like her.

But then another crooked grin slid across his lips, obliterating the last of her monumental efforts to hate him, and her vampire captor squeezed her hand, whispering the word into her ear like a promise. "Partners."

CHAPTER TWENTY-SEVEN

The red silk dress slid over Jaci's curves like water, setting off her blue eyes and silvery hair in a way her usual black garments did not. Standing in front of her bathroom mirror, she applied a final coat of mascara, then took a step back, admiring her efforts.

Bubbles fizzed through her stomach—partly because of the danger she was about to throw herself into.

But the rest of those damn bubbles were all for Gabriel. The other night, after they sketched out the plan for Shimmer, he'd walked out of her apartment with no more than a whispered goodnight, leaving her pent up once again, tossing and turning and dreaming about his wicked mouth. They continued to orbit each other at Obsidian, exchanging pleasantries and talk of liquor orders and music selections. But he didn't visit her apartment again. Didn't scold her for walking to work without an escort. Didn't linger as she flirted with her demon contact, feeding him lies about her so-called friend getting excited for Saturday's meeting at Shimmer.

But always, Jaci felt his eyes on her. Watching. Assessing.

Satisfied she looked as hot as she was going to get, she stuffed the makeup into her purse, along with her Tarot cards, phone, and a few other essentials, and headed out to the living area.

She heard him approach. Saw him through the peephole, dashing in his black suit, sky blue shirt, no tie. His dark hair was stylishly messy, and she curled her hands into fists, resisting the urge to whip open the door and run her hands through it.

He stood just outside the threshold. Checked his phone. Smoothed his jacked. And then, for the first time in the history of their odd arrangement, he actually rang the bell.

Jaci gasped. Again the bubbles rose inside her, heating her cheeks.

But when she finally opened the door to greet him, all those fizzy little bubbles popped.

Gabriel didn't say a word as his eyes traveled down the length of her body, then back up, so slowly she thought she might pass out from the torture of it. When he finally met her eyes again, his gaze was completely inscrutable. The only sign that he'd even formed any opinion at all was that telltale tick of his jaw muscle and a deep, heavy sigh that could only mean one thing.

Disappointment.

"Is this… not all right?" Fire spread from Jaci's cheeks

down to her chest, and she ran her hands over the front of her dress, fidgeting. Was it wrinkled? Was it her hair? Had she gone too heavy on the makeup? Too light?

And why the fuck did she suddenly care so much what Prince High Horse thought of her outfit?

"Listen, Prince," she snapped. "It's not like I had a lot of time to throw something together. I just—"

"Jacinda." He stepped into her apartment, sucking up all the air in the room. He placed a hand on her lower back and leaned in close, lips brushing her cheek, his whispered words unleashing a new flurry of bubbles. "You look... bloody hell."

When he finally pulled back, he stared at her again, his gaze dark.

He swallowed hard. "I thought we were waiting on the glamour magic until we got closer? So it would last longer?"

"We are. What do you mean?"

"Nothing. I just... it's..." He closed his eyes and shook his head. When he finally looked at her again, his crooked smirk was back in place, cool and confident once again. "Right, then. Shall we?"

CHAPTER TWENTY-EIGHT

"Why the Moon?" Gabriel asked.

After the nearly endless two-hour drive, they'd parked Gabriel's BMW in a nondescript public garage about a block away from the club, hidden in the shadows on the bottom floor.

The Moon card sat on the center console between them, a spectral vampire woman in a white lace dress and veil, clutching a bloody scythe. A full moon hovered behind her, massive and luminescent, casting its light on the ruins of an ancient cemetery.

"The Moon is often associated with illusion and deception," Jaci said, "which makes it the perfect conduit for glamour magic."

"I'm beginning to think Aiden was right about you." Gabriel laughed, soft and intimate in the small space of the car. "You *are* a bit spooky."

"More than you know. Now hold still, and don't say a word."

"Will it hurt?"

"Only if you don't shut your sexy mouth."

Gabriel bit back another smile, and Jaci got to work, envisioning new appearances for them both, drawing on the energy of the Moon card to bring the illusion to life.

Taking Gabriel's hands in hers, she chanted her spell.

> *By the magic of her light*
> *The moon shall make our shadows bright*
> *When daylight fades and darkness gleams*
> *Nothing now is what it seems*

Silver mist filled the car, enveloping them both in its cool touch. Gabriel's eyes widened in surprise, but true to his word, he didn't speak. Just sat in stunned silence as the mist caressed his skin, slowly transforming him from the sexy vampire she knew to a slightly more understated, slightly more blond man who could easily pass as a mage. When he met her gaze again, his eyes were a soft brown, no trace of the green left.

The mist tingled across Jaci's skin, turning her silver hair dark, her blue eyes hazel, adding new wrinkles around her mouth. When she'd conjured the image in her mind, she'd hoped adding a few years to her face would make her look a little more experienced, a little more wise.

A little less naive.

She *wasn't*, of course, but that didn't matter. Glamour

magic was all about the illusion, and this one was damned convincing.

If not for the familiar glimmer of mischief in Gabriel's brown eyes, she might not have recognized him at all. And judging from the way his jaw hit the floor when the mist finally retreated and revealed her new form, he didn't recognize her either.

Transformation complete, Jaci shoved her purse beneath the passenger seat, taking only the essentials with her—a tube of lipstick and a Tarot card, the Lord of Scepters. It was a fiery image, a horned king brandishing a flaming scepter, his fire-breathing stallion carrying him through a storm of blood and lightning.

Her demon friend had told her the Keepers of the Dark Flame used it as a sort of calling card. She hoped he was right. The fact that he badly wanted to fuck her—and hadn't yet—was the only reason she was trusting his word.

Never underestimate the power of a desperate dick on a feeble mind…

The moon had already risen as Jaci and her "mage" companion walked the short distance to the club, its bright face winking at them over the ocean. The plan was fairly straightforward—while Gabriel waited at the bar in case of trouble, Jaci would charm her way into the meeting, sniff out clues about Renault's whereabouts, and slip away long before the mages suspected a thing.

"Remember, little moonflower," Gabriel said now, stopping just outside the doors. He leaned in close, the low vibration of his murmured warning sending tingles across her scalp. "You can work your mysterious ways on these mages all you'd like, but at the end of the night, you're coming home with *me*."

"Still with the possessiveness, Prince?" Jaci laughed, doing her best to hide his effect on her. "Maybe you should get a cattle prod and brand my tits with your initials—Property of GR. Oh, but wait. You should do them backward, so when I look in the mirror I don't get it mixed up and go home with the wrong dickhead. Reginald Green, perhaps? Renato Goldsmith?"

Gabriel shot her a warning glare, but that mischief still sparkled in his now-brown eyes. "Save the fireworks for the show, witch."

"And you, Prince… Lose the accent. Anything that can peg you as a Redthorne gets left at the door."

"Perhaps I won't speak at all."

Jaci grinned and opened the door, the opulent white light of the club washing over them both. "Even better."

"Welcome to Shimmer, friends." The bartender set two cocktail napkins on the bar, giving the newcomers a quick assessment. Suspicion flickered in his gaze.

Jaci forced her nerves to settle. She had every confidence in her glamour magic. The guy was just doing his job, checking out the unfamiliar faces, trying to decide whether they were friends or foe.

Nothing to worry about.

"What can I get for you?" His eyes were on Gabriel, the barest hint of a challenge in his tone.

Gabriel didn't say a word.

"Not much of a talker, huh?" the bartender said.

"Go easy on my brother," Jaci said with a smile. "Small words, no fast movements." She leaned across the bar and tapped her temple, dropping her voice to a whisper she knew damn well Gabriel could still hear. "Too many hallucination potions in his formative years. Cooked up his brains like scrambled eggs."

"I see." The bartender laughed, his suspicious gaze warming a bit.

Next to her, Gabriel seethed, but didn't deny the charge. That would require speaking, and he was too damned stubborn to cave in now.

She ordered him a vodka tonic, just to piss him off, then flashed another smile at the bartender.

"Reggie here is good with the VT, but I'm actually looking for some friends?" She retrieved the Lord of Scepters card from the front of her dress where she'd strategically stashed it. It was still warm from her body, and when the bartender took it between his fingers, his breath hitched.

A low growl rumbled in Gabriel's chest, but he sipped his drink as if he weren't paying them any attention.

The bartender handed the card back to her, then pointed toward the vast ocean-view windows stretching out behind them. "Follow the windows to the end. The third door on your left—that's where you'll find your friends."

"Thank you." She tucked the card back into her dress, winked at the bartender, then turned back to Gabriel. He circled her wrist with his fingers, his thumb brushing her skin.

"I've got a meeting, *Reggie*," she said. "But I'll be back before you know it. Be good, okay?" She stretched up on her toes and kissed his cheek, barely resisting the urge to pat his head.

Gabriel tightened his hold on her wrist, his whisper so soft she nearly missed it. "Watch yourself, witch. First sign of trouble, I'm taking you out of here."

"*Second* sign," she whispered back. "The first sign will just be me, setting the mood."

CHAPTER TWENTY-NINE

"We've been expecting you, witch." The hooded mage stood before the open door and bowed as if he'd been waiting for her. He didn't even ask to see her card.

"You have?" Jaci asked, putting a little smolder into her voice. It was just as she'd hoped—the loose-lipped demon had already spread the word.

"The Dark Priestess granted us a shared vision. We saw your arrival some days ago."

Dark Priestess? Shared vision? The scent of bullshit was so strong she nearly wrinkled her nose, but Jaci kept her smile firmly in place, nodding a silent acknowledgment as she followed him into the room.

It was nothing special—the kind of meeting room you'd expect in a hotel or restaurant, a long conference table at the center, a whiteboard on one end. Just beyond the uninspiring beige walls, the ocean roared against the shore, but unlike in the main room, there were no windows here to let in the stunning view.

Eleven mages sat around the table, not a witch among them. All of them wore the same black hooded robes, faces hidden mostly in shadow, only their grim mouths showing.

Jaci fought off a shiver. Cults always gave her the fucking creeps.

Two empty chairs waited at the head of the table, and the mage who'd met her at the door directed her to take one. He took the other.

No one spoke.

"So, um, hi. I'm... Demetria," she said, blurting out the first name that came to mind. Sitting there among the somber hooded mages, she felt like an over-caffeinated bimbo in her red dress, her voice too high, her gestures too jittery.

So much for wise and experienced...

"I'm not really sure how this works," she continued, barreling on and hoping like hell something logical would eventually fall out of her mouth. "My friend thought I might be able to find work here."

"Why have you not found work elsewhere?" the head mage asked.

Jaci blew out a sigh of frustration. "Ever since the royal vampires made their power play, it's almost impossible for a girl with my talents to find work."

"What sort of talents?" he asked, his hood falling back to reveal pale gray eyes shining with a dark malevolence— a malevolence she was counting on.

His interest bolstered Jaci's confidence, setting her back on track.

With a sly grin, she shrugged and said, "The kind that would cause a love-and-light mage to run scurrying for the nearest purification bath."

He laughed, then looked at each of the others in turn. They nodded, one at a time.

The cult-vibes crawled across her skin again, and Jaci rubbed her arms.

"You've come to the right place," the mage said. "Why don't you tell me more about the sort of work you're interested in?"

"But... here? With... everyone?" Jaci made a show of looking nervous and mistrustful.

Gray-Eyes nodded sagely. Compassionately. Resting a hand on her shoulder, he said, "None who carry the Dark Flame would betray the trust of a fellow mage. Or, in your case, a witch." He laughed again, his fingers tracing soft circles on her shoulder.

She bit back a gag and forced a grateful smile. "Well, I'm not the biggest fan of the royals, as you might've gathered. I'd heard there might be some... alternative groups working to set things right? To part the veils, rebalance the scales, so to speak?" She held his gaze, hoping he got the metaphor. She was the stranger here—coming out swinging with "Hey, I'm a necromancer and I hear Renault Duchanes is a hell of a guy" was probably a little too ballsy, but that was the message she wanted to get across.

Again, Gray-Eyes took the bait. "There's a vampire

working on some new methods. He might be able to use your expertise."

Jackpot.

"A vampire?" Not wanting to seem too eager, she shrugged and wrinkled her nose. "I was hoping to connect with some mages or witches."

"You don't like vampires?"

"I don't like them, I don't trust them, and I don't appreciate their smug sense of superiority." She furrowed her brow, pretending to mull it over. "I'm willing to compromise for the right opportunity, but the biggest challenge I've found with vampires is they're so damn limiting."

"How do you mean?" he asked.

"Most of the vampires I've worked with over the years have extremely restrictive views on witches. On what we can do for them. My talents are wasted on magical tattoos and the occasional hex. I'm looking for something a bit more…" She flashed a dark grin. "Challenging."

"Renault Duchanes is not your typical bloodsucker. His needs are as exceptional as his vision."

Renault? A visionary?

Wow, this guy is really *drinking the Kool-Aid…*

"Renault Duchanes?" she said, letting her genuine revulsion shine through. "I thought he took the coward's way out after the attack on his old club."

"He's simply gathering new assets. Re-assessing. Rebuilding. He just purchased a warehouse property in Newark," the mage said proudly, defensively, as if he couldn't bear the thought of anyone thinking his friend

Renault was a cowardly loser who'd run away screaming at the first sight of enemy fire.

"And you think I can help with this... rebuilding effort?" she asked, pretending to consider it in earnest.

"Oh, I *know* you can." Those gray eyes assessed her. Dissected her. There was death in those eyes, she realized suddenly. An emptiness she hadn't noticed before.

"In fact," he said, and the rest of the mages rose as one, slowly closing ranks around her. "You can help *all* of us, witch-demon."

Witch-demon...

It was just like the demons outside the hospital that night.

How the fuck did they know?

The mage laughed—a greasy, throaty sound that slithered down her spine, settling in her stomach with cold dread.

She bolted to her feet, but there was nowhere to go. The mages surrounded her, terrifying in their hoods and shadows.

Fuck staying calm. Fuck staying in character. It was time to roast those motherfuckers.

Jaci lifted her hands, calling up her hellfire.

Nothing happened.

She took a deep breath, visualized the fire, the smokey taste in her lungs, the heat, the sparks.

Still, nothing fucking happened.

"Save your energy, witch-demon. You're going to need it." Gray-Eyes dangled a talisman before her eyes, a small silk pouch full of herbs and stones.

Jaci didn't have to ask what was inside. Likely a lock of her hair, stolen from the demon who'd been chatting her up. She knew a proximal binding spell when she saw one.

Shit. It didn't matter that she was half demon. Witch magic, hell magic… whatever spell they'd concocted, it fucking neutered her.

Dread turned to rage, lighting her up inside in a way her neutered hellfire did not.

The mages had fucking played her. The demon had played her. And she'd walked right into it.

Devil's balls, that vampire was making her soft. Stupid.

"Need it for *what*?" she asked, though she suspected she already knew the answer. Group of deranged men, secret rooms, trapped witch. What the fuck else could it be?

The mages only stared at her.

"Seriously, boys?" She folded her arms across her chest and rolled her eyes, as if the weapons of wit and sarcasm were just as effective as hellfire. "Does this whole D&D charade actually work? This is a bar, for fuck's sake! If you're looking for some action, I'm sure there are plenty of witches out there just dying to throw a drink in your face."

"We're not interested in tainting ourselves with your flesh, witch-demon. It's your blood we're after." Gray-Eyes hit a button on the wall, and the conference table—which she now saw was built on a platform attached to a mecha-nized track—slid forward, revealing a dark stairwell that smelled like seaweed and dead fish and undoubtedly led to some dank, unnameable hell Jaci had no interest in exploring.

"Well, thanks for the offer," she said, "but that's a hard pass. I—"

He shoved her down the stairs, the others crowding in close behind. She'd just gotten her footing when the conference table slid back into place, blotting out the last of the light from above, sealing her in a fucking tomb.

"Move." Gray-Eyes—at least, she thought it was him— pushed her down a long hallway, nothing but bare rock walls slick with condensation. The fish smell grew stronger, the sound of the sea louder. After a few twists and turns, they arrived at the mouth of another chamber, no more than a small cave, the interior lit with hundreds of black candles tucked into its grooves and hollows. The floor was bare save for a sigil painted in red and surrounded by a circle of salt.

Pure, undiluted fear shot through her body, turning her legs to Jell-O.

Jaci knew the sight of a ritual sacrifice when she saw one.

And worse, she knew the sigil of hell's oldest succubus.

Her fucking sister.

The other mages filed in behind her, each one choosing a candle, then gathering around the circle. Hoods drawn low, they began to chant in Latin, too softly for Jaci to make out the words.

"What the hell is this?" she breathed, her voice a shaky whisper.

Gray-Eyes shoved her to her knees and fisted her hair, yanking her head backward. Then, pressing an athame to her throat, he said, "Viansa, Dark Priestess of the realms, She Who Carries the Dark Flame, She For Whom the Gates Will Fall, sends her regards."

CHAPTER THIRTY

Over the bloody awful taste of his third vodka tonic, Gabriel nearly missed the scent of trouble. When it finally hit him, he knew it wasn't the mood-setting sort, but the deadly one.

It was his witch. Her blood. Her fear.

Gabriel didn't think twice about breaking his glamour. Didn't spare a single fuck for the bartender, the servers, the other witnesses.

The moment that scent reached his nose, he was gone, blurring past the windows, crashing through the third door on the left, shocked to find the room empty.

Yet she was there. *Somewhere.* The scent of her fear was unmistakable. Sharp and metallic, crashing over him in hot waves.

He felt along the walls in search of another door, snatched the whiteboard from its mount, only to realize the scent was coming from… the conference table?

He tried to flip it. Noticed it was attached to some sort of platform. Wrenched it from the bloody tracks, revealing a dark stairwell beneath. He blurred down it, leaving the tittering mages behind him in the dust, no thought for what he might find there, only that it had better be his witch—alive and fucking unmarred.

No one followed.

The images came to him in flashes.

Hundreds of candles.

Hooded monsters.

His woman on her knees.

Red dress in the dirt.

The gleam of a blade against her pale throat.

And that was the last thing Gabriel consciously processed before everything turned red.

The taste of blood filled his mouth, warm and salty, divine retribution as he tore out the mage's throat with his fangs. The others charged at him, throwing their useless candles, calling up ancient spells, praying to their demons, but Gabriel was too fast for all of them, nothing but a blur of broken spines and severed heads, bodies cleaved, rivers of blood washing away the salt, washing away the sigil, washing away the sin.

Unlike vampires, mages didn't turn to ash and blow away. They died like men, bleeding and shitting, a carcass of rot and ruin left to mark their passing.

When the last one uttered his final cry, Gabriel knelt before his witch on the blood-slick floor. Her glamour had shattered, but once again she wore a mask of blood and violence. One he'd put upon them both.

Wordlessly he picked her up and rose above the filth, carrying her out of that death chamber, holding her tight against his chest as he marched up the stairwell, steadying himself with the rhythmic beat of her heart.

Still gathered in the conference room, the bartender and other staff members gaped, muttering about calling the authorities, calling an exorcist. Gabriel had no idea if they'd known about the cave, known that they were harboring a sacrificial cult. He didn't care. Right now, there was only his witch.

Jacinda trembled in his arms, but it wasn't fear Gabriel sensed. It was rage. So much of it swirling through her, he marveled she could even contain it.

"Tell me what you need, little moonflower," he whispered into her blood-drenched hair. "Name it."

"The… the beach."

He nodded and carried her toward the exit, past the windows stretched out before the sea, past the bar where she'd called him Reggie.

Outside Shimmer, he tightened his hold on her, taking a deep breath of ocean air.

"Prince." She dug her nails into his arms, her eyes full of fire, magic crackling all around her. "*Hurry.*"

CHAPTER THIRTY-ONE

Jaci was a ticking time bomb.

Magic and emotion roiled inside her, none of it hers, all of it looking for a way out. If she didn't get to the shore in thirty seconds, a lot more than a dozen crooked mages would be dying tonight.

"Prince," she demanded, clutching his arm. "*Hurry*."

Without another word, he blurred them to the moonlit beach. She leaped out of his arms, and then she was off, charging straight into the icy water. She sensed her vampire behind her, but she had no time to turn around, no time to warn him.

The sea turned darker than midnight, frothing mad at her intrusion. Waves crashed over her feet, her calves, her thighs, her waist, and still she trudged in deeper, the water so cold it stole the breath from her lungs. But she hadn't gone far enough. Not yet.

"Jacinda! Wait!" Gabriel waded in after her, the wild

waves having little effect on his vampire strength. But when it came to his safety, it wasn't the water she was worried about.

It was her.

She was up to her neck now, water sloshing into her mouth, already tugging at her. Clawing.

The darkness inside her churned and bubbled.

"Jacinda!" he cried out for her, his voice a million miles away, even though he'd waded so close she could see those green eyes flashing, so close she could reach out and touch him.

"I'm sorry," she whispered.

Then Jaci lifted her arms, tilted her head up toward the moon, and opened her mouth.

A vicious roar clawed its way from the depths of her soul, exploding out of her with all that stolen rage, all that darkness. The sea swirled into a vortex, trapping her and Gabriel inside, rising above them in an endless funnel that stretched up toward the stars, suspending them in a tiny circle of calm.

Lightning crackled across the sky, flickering in Gabriel's eyes, one bolt after another chased by thunder so deafening it seemed as if the sky itself would shatter. The ocean continued to churn around them, Jaci's arms trembling with the effort of holding it at bay.

If she let go for even a moment, she and her vampire would be swept out to sea.

Gabriel reached for her face, closer than she realized,

fingers skimming her cheeks. "Come with me," he whispered, almost begging. "I can protect you."

But he didn't understand. She wasn't the one in danger. She held the power of the sea at her command, a tempest that swirled around her, *for* her, crackling with energy and black magic and fury and wrath, all the darkness unleashed by the slaughter of the mages channeled directly into her soul.

She'd never felt so fucking powerful.

But it was too much. Magic, rage, lust, all of it still coursing through her blood, feeding the angry ocean just as the ocean fed it right back to her.

As powerful as it made her feel, she couldn't contain it. She was losing control, arms trembling, her body close to giving out.

Jaci opened her mouth to warn him, but he was already there. *Right* there, drawing her close, holding her against his chest, steadying her.

"Let it go," he murmured in her ear. "Whatever happens, I'm with you. Let it go."

"Gabriel!" she shouted, and all at once her body broke, like a rubber band stretched too far and finally snapping. The water crashed down around them, the sound like the end of all things, the force of it sucking and tearing, demanding, claiming.

But somehow, Gabriel was stronger.

He blurred them out of the tempest, out of the angry sea, a massive tidal wave forming in their wake. They stopped to catch their breath on the shore, rain pelting them, lightning blasting across the sky, and still the vicious water chased them, the wave cresting so high it cast a shadow over the beach.

They saw it at the same time—a rickety structure set off in the distance, no more than an old boathouse perched at the end of an ancient pier. Gabriel swept her into his arms, and the world spun out of focus, the sudden weightlessness making her dizzy. When she opened her eyes again, they were inside the boathouse.

Gabriel pushed her against the wall, shielding her body as the tidal wave crashed over the top, spilling through the cracks, shaking the foundations, calling to the darkness still festering inside her, seeking her, chasing her. The wind howled against the walls, wave after wave crashing, smashing, tearing.

Then, just as quickly as it had risen, the magic inside her fizzled out and the vengeful black water receded, slowly crawling back out to sea.

Gabriel stepped back, taking her face in his hands. "Are you all right?"

Jaci's lungs pulled in deep gasps of wet, salty air, her heart jackhammering, the roar of the ocean still echoing in her ears. The boathouse was dark and musty, rotten with disuse, dripping with cold, wet water.

The bleakness of it, the smallness, the death, the way the darkness ate up all the light… It reminded her of the cave. Of all the dark, dangerous places where she'd been shoved. Tortured. Left to die.

She fisted her trembling hands in his wet shirt, unable to speak.

She was supposed to hate him. Her captor, her tarnished prince, the monster.

The monster who'd seen the darkness inside her and didn't run from it.

The monster who'd tried to save her from herself.

"Gabriel," she breathed, and a new fire rose, a fury that had nothing to do with dead mages and everything to do with his hands. His mouth.

She tore open his wet shirt and ran her hands up his chest, then brought her mouth to his smooth skin, licking his nipple, tasting the salt of the sea. Gabriel shivered, his dick hard, his breath turning ragged.

He lifted her off her feet, and in another dizzying blur, he pushed her against the wall, pinning her with his muscled body, heat cresting between them.

He shoved the dress up around her waist, and she wrapped her legs around his hips, his wet pants cold against her bare thighs. She gripped his shoulders and held on, her heart beating so loudly for his touch, it drowned out the memory of the pounding surf.

Gabriel fisted her hair, his chest pinning her in place, his other hand sliding between her thighs, fingers seeking her wet heat.

Mouth hot and close to her ear, he growled another warning. "*No* one touches you but me. Monster, mage, or man, I will bleed and burn them *all* for you, Jacinda Colburn."

He kissed her neck, her jaw, dragging his lips to hers, and for a minute she thought he might finally kiss her, despite all her earlier refusals. But then he lowered his mouth to her throat instead, her skin searing beneath his ravenous kisses.

Gabriel freed his dick from his pants, shoved aside her underwear, and thrust inside her, filling her, claiming her, stealing her back from the sea that had tried to take her, his touch so hot and fierce and alive it made her weep.

Jaci rode him hard as he held her close, the rain crashing down all around them—the whole damn *world* crashing down. Her back rubbed against the rotten wood, shoulder blades scraped raw from the force of his wild thrusts, the salt of the ocean filling her mouth and nose, mixing with his evergreens-in-winter scent until she felt the rest of the world evaporate, leaving her alone in the wild with her vampire, no secrets between them, no lies, no wars or alliances. No ice.

Only heat. Only passion. Only fire.

It felt as if hours had passed, Gabriel plunging into her again and again, bringing her back, marking her, owning her. When she finally came, it happened in a sudden gasp, a burst of light and heat that snuck up on her, exploding in a storm of chaos. She cried out for him, fingernails digging into his shoulders, and when she drew back and looked into his eyes, in their stormy green depths she saw her nightmares, the darkest evil that haunted her steps. Whether it was a mirror or a premonition or a glimpse into his own private hell, she had no idea, but it bound them in a way she couldn't describe, a way she knew they both recognized but would never speak of.

Gabriel's thrusts intensified, and then he came inside her, trembling and hot, slamming her against the wall, holding her so tight she feared death had finally found her.

CHAPTER THIRTY-TWO

They left the boathouse in silence. The ocean murmured softly now, a petulant child who'd worn herself out with a tantrum. Jaci understood the feeling.

The vampire walked a few paces ahead, Jaci's footing uneven on the cold sand, one foot bare, the other aching in the shoe that had somehow survived the storm.

Gabriel stopped. Turned around and looked at her. Turned back and stared out across the sea, as if its blue depths held the answers he sought.

Jaci couldn't even imagine what he was thinking. Other than a few spells and the time she'd killed those grays near the hospital, she hadn't shown him a whisper of her real magic. Of the darkness that churned inside her. The power.

He'd never even asked. For all the time they'd spent together, all the hours he'd stalked her every move, when it came to her witchcraft—the very magic that made her tick —he'd only ever *demanded*.

Tell me about the grays, witch. Find the source of this curse, witch. Don't get emotional, witch. Don't forget who owns you, witch.

Even now, when she caught up to him on the shore and he spoke for the first time since the boathouse, he said only, *"Duchanes."*

The name burned through his lips, burned into her chest like an accusation.

She shook her head, and he turned toward the sea, pacing the shoreline once more, back and forth, back and forth, muttering to himself. To her. To the sky.

"What the fuck *was* that?" he asked. "The mage... He touched you, and the chanting... The blood and the salt... There was a storm, and you... You just..." He shoved a hand through his wet hair. When he finally stopped pacing, he glared at her, his face tight with confusion and dread.

"What the fuck *was* that?" he repeated. This time, it was only a whisper, but it burned her just the same.

Jaci closed her eyes, the tears already stinging. But what did she expect? Gabriel was a vampire prince, brother to the king she'd helped to poison, the family she'd been working against. He didn't care about her. Why would he?

No one touches you but me. Monster, mage, or man, I will bleed and burn them all *for you, Jacinda Colburn...*

That's all she was to him. All she'd ever be. Gabriel had slaughtered a dozen mages all because they'd touched his property. All because he needed to send another fucking message.

The fact that he'd saved her life? That he'd brought her

back from the darkness? She was a fool to think it had anything to do with her.

"I botched the Duchanes intel," she answered, as if that explained it all.

Gabriel shook his head and sighed, his eyes veiled. "And the storm? The wave?"

Jaci's heart sank. He didn't care what that kind of magic did to her. How it left her buzzing and raw, her insides scraped hollow. All he cared about was that she'd somehow fucked up their simple plan. That the dark mages who damn near sacrificed her life had dared to put their hands on his fucking property.

Anger rose inside, a black and twisted thing that burned all the raw nerves the magic hadn't reached.

Somewhere in the back of her head, a dim voice told her she was misunderstanding. That the shocking intensity of the events they'd witnessed, caused, and endured had rattled them both. That she needed to tell Gabriel about Viansa, about the curse, about her lineage, about her deception.

About all of it.

But in the midst of her quiet rage, her pain, all Jaci could do was attack.

"For all your bloodlust," she spat, "for all the people you've tortured and killed, you have no idea what happens when you unleash so much violence on men, do you?"

Confusion knit his brow, and he gaped at her, completely oblivious.

"Mages are human, and human emotions are energy

forms," she said. "When you killed them, all their anger, their trauma, their fear, their pain—all of it exploded in an instant. And where do you think it went?"

"Jacinda, I don't know what you're talking about. All I know is what I felt. What I scented—your fear. And when I stepped into that cave and saw a mage with a knife at your throat, his hands on you—"

"You slaughtered them!" she shouted, as if he'd somehow forgotten. "And I sucked up all the bad mojo like a Hoover, turning myself into a bomb. That's what you saw. That's what brought the storm and the sea. That's what nearly finished us *both* off."

Gabriel shook his head, incredulous. Disbelieving. She saw it in his eyes—a cold revulsion where moments earlier there had only been heat.

Inexplicably, he reached for her face, but she didn't want his placating touch now. She pulled back, shaking her head.

A flash of guilt and sorrow shot through his eyes, but then he closed himself off again, putting her on the other side of a wall of ice.

In a cool, detached voice, he said simply, "Coming here tonight was a mistake."

Unbelievable.

She shoved his shoulder, damn near ready to rip his heart out right there. "You are *such* an asshole."

She waited for him to call her on it. To wrap her in his arms and pin her down on the beach, claiming her once more in all the filthy, vicious ways only Gabriel could.

But in the end, he only shook his head, a heavy sadness settling over his shoulders.

Oblivious to their arguing, the sea whispered against the shore. Demons and vampires might be immortal, but they had nothing on the timelessness of the tides, endlessly reshaping the world while the rest of them pretended they were anything but a passing fart from the universe.

Salt stung Jaci's eyes. Her legs began to quiver with exhaustion. The insanity of the night had finally caught up with her, and she swayed on her feet.

Gabriel darted forward to catch her—instinct more than heart, most likely—and she pushed him away, straightening herself before she face-planted. Then, because even her wet hair was warmer than the absence of her vampire's touch, she pulled the sopping mess over her shoulders and ducked his gaze.

It was too intense. Too accusatory. And if she didn't know better—too worried.

But Jaci *did* know better. If the vampire was worried, it was only about his precious intel on Renault. The yet-to-be-determined cure on his family curse. All the many grievous mistakes his "property" had made tonight.

Her guilt bubbled up, bleeding into her longing and fear and desperation until she could no longer tell where any of them ended and any began.

Gabriel opened his mouth to speak, but she held up her hand and shook her head. In a soft, defeated whisper, she said, "Take me home, Gabriel."

CHAPTER THIRTY-THREE

Gabriel.

Not Prince. Not vampire. Not dickhead.

Bloody hell, he'd never hated the sound of his given name as much as he did at that moment. It was empty. Distant. A door slamming in his face.

Gabriel.

They got back to the car, and immediately he started it up and cranked the heat. Jacinda was pale and shivering, her lips nearly blue.

Gabriel.

He got out and closed the door. Headed for the trunk. There was some dry cleaning shoved back there, and he tore open the bag, retrieving one of his suit jackets.

Gabriel.

Back in the front seat, he draped the jacket over her shivering form, expecting her to resist. Preparing for the fight. He'd pin her down if had to, tie her up, force her to let him take care of her.

Instead, teeth chattering, she clutched the jacket tighter.

He didn't know whether to be relieved or worried.

"Jacinda," he whispered, a broken man with a head full of confusion and a heart full of thorns.

He reached for her face, but she turned away, tears cutting through the salt staining her cheeks.

Gabriel.

With nothing else to do but drive, he navigated them out of the parking lot and did just that.

"We were right about Renault. He's not far from the city at all."

Gabriel had gotten so used to the muted hum of the tires on the highway that it took him a few beats to realize the words had come from Jacinda's lips and not his imagination.

It was the first she'd spoken since they'd left Montauk an hour ago.

"Jacinda," he breathed, more relieved than he cared to admit. He glanced at her across the dim space of the car, a pair of passing headlights illuminating her face, then throwing her back into darkness. "Are you all right?"

"Working out of a warehouse in Jersey," she continued, as if Gabriel hadn't said a word. "Newark, if the dead mages can be believed. But, you know what they say—"

"Jacinda, please listen. I—"

"Dead men tell no lies." Laughter bubbled up, but it wasn't warm and soft. Wasn't hers.

"I don't care about bloody Duchanes. I only care that you're safe."

"Sure I am." Another laugh, wild and wicked. Crazed. "Safe as any witch who just fled the scene of a mass mage murder—hey! Say that ten times fast! Mass mage murder. Mass murder of magical… mass… mages. Murdering murderous mass—"

"*Jacinda*."

She clamped her mouth shut, but she still wouldn't acknowledge him. Wouldn't even look at him.

He tried again, his voice low and soft. "Jacinda, we need to—"

"*Stop*."

The sharp, sudden command rose up between them like a solid wall, smashing right through him.

In all their arguments, all their threats, all their bloody games, it was the one word she'd never uttered. The word they both knew held more power than a spell to put Gabriel back on ice.

"I can't do this with you anymore, Gabriel," she said, the sound of his name just as grating as it had been on the beach. The crazed laughter was gone, leaving only exhaustion in its wake. "I get that we're not exactly… friends. I don't know *what* we are. And you've got a million reasons not to trust me, which I also get, and there's so much more I—"

"This has nothing to—"

"Let me finish."

He clamped his mouth shut, knowing he didn't have the right words anyway. Hadn't he already proven that on the beach, sending her into a tailspin with his questions? Hurting her more with every word?

"All we're doing is pretending," she continued, the words slicing through his heart. "In your eyes, I'll always be a dark witch. That's what you see first, before you see the woman—the person—beneath. Sure, you're attracted to me. The sex is… fucking epic. And maybe you even *like* me, despite yourself. But you don't know me. Not at all."

He waited a few beats, not wanting to interrupt. When it was clear she had nothing more to add for the moment, he said softly, "But I *do* know you, little moonflower."

She winced, as if the name he'd been calling her for months—the name he whispered even when she wasn't there, just to bring it to his lips—physically hurt.

"The fact that you believe that only proves my point, Gabriel. It means you can *never* know me because you're already so sure you've got it all figured out. There's no room for curiosity. For exploration. There's no room for anything but assumptions and the lies you tell yourself to justify your attraction to me. Because how terrifying would it be if the Redthorne prince—the vampire who *despises* witches—actually had feelings for one?"

His heart thudded, his mouth filling with the taste of salt and bitterness.

She fucking nailed it.

Gabriel *was* terrified. No, maybe he didn't know her. Maybe he never would. Maybe she held secrets so dark, so deep, no man—mortal or immortal—would ever unearth them.

But he *wanted* to know her. Not as a witch. Not as a woman. Not as whatever else lie deep in that fiery heart of hers. But as everything, all of it, all at once, everything that made her the woman who'd set his soul on fire.

"Jacinda, I… You… There's so much, and…" He fumbled for the words again, the right ones this time, the simplest expression of the most complicated fucking thing he'd ever experienced, yet there on the dark stretch of highway, heart jammed in his throat, none of them came.

So he reached for her instead, brushing his knuckles along her jaw, hoping the tenderness in his touch conveyed what his broken speech could not.

Jacinda shook her head and turned away from him, her rejection crashing over him like the ocean that'd nearly drowned them both.

Gabriel waited for her to speak. To shout. To climb over into the driver's side, take his face in her hands, and finally kiss him, confirming that he wasn't alone in this fathomless ocean after all.

But his feisty, fiery, sassy witch was all out of words. All out of everything.

With a heavy sigh, he turned his eyes back to the road, following that cold black ribbon home.

By the time Gabriel pulled into the underground parking garage back home, Jacinda was sound asleep, mouth parted, her breathing deep. After everything they'd been through tonight, Gabriel didn't have the heart to wake her. As carefully as he could, he extracted her from the passenger seat and hauled her close, bumping the door closed with his hip.

She'd asked him to take her home, but she wouldn't be going to her place tonight.

She'd be going to his. His penthouse. His bedroom. His bed.

He wasn't letting her out of his sight.

Up on the fifteenth floor, the moon shone like a jewel through his windows, casting the normally dark gray bedroom in a wash of light. In the quiet peace of his room, it seemed impossible that the moon that hung in the city sky now was the same moon that had watched them cheat death hours earlier.

Gabriel set Jacinda on the bed, gently rolling back the blankets. Her dress was dry now, crusted with salt, but no longer ice cold. He unbuckled and removed the one shoe, the jewels from her neck, the few clips that still clung to her hair. Silvery locks spilled down over her shoulders, unleashing the salty scent of the sea.

Memories crashed over him like waves, dark and dangerous, filling his chest with sharp, jagged fear.

But that's all they were. Memories. Ghosts, just like all the rest. Jacinda was safe. They were both safe. From mages, from magic, from rogue waves, from demons and darkness.

He figured she'd be more comfortable in his shirt, but he didn't think he could take the dress off without unleashing his own desire, a raging thing she'd dug out of the ice and brought back to life with the fire of her touch.

So instead, he left her clothed, pulling the blankets up to her neck and tucking them around her body.

She murmured slightly, but her eyes never opened.

Gabriel sat on the edge of the bed and held her hand, watching her sleep for a long time, fighting back the images of that cave.

Frantically searching for her in the conference room, he could hear her heartbeat. Scent her adrenaline. And when he finally blurred into that cave and found her kneeling on the floor, the mage touching her, he'd seen it—that look. It was the same look he'd seen in every monster he'd ever tormented. In the end, they all knew when death was near. And no matter how terrible they'd been in life, no matter how much death they'd meted out themselves, they always feared its arrival.

And in that moment, when he saw that look in *her* eyes, for the first time in his pathetic immortal life, Gabriel felt that same fear chewing through his fucking heart.

Now, the moon his only witness, he whispered his confession.

"I didn't kill those mages for touching my property, Jacinda." He ran a hand over her hair, looping a fat curl around his fingers. As always, it reminded him of a flower petal, a delicate bloom hiding the thorns beneath. "I did it because you were terrified. Because *I* was terrified. I thought… I thought I was going to lose you."

She didn't respond—didn't even hear him, which was just as well. It was more than he should've said anyway.

He dropped her silky curl.

Brushed the salt and sand from her pillow.

Pressed a tender kiss to her forehead.

And left her to the darkness of dreams he had no business invading.

The wolf shifter answered on the first ring. "What can I do ya for, Little Red?"

"Cole. You up for a bit of scheming, mate?"

He could practically hear the wolf's grin stretching wide.

"Ask not what you can do for your wolf," Cole said with a snicker, "ask what kind of shit your wolf can stir up for you."

"I don't… What the bloody hell are you on about?"

"Sorry. Got into the green a little early tonight. Potent batch, this one. You know, after all these years hiding out like a damned hermit, I think I got me a case of cabin fever. And it ain't actually a fever, if you can believe it, but more like a—"

"For fuck's sake, Cole. I don't speak stoner. Translate."

"All right, Little Red. Here's your translation." Cole

blew into the phone—a plume of marijuana haze, no doubt —then snickered again. "Hell yeah, bloodsucker. Where and when, and how many pairs of pants should I bring?"

"Newark. Soon as you sober up. And make it two pairs, just in case." Gabriel scrubbed a hand over his jaw. "I need you to track down a lead on Duchanes."

CHAPTER THIRTY-FOUR

Dark walls. Dark sheets. Dark thoughts.

Jaci sat up in bed—not hers, she realized. Gabriel's.

The red dress still clung to her, stained and crusted with salt, but the vampire's scent was all around her, cool and crisp, masculine, making her ache for things she was pretty sure she'd destroyed last night.

Memories flooded her mind—the mages, the sea, the boathouse, the arguments, the darkness.

The regret.

There was so much she had to tell him. So much she had to explain. So much she was still trying to understand herself.

The Keepers of the Dark Flame had known who she was from the very start, and they'd intended on sacrificing her —that much was obvious. But had they really communed with Viansa? Was the sacrifice supposed to help her manifest? Had her sister grown so powerful that she could command a legion of dark mages?

And what about Gabriel's curse? And her father's soul?

Jaci closed her eyes, the breath leaving her lungs in a hot rush. She had to tell him. All of it. He'd hate her for it, but he deserved to know. And maybe, even if he couldn't forgive her, he could help her find a way through it.

"Good morning, Jacinda."

She startled at his voice, a soft, sexy rumble in the morning calm. She opened her eyes to find him standing before the windows, dressed in low-slung gray sweatpants and a black T-shirt that clung to his chest.

Her mouth filled with the taste of salt, the memory of her tongue on his smooth skin.

Gabriel smiled. Uncertain. Warm. Terrified.

He held a mug of something hot in his hand, the steam curling up around him.

"Is that tea?" she asked, catching the scent of mint and vanilla.

He joined her on the bed, sitting next to her and handing it over. His eyes were a brighter green today, no touch of last night's storm, only a slight frost clinging to the edges. She gazed into them now, trying desperately to remember why the fuck she'd ever hated him. How it was even possible.

"I'm afraid we're going to have to start rationing the mint," he said. "Last time, I bought out the bodega's entire supply. The owner accused me of trying to impress a woman."

Jaci rolled her eyes and laughed. "And what did you tell him?"

"I told him you're *not* a woman, you're a witch, and therefore infinitely more difficult to impress."

"Did he believe you?"

"Mortal men never do. That's the fun of it." He cupped the back of her head, touching his forehead to hers, his words a teasing whisper against her lips. "You're my dirty little secret."

Jaci let out a soft hum, but she knew Gabriel Redthorne's *real* secret now.

He wasn't the cold, ruthless vampire he pretended to be. Deep down, beneath all the ice, was a core of molten heat that had awakened her and challenged her and saved her in ways she was still trying to understand. To accept. To allow.

"I'm sorry about last night," she blurted out, unable to accept another moment of this peace, this warmth. It felt like borrowed time, and the thought of losing it already filled her heart with a deep well of sadness. "I wish I could've gotten more information about Renault, but things went sideways fast, and I just... It all fell apart."

Gabriel shook his head. "None of it was your fault. I should've gone in with you. I should've..." His jaw clenched tight, and he sighed through his nose. "Anyway, you *did* get information. Good information. Cole is already looking into recent warehouse purchases in and around Newark. If the mage was right about that, we might be able to track the exact location."

"And then what?"

"Cole will let us know, and we'll make a plan."

Us. We'll. The words were a balm on her aching heart. Temporary, but soothing nevertheless.

"Jacinda, last night... *I'm* the one who should be apologizing. I was so confused about what happened, about the magic, the storm. Everything just... It all came out wrong. I made a right mess of things. I had so many questions—I *still* have questions—and I don't know how to ask them."

He fingered a lock of her hair, tugging the curl straight, then releasing it, watching it spring back up, fascinated.

"What *was* that?" he whispered, and she knew he wasn't talking about her hair.

"You're familiar with empathic witches?"

Gabriel nodded. "Like Isabelle."

"Think of my magic sort of like that. Not empathic, but empathic-adjacent."

"What do you mean?"

"Empathic witches sense emotions. The more sensitive the witch, the greater that sense becomes. Some witches can use their gift to understand people, to help them. Others have trouble knowing whether something they're feeling is their own emotion or someone else's—they basically take on the emotions of everyone around them." She sipped her tea, letting it warm her from the inside out. "A witch like Isabelle, with all her experience, probably doesn't struggle with it so much. But the way my empathic magic works is different. Even with time and experience, I *can't* separate myself from it. It's not possible."

"So when you sense emotion, you always feel it as if it's your own?"

"I don't *sense* emotions. I *absorb* them. Fully. I know they're not mine, but I can't stop them from invading my body and making it react as if they *are* mine. It only happens with humans—not other supernaturals—but that's still a lot to deal with."

"It's constant? You're always picking up human emotion?"

Jaci nodded. "Normally, I can ground myself and the energy just dissipates. But there were so many mages last night, the moment so intense, and when you killed them, their emotions—the darkest, worst parts—had nowhere else to go. They filled me right up, fused with my magic, and turned me into a bomb. That's what you saw on the beach. I detonated."

"Bloody hell, Jacinda. Has anything like that ever happened before?" His eyes filled with terror. With wonder. With compassion.

Jaci lowered her gaze, unable to bear the weight of his. The sincerity. She couldn't answer him. Didn't want to go back there, back to hell and the vicious experiments her so-called family had put her through.

Thankfully, Gabriel didn't push.

"That was smart thinking," he said, looping another curl around his finger. "About the beach."

"There are few things that can contain energy like that without causing mass chaos. Even the ocean had a hard time with it, but in the end, I knew she'd be able to handle it."

"Just like you." Gabriel smiled, soft and warm. Then, his voice falling to a whisper, "I still don't know the right thing to say, Jace. But when I see the pain in your eyes, I want to erase it."

Jace. The casualness. The comfort. She wanted to wrap herself in it, to fall asleep in its arms knowing it would still be there when she woke up again.

But she'd given up on those kinds of fairy tales long ago.

One sweet morning with tea in bed and his hands in her hair didn't change that.

Jaci set her mug on the nightstand and forced a smile. "Don't take this the wrong way, Prince, but... Thanks for—you know. Saving me. *Again.*"

Gabriel didn't smile. Didn't laugh. He shook his head, guilt filling his eyes. "I never should've allowed you to put yourself in that situation in the first place. I should've known better than to trust a demon."

"That's on me."

"No, it isn't." He cupped her face, his brow creased with pain and regret, his touch as soft as a feather. "I warned you I would destroy you, little moonflower."

His voice was a broken whisper, but whatever Gabriel felt guilty about, whatever pain he'd inadvertently caused her last night, whatever pain he thought he could've prevented, all of it paled in comparison.

Jaci—vile, wicked, evil—had actually considered carving out his heart. That was her grand plan. The Hail Mary that would somehow save her father, consequences be damned.

The image flashed through her mind's eye, Gabriel's heart beating in her hand, dark blood running between her fingers, warm and wet. His body, resurrected before it turned to ash, an empty husk staring back at her with vacant eyes, his own bloody heart calling to the unfathomable hunger inside him.

Deep down, she knew she couldn't have gone through with it—not even in the vampire's most hateful moments. Not when push came to shove, and blade came to flesh.

But the fact that she'd even considered it? It filled her with a shame so dark and heavy, it nearly drove Jaci to her knees.

Not because she was a good person. Not because she'd seen the error of her ways. Not because she wanted redemption and forgiveness for a sin she hadn't even confessed.

But because somehow, through all the threats and fights and teasing and touching and heat, through all the risks, through all the dark magic and epic, life-saving heroics, Jaci had fallen in love with the vampire prince.

The realization drew her up short, making her gasp, making her ache, making her hollow.

"Tell me what you're thinking, little moonflower," he whispered.

Her tears blurred him into two versions, her dark

vampire captor and her white knight, both of them filling her heart.

"Kiss me," she breathed.

Gabriel's eyes widened, his sharp intake of breath audible. He knew what it meant—so much more than a kiss, so much more than a dare—but Jaci was done pretending. Maybe it would all crash and burn the moment she told him about Viansa and the curse, about who she really was, all the secrets he thought he already knew. Hell, maybe it would crash and burn right now, before their lips even touched. Maybe he'd turn his back on her, shore up those walls of ice, and never let her find another crack.

But just as he'd slaughtered her enemies, just as he'd waded into the sea to save her, those were the risks she was willing to take.

Trembling before him, Jaci held his gaze, awaiting his answer, terrified of what it would mean if he kissed her. If he didn't.

Finally, after a thousand lifetimes, Gabriel cradled her face, his touch kind and gentle and warm, as if he were afraid she was a bubble he might burst. The pad of his thumb arced back and forth across her lips, and she sighed at the intimacy of his touch. She'd never felt anything so soft, so erotic. Never allowed it.

"Tell me to stop, Jacinda Colburn," he whispered, his eyes full of some new fire. Gone was the frost, replaced now with the tender greens and golds of new spring buds after a lush rain.

Tears spilled down her cheeks, but Jaci smiled. In a

trembling voice, she said, "Don't stop. Just kiss me, Gabriel Redthorne."

He brought his mouth to hers, lips brushing lips, soft as a delicate breeze, teasing, hopeful. He drew her closer, sliding his hands into her hair and finally, blissfully, beautifully, pressing his mouth to hers.

Jaci's eyelids fluttered closed, and she parted her lips, drinking in his warm breath, shivering at the gentle exploration of his tongue, hot and velvet-soft, tracing her lips, then slipping between them, tasting and teasing.

A low, desirous moan rumbled through his chest, and she opened wider. Gabriel deepened their kiss, his tender teases quickly growing urgent, hot, devouring. Pleasure arced down her chest, down to her belly, down to her core. Gabriel's fingers tightened in her hair, and he guided her back against the pillows, slowly climbing on top of her, never once breaking the kiss.

When their mouths finally parted for breath, Gabriel looked bewildered, his eyes glassy, a smile curving his lush mouth. He was hard for her, his dick pressing urgently against her thigh, making her shamelessly wet.

"What are *you* thinking, Prince?" she teased, tears still brimming in her eyes. Happiness. Fear. Shame. New love. So much she couldn't contain it.

"I'm thinking about extending that overdue invitation into my bed." His smile turned devious, and his earlier threat whispered through her mind.

If I ever invite you into my bed, the things I'll do to you there will not be quick. They'll not be polite. And you can call it a one-

and-done deal all you'd like, but I promise you, witch. The only word you'll be uttering when I'm through with you is more…

Desire flooded her body, her nerves on fire, her breath shallow. She reached for his face, running her fingers along his stubbled jaw. She'd never wanted anything so badly.

But she couldn't have it. Not until she told him all the things she needed to say.

"Gabriel, I—"

His eyes went wide. Pained. He collapsed on her chest, a heavy weight crushing her into the mattress.

"Gabriel?" She pushed against him. He didn't move. Didn't speak.

"Prince?" she tried once more. Desperate. Terrified.

And then…

A sound from across the room. A flicker of light. A change in the air currents.

Panic rushed through her body, tingling in her limbs, making her hot and prickly. Jaci slid out from beneath him and lifted her head.

And there, just beyond the foot of his bed, an old foe slithered from the shadows, her blue eyes bright, her black-painted mouth twisted into the scowl that had haunted Jaci's nightmares for her entire life.

"Hello, Lab Rat," the cruel mouth said, stretching into a grin. "Sorry to interrupt this portrait of domestic bliss, but… Wait! Actually, I'm not sorry at all." She hopped onto the bed at Jaci's feet, bouncing on her knees like a child. "Didn't I tell you the reunion would be epic?"

CHAPTER THIRTY-FIVE

The doors to Obsidian opened, ushering in the cold December wind and giving Gabriel a glimpse of the wasteland outside. The skeletal remains of St. Mark's Place jutted awkwardly from the ground, snow collecting on their rusty bones. Silence whispered across the barren streets.

From his seat at the bar, he turned toward the newcomer, hope rising.

Jacinda?

But… no. It wasn't his witch who'd finally found her way home. It was a woman he'd never seen before—tight gold dress, glossy black hair, a painted smile to match. The dark lipstick made her teeth look exceptionally white. Exceptionally sharp.

She wasn't human, wasn't a witch, wasn't a vampire or shifter. He couldn't quite get a read on her.

"We're closed," he said gruffly. He went back to his glass of bourbon, but the liquor transformed from auburn to black before his eyes. When he tried to drink it, it turned to ash on his tongue.

"Please, Mr. Redthorne. It's so cold out there. So lonely. I just need a warm place to wait for my ride. Maybe a drink?"

Gabriel scoffed, spitting the ashes from between his lips. If she thought her painted smile would work on him, she was in for an even colder night than the one she'd left outside those doors.

But he didn't see the harm in letting her have a drink.

He went around behind the bar and grabbed two clean glasses. Opened a fresh bottle of bourbon and poured one for each of them, not bothering to ask what she wanted.

The scent of the alcohol hit him, familiar. It was the right color too, no ash. But… something was wrong.

Obsidian was his club, but why was it closed? Where were the patrons? Where were the bartenders? The staff? The one with the silver hair… What was her name?

"Something wrong, friend?" the woman asked, so close to him now he could feel the heat rising off her body. She smelled like fire. Felt like it too.

Gabriel blinked, his vision blurring, then righting again. "Do I… know you?"

"Not yet." Again with the black smile. "But I'd like very much to change that. Wouldn't you?"

Gabriel scratched his jaw, considering. Would he? How long had he been sitting here? Where were his brothers? His associates? That woman with the silver hair? Jennifer? Was that her name? Jeanette?

The raven-haired woman lifted her glass, touched it to the rim of his. "To new friends."

Gabriel nodded and took a drink. It burned, just as he thought it should.

She downed hers in a few quick gulps. Then, leaning in close, "Maybe I'll stay for another. No one wants to be alone on a night like this."

Gabriel nodded. He couldn't argue with that.

He poured another round, then another after that. In the darkest recesses of his memory, something scratched, a trapped thing trying desperately to free itself, but if he was supposed to do something that day, or meet someone, it was too late now.

He turned toward the woman. Heat made her image waver. Made him thirsty. Made him tired.

"You look like you could use a hug," she said, reaching for him.

"Why not?" Gabriel leaned into her embrace. She felt hot and suffocating, but suddenly he didn't have the strength to resist her. To wonder if he even should.

"That's better, isn't it?"

Gabriel nodded. It *was* better. Soft. Warm. Tired.

She threaded her fingers into his hair, stroking him. Humming. Sounded like an old song his mother used to sing.

The woman tilted his head back. Leaned in close.

Her black lips grazed his mouth, then pressed closer…

No. The kiss was all wrong.

Everything about this was wrong.

Shaking out of the lull, he wrapped a hand around her throat and shoved her away, holding her at arm's length.

"Who the bloody hell are you?" he demanded.

Her mouth stretched into a wide, hideous grin, her eyes turning demon black. "I'm your worst nightmare, vampire prince. And I've come to—"

Hellfire exploded around her, enveloping her in a silver flame that reeked of brimstone.

Gabriel released her and leaped backward, slipping and smacking his head on the bar, landing on the floor with a crash, everything spinning.

When the room finally righted itself, the bar vanished.

Gabriel was back in the penthouse, sprawled face-down on his bed, his head throbbing.

Just a nightmare. A hallucination.

He rolled over onto his back. Sat up slowly.

And watched the nightmare come to life.

Across the bedroom, the woman with the raven hair leaned back against the wall with her hands raised in mock surrender, a cruel laugh cutting through the ringing in his head.

Just a few feet away, Jacinda held her hands out, a ball of silver hellfire roiling between them.

Hellfire she controlled.

Hellfire she conjured.

Gabriel sucked in a breath. Squeezed his eyes shut. Opened them.

The hellfire grew brighter at Jacinda's command.

Gabriel tried to fight the logic, tried to mute the alarm clanging in his head.

But it was no use.

He watched in stunned horror, his heart shattering, his head spinning, his life spiraling.

The woman—the one he was pretty damn sure he'd fallen for—wasn't just a witch.

She was a fucking demon.

CHAPTER THIRTY-SIX

Viansa's laughter filled the bedroom, crawling across Jaci's skin like fire ants.

"The Lab Rat has sharpened her teeth!" The bitch sneered at her, taunting her with wild, crazy eyes. Eyes the same shade of blue as Jaci's. The same as their demon mother's.

"Stay out of his head!" Jaci ordered. The hellfire in her hands grew brighter. The tips of Viansa's hair were already singed, her gold dress stained black. But the attack hadn't hurt her. *Nothing* could hurt her.

"Don't tell me you're carrying a torch for that bloodsucker." Viansa rolled her eyes, as if the very idea were a major inconvenience to her plans. "Honestly, Jay. Drop the fire. I'm your sister, for devil's sake!"

"Half-sister, and I think I'll keep it, thanks."

Another eye-roll. A huff that made her sound fifteen

years old instead of fifteen millennia old. "Oh, look! Boyfriend's awake! That's... unexpected."

Jaci didn't dare take her eyes off the demon. In her peripheral vision, she caught the movement on Gabriel's bed. Heard the groan of confusion as he came to consciousness.

"You actually listened to me?" Jaci asked, wondering what the trick was.

"Hell no. Boyfriend broke free all on his own."

Jaci gasped. It should've been impossible.

As a succubus—an extremely powerful one at that—Viansa could trap people in her thrall, wreaking havoc on their minds while their bodies sat in stasis. Since Viansa was the one who'd bound the Redthorne curse, she had a direct connection to Gabriel through his blood—like a GPS signal she could theoretically follow anywhere. It would also enable her to dig that much deeper into Gabriel's head.

What Jaci couldn't figure out was how the fuck she'd finally manifested here, and how Gabriel managed to break the thrall.

As far as she knew, no one had ever done it before.

Viansa knew it too. And though she was doing her best to hide it, it fucking terrified her.

"Anyway," she said with a dramatic sigh, "I brought a message from Demetria. She really wanted to be here herself, but she couldn't. Got a little... tied up."

Viansa reached into her purse and hauled out something purple, tossing it at Jaci's feet.

It glistened up at her, sending her stomach into free fall.

A tangle of purple hair torn from a scalp, gruesome and bloodied.

It's a lie. It has to be a lie. If Meech were dead, I'd know it. For sure I'd know it…

Swallowing her fear, Jaci repeated the mantra in her head, keeping her hellfire hot.

If there was a single bright side to this monumental shit-show, it was that the bitch was now topside, which meant Jaci had a chance of binding her.

Assuming she could survive the next five minutes.

Assuming she could find another spell.

Assuming a lot of things.

"Aww, what's wrong, baby?" Viansa made an exaggerated pout. "Did my unexpected arrival throw a kink in your plans to ride off into the sunset with your vampire boy-toy? I mean, I get it." She glanced at Gabriel, still struggling to get out of bed, and let out a low whistle. "I would *absolutely* hop on that cock if he were mine. Actually, what am I saying? He *is* mine!"

She stripped out of her dress and sauntered toward the bed, but Jaci was faster, hitting her with a blast of hellfire that sent her sprawling.

Bad idea.

Viansa was on her feet in a heartbeat, her own hellfire flickering black in her hands as she charged toward Jaci with a look of vengeance Jaci knew all too well.

But once again—impossible, beautiful, jaw-dropping—Gabriel was faster. He blurred between them, slamming Viansa into the wall so hard the plaster cracked.

"You won't touch her again, *demon*." Gabriel pinned her by the throat, her feet six inches off the ground, her naked flesh glimmering with a sheen of sweat.

"Mmm, you like it rough, vampire? I can teach you a thing or two."

"Leave him alone," Jaci said, ready to lay into her with another fireball, but Gabriel pushed her back, keeping her tucked behind him with one hand, the other still wrapped around Viansa's throat.

"How the fuck did you get here, demon?" he demanded.

Still pinned to the wall, Viansa shrugged her shoulders and let out a high, false giggle. "Lab Rat didn't tell you? Jacinda! Secrets and lies aren't the way to start a new relationship!"

Gabriel turned to look at Jaci over his shoulder, but she didn't have the answers, only speculation. Was it the mages? Some other scheme her sister had been cooking up? Something to do with Meech?

"She summoned me, silly!" Viansa said. "A splash of your blood, a few Tarot cards, demonology 101 really. I mean, there were some other steps after that—a few human sacrifices, a bunch of dark mages doing my bidding, a vampire who can't say no—but it all started with your blood. Poetic, right?"

Gabriel dropped her, letting her hit the ground. "Explain."

Viansa laughed, sending shivers down Jaci's spine. "Nah, I think I'll let her do it."

Gabriel turned to look at Jaci again. The moment he took his eyes of Viansa, the succubus charged at Jaci, knocking her to the floor.

Her vampire reacted fast, but this time, Viansa was faster. The bitch hadn't even moved, hadn't even glanced in his direction, but suddenly Gabriel was immobilized, dropping to the floor in a graceless heap.

"Let him go, Viansa," Jaci demanded, scrambling to her feet. "You're here for me. So fucking end it. End it!" Her voice shook with rage, with all the things Viansa had put her through, with all the terrors she had yet to unleash. Jaci couldn't beat her here, not without the right magic. Not without backup. *"End it!"*

Viansa glanced at her red-lacquered fingernails and shrugged as if Jaci had just asked her what they should order for lunch.

After an endless sigh, she finally looked up and said, "You know, it's the funniest thing, Jay. All this time, I had a plan. Get topside. Turn boy-toy's mind to mush and fuck him until he turned to ash, then do the same thing to every one of his royal brothers and their sirelings, then drag you back to hell and spend the rest of eternity repaying you for leaving me."

"Leaving you? Viansa, you—"

"But now that I'm here," she said, "I think I might hang out a bit. Check out the sights, see what I've been missing out on all these millennia." She picked up her dress, slithered back into it. Did a little shimmy. "Damn, it feels so good to stretch my legs."

"Hang out?" Jaci asked, incredulous. Her half-sister was already headed for the door. "*Hang out*? Check out the sights? Viansa, where the *fuck* are you going?"

"Nowhere. Everywhere. I don't know." She turned to flash one more cruel grin, dropping her voice to a menacing whisper. "But I'm sure we'll catch up again *real* soon. Ta!"

The moment she was gone, the thrall broke, and Gabriel got to his feet.

Jaci ran to him, reached for him, but he held out a hand to stop her.

And in that one gesture, that one small movement, Jaci saw the end of it all.

"The demon said she'd let you explain," Gabriel said, cold and detached. "I suggest, little moonflower, you make it compelling."

It took Jaci twenty minutes of pacing the bedroom before she could form a coherent sentence, and when she finally rediscovered the ability to speak, the first thing that fell out of her mouth was, "Viansa is a succubus."

"A demon," Gabriel clarified.

"Sort of."

"Sort of?"

"There are common demons—like Rogozin and his crew. Dark essences who possess human vessels. Then there are *demons*. Like, O.G. demons whose essences are bound to hell. They don't need vessels because they can take any form they want. Viansa's always favored that one."

"How long is always?"

Jaci blew out a breath. "Near as I can tell, somewhere between twelve and twenty thousand years." She met Gabriel's stern glare. "She's the first succubus, Gabriel."

"How the fuck do you know her? Whose purple hair is that? What did she mean, you summoned her? What the *fuck* did she do to my mind?" He shoved a hand through his hair, his questions coming at her rapid-fire, anger rolling off him in waves.

It was no less than Jaci deserved. In fact, she deserved worse. Way worse. And she was pretty damn sure she was going to get it.

Still, she owed him answers. As many as she could give him.

"Viansa has the power to control thoughts. She can make a man relive his worst nightmares, bring his fears to life, or create a complete illusion in your mind. It immobilizes you while it's happening, and your mind has no idea the illusion isn't real."

"For fuck's sake. How did she get here?"

"I'm not sure. She's an original hellbound demon. She wasn't supposed to be able to manifest here."

"She said you summoned her. With my blood."

"If that's true, it was unintentional. Gabriel, I..." Jaci dropped onto the edge of the bed, no longer possessing the strength to stand on her own two feet. "Viansa is the demon who bound your curse."

The look in his eyes was murderous. "How long have you known?"

She blinked. Sucked in a breath. Tried to gather her thoughts. Her strength.

"*How long*?" he shouted.

"Since… since that day I did the blood spell in my apartment. She possessed your body, just for a minute, and I knew it had to be because of the connection to the curse. It was the only explanation."

"And you recognized her?"

Jaci nodded.

He lowered his head and sighed, still trying to piece together the puzzle, to find the explanation that would make any of this craziness sound real.

"How the *bloody* hell do you know her?" At this, he looked up, captured her gaze. She could see the gears turning behind his eyes, keys sliding in and out of locks, pieces filling in the holes.

But she held the final pieces.

"Viansa is my sister. Half, anyway."

"Your sister. That means you…" He shook his head as if he couldn't bear to let the thought stick. The truth. "I saw your hellfire. I saw you cast it. You… You're… You're a…"

This was it. The last piece. The final stake through the heart of whatever relationship she'd stupidly thought they could have.

"I'm a hybrid, Gabriel. Half witch, half demon. Created in hell, born of an unholy union between a drugged mage and a vicious demonic bitch, bred for one purpose."

Time stopped.

Heartbeats stopped.

Lungs stopped filling, blood stopped moving, clouds stopped passing before the sun.

And in those bleak, brutal moments—far too late, far too feeble—Jaci tried to make her full confession.

She told him about her life in hell, how her mother and sister had tortured her, experimented on her, forced her to perform like a circus monkey, beating and starving her when she couldn't produce the desired results.

She told him how, when she turned eighteen and still hadn't manifested the dark powers her mother had expected, the demon bitch had planned to kill her.

She told him how her father had bargained his own soul away to set her free. Told him how she'd brought his body back from the dead, spending the last seven years searching for a way to save him.

And then she told him the worst of it.

The Redthorne curse. Her discoveries. The resurrection. The heart.

Vita mutatur, non tollitur.

Life is changed, not taken away. The dead shall rise. The dead shall return.

Three of Knives, Death, Ten of Knives.

Blood and vengeance. A severed heart.

Death. Resurrection.

Blood on the sheets. Betrayal.

The dead shall rise. The dead shall return.

Vita mutatur, non tollitur.

Blood on the roses. Blood on the sheets. Blood on the snow. Blood on the grave.

The dead shall rise. The dead shall return.

All of it spilled from her, a torrent of pain and deception, of fear. Of sorrow. Every word seemed to slice a little deeper into Gabriel's chest, to put another block of ice around his heart, to suck the new warmth from his eyes until there was nothing left but barren snow.

Finally, drained of all her words, every confession wrung free, every fear laid bare, she waited for her vampire to roar. To lay waste to the bedroom. To kill her.

But in the end, all he said was, "*What* purpose, witch?"

Witch. Cold as frostbite. Cold as death.

"For what purpose was the hybrid hellspawn bred?" He looked right through her, right past her.

Jaci rubbed the chill from her arms, her heart bleeding, her soul in tatters. "Destroying vampires and ushering in the eternal rule of hell on Earth."

CHAPTER THIRTY-SEVEN

Gabriel's world had never felt so small. So dark.

A demon. A bloody demon. One who'd lied to him, manipulated him, and used him to summon an even greater danger to their world, setting an ancient succubus loose on a city whose residents had no way to protect themselves and needed very little encouragement toward abject depravity.

And that wasn't even the worst of it.

Jacinda Colburn, his silver-haired little moonflower, his witch, his partner, the woman who'd set his soul on fire, had been plotting to turn him into an undead ghoul. To carve out his heart and leave his body to waste away, feeling every bit of flesh rotting off the bone, every sunbaked blister, every hollow pang of desperate, unquenchable thirst until the slow march of time finally trampled him into dust.

"It didn't work, Gabriel," the witch—rather, the *demon*—

said now. "I was a complete failure in their eyes, and they almost killed me, but then my father made the deal and sacrificed himself to—"

"Don't." He held up a hand, unable to hear another word out of her filthy, lying, conniving mouth. "Don't speak to me of fathers and sacrifices. Any man foolish enough to bed a demon deserves what he gets."

Including Gabriel, he realized. And he'd be paying for *that* mistake for a long time.

"My father was innocent," she said.

"My father was not. But he did teach me a hard lesson. Fucking gutted me at the time, but it stayed with me, a shadow in the corner of every nightmare. And now, two hundred fifty-odd years after that wretched, soul-crushing day, it comes back to taunt me." He took a step toward her. Another. "Do you want to know what it was, little moonflower?"

She shook her head, tears gathering in her eyes, but Gabriel was done catering to her emotions. Done carving out his own damn heart and handing it over like a fucking whipped dog.

"My father was a scientist, above all else," he said. "Constantly curious, constantly experimenting. *Dissecting*."

The word made her shiver, her face turning deathly pale, but Gabriel pressed on.

"His work drove him to madness. To isolation. Dorian and the others dealt with it better than I—always off on one adventure or another, leaving me behind. For most of my childhood, my only friend was a blind, deaf goat we'd aptly named Nuisance, for all the trouble she caused. It was a wonder my father hadn't sold her off for meat years earlier."

Gabriel shook his head, a sad smile touching his lips as he remembered the damn goat, chewing through the leather tack in the stables, kicking down her stall door, following Gabriel like a shadow, sticking her nose in all the myriad places it didn't belong.

"One day, when I was maybe seven years of age, I'd been left home alone, forgotten in one of the usual chaotic departures of a family trip to London. I was tired of talking to that deaf goat and decided I needed to find a more stimulating activity. Something that might impress my father."

"Gabriel, you don't have to tell me this. I—"

"My siblings and I were expressly forbidden from entering his study, but on this day, I convinced myself he'd forgive me once he realized why I'd done it. Once he saw the budding genius in his midst. Alone in that big, empty manor, I broke into his study, retrieved his medical bag, and scanned the shelves of preserved organs and fetuses, looking for inspiration."

The memories came back to him easily—the smell of the formaldehyde, the weight of those heavy glass jars, the sound like a wet slab of meat as he removed the fetal pig from the jar and dropped it on a piece of newsprint.

An operation, he'd called it. Cutting and slicing, rearranging, making careful notes and sketches just as he'd seen his father do a hundred times as he and his brothers took turns gazing through the keyhole, desperate for the barest glimpse of the man they hardly even knew.

Jacinda's face grew paler with every word, but Gabriel wouldn't stop. Not until he got to the lesson.

"I was so convinced my father would be proud, impressed even, that when he returned from the trip and responded to my operation with silence, with nothing but a graying of the face and a shake of his head, I was heartbroken and confused. Perhaps something had happened in London, I thought, to sour his mood. Perhaps he and my mother were locked in another of their infamous battles.

"Three days and nights passed, and I didn't see my father. Not once. On the fourth night, I awoke to a terrible screaming—the sound of one of our mares in labor. Her shrieks terrified me. I hoped she and the colt would survive the night."

Gabriel closed his eyes and took a deep breath, the memory of those screams rattling him even now.

"The next morning, I went outside to check on the mare, to see if I might be allowed to name the new colt. But instead of a baby horse, I found my father, standing in the very last stall, six inches of blood-soaked hay covering his boots. Nuisance lay slaughtered at his feet."

Jacinda gasped, and Gabriel opened his eyes, forcing the ice back into his tone, back into his heart, shutting it all down once more.

"My father *eviscerated* that poor animal, Jacinda. An animal with no vision, no hearing, no concept of what evil had befallen her. And that man waited through the night, through the dawn for me to come. When I looked up into his face, there was no anger, no rage, no sign of a crazed murderer. Only the cold face of my father, a man I thought to impress with my cleverness. He handed me a shovel and ordered me to clean up the mess as calmly as if I'd spilled a glass of water at dinner.

"He watched me shovel up her remains, bits and pieces of the only friend I had. Watched me scrub out the stall, my hands raw, her blood staining my clothes. And for every whimper or tear that fell, he lashed me with a saddle strap, the scars ensuring I'd never forget the lesson."

In the shocked silence that followed the telling, Gabriel heard Jacinda's heartbeat. Heard her breath. Heard the echo of the old man's voice, still haunting him. *Taunting* him.

To be weak is to be a victim, Gabriel. You find me cruel, perhaps, but strength comes from learning to control your emotions. To hide your weaknesses until they become so dark and small, they simply vanish...

That was the day Gabriel learned how to turn his heart to ice.

Later, when his brothers asked why he was limping, when they asked what had happened to Nuisance, when they asked why their father had locked them all out of the stables that day, he lied, swiftly and easily, telling them only that he'd fallen and she'd died of old age.

And later still, when he crept out to the ditch behind the stables and found her remains in the hole where he'd left her, flesh and bones crawling with flies, he buried her properly, and with every shovel full of dirt, he found he could no longer cry.

That he no longer cared.

His emotions—his weaknesses—had truly vanished, just like his father had promised. And in the void left behind, a new power swept through him. A coldness no one could touch. A wildness that set him free.

Now, he gripped the demon's jaw, the menace in his touch matching the menace in his heart, and repeated his father's final words, the harshest words, wishing he'd heeded them sooner.

"Be *merciless*, Gabriel Redthorne, or you will find yourself at the mercy."

The old king's voice cut across the centuries, the continents, trembling in Gabriel's own voice now, in his touch, in the eyes of the woman who'd betrayed him.

"What happened between us was the result of a distraction," Gabriel said. "A weakness I nearly let drive me to ruin." He released her jaw. Turned his back on her. "It won't happen again."

He felt the ache of her loss, heard the hard thump of her heart. His own echoed the same miserable beat, but he ignored it. Shoved it down. Wrapped it in ice, just like his father had taught him.

"But… Viansa," she said, desperation leaking into her voice. "We can't let her run wild here, Gabriel. She'll destroy the city, and then she'll move on to an even bigger target. She won't quit until she figures out how to break down the hell gates for good. We have to stop her."

"You're right. We do." He turned to face her once more. "We will."

Seconds passed. Maybe more. Hearts thudded. Outside, a car horn blared. A front door slammed. Someone dropped a thing made of glass, shattering it on the pavement, and two children began to wail.

"Partners?" Jacinda held out her hand. It was no more than a whisper, that one-word question, but the fresh hope in her eyes—the bloody *audacity* of it—was deafening.

The children wailed. The goat's cries echoed in his mind. The smell of the blood. The wet thwack of the shovel as he'd shoved it into the hay and guts, again and again, his father looming over him.

Gabriel stared at her outstretched hand as if it were a dead thing, a dark and poisonous flower he wouldn't dare touch.

"I will tolerate your presence as long as the task of eliminating your sister binds us," he said, meeting those devastating blue eyes one last time. Then, in a voice so bitingly cold it terrified even him, he said, "But the day I make a deal with a *demon* is the day you'll taste the last of my bitter ashes."

It's not over yet! Gabriel and Jaci's story continues in Heart of Fury!

With Viansa running amok in Manhattan and the curse

wreaking havoc on the royal vampires, can Gabriel and Jaci overcome the bitter sting of betrayal and hunt down the succubus from hell before it's too late?

In the immortal words of our favorite little witch-demon, "Don't stop!" Find out what happens next in **Heart of Fury, book two of the Vampire Royals of New York: Gabriel series!**

Vampire lovers! If you loved reading this story as much as I loved writing it, please help a girl out and **leave a review on Amazon!** Even a quick sentence or two about your favorite part can help other readers discover the book, and that makes me super happy!

If you really, *really* loved it, come hang out with me and the other amazing Vampire Royals of New York fans in our private Facebook group, Sarah Piper's Sassy Witches. Pop in for sneak peeks, cover reveals, exclusive giveaways, book chats, and plenty of complete randomness! We'd love to see you there.

XOXO
Sarah

Paranormal romance fans, I've got even more sexy books ready to heat up your bookshelf!

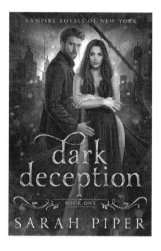

VAMPIRE ROYALS OF NEW YORK: See where it all began with Dorian and Charley's series—a scorching paranormal romance trilogy featuring a commanding, dirty-talking vampire king and the seductive thief who might just bring him to ruin… or become his eternal salvation.

TAROT ACADEMY is a paranormal, university-aged reverse harem academy romance starring four seriously hot mages and one badass witch. Dark prophecies, unique mythology, steamy romance, and plenty of supernatural thrills make this series a must-read! Read on for a taste of book one, Spells of Iron & Bone!

TAROT ACADEMY 1: SPELLS OF IRON AND BONE EXCERPT

CHAPTER ONE

There's no problem a proper cup of tea can't fix.

It says so right on my work apron, just beneath the Kettle Black logo Mom designed decades ago, back when the café only existed in her dreams and sketchbooks. It says so on our menus and the shirts we sell to tourists. And it says so on the Mother's Day mug I painted when I was six —a black-and-gold one that sits next to the cash register, holding all the pens.

There used to be a plaque on the wall, too, but that came down years ago, buried in a box with the ashes of Connor and Melissa Milan, resting beneath a granite headstone in Los Pinones Cemetery.

Devoted parents and friends

May their eternal light shine as a beacon for all who loved them…

If you squint at that part of the wall now, you can still make out the square of plum-colored wallpaper, slightly darker where the plaque used to hang.

Anyway, as far as truisms go, the tea thing always felt like a good one. For the first eighteen years of my life, the simple brew healed all manner of wounds, from scraped knees to bruised egos, from mean-girl dramas to the fathomless ache of unrequited love.

And later, when I lost my beloved parents, when even the shrinks and social workers had given up on me, when my days turned so dark I feared Death himself would come and snatch me right out of my bed, two things brought me back from the abyss:

My best friend Jessa Velasquez and some good, hot, life-affirming tea.

There's no problem a proper cup of tea can't fix, my mother's voice echoes again now.

It's funny how badly I still want to believe it.

But there's another truism—bigger, all-encompassing—one my parents forgot to mention before the river swept them down the Lost Canyons of Arizona, dashing their skulls against the rocks before the water could even finish drowning them:

There's nothing the universe loves more than a chance to show us how truly breakable we really are.

CHAPTER TWO

I've never seen a sky as wicked as the one that just blew in over Tres Búhos.

It's a mean one alright, full of ire and vengeance. And while I love a bone-rattling Arizona storm as much as the next witch, I'd rather not be sitting on top of the tallest rock in the desert when Mother Nature goes balls-out ballistic.

She's kind of an asshole sometimes.

I'd also rather not be dressed like a human lightning rod, but considering I can't make the two-hundred-foot descent without some serious hardware, looks like that dream's dead on the vine too.

I glare up at the sky. All morning it was clear and calm, the perfect day for a climb. But the second I get settled on top, light the palo santo, and whisper a few words of my mother's magick...

"Message received," I grumble, keeping the *asshole* bit to myself.

In response, the oil-black clouds flicker with a preview of what's to come, and a burst of hot, gritty wind rifles through the old grimoire on my lap. The faint smolder of palo santo dies, its sweet fragrance replaced with the scent of ozone.

That sky is ready to burst.

I close the spellbook, resigned. My attempt at magick—if you can even call it that—was destined to flame out anyway. Sure, I can sense people's energies, and my body has an uncanny ability to heal itself quicker than most, but as far as active powers? Other than casting witchfire, my magick is basically nonexistent, just like my parents wanted it to be.

Just like I promised to keep it.

Guilt surges anew, making my skin itch.

"Forget magick, Stevie. It's a curse…"

They weren't Mom's *literal* last words—those would come in the hours that followed, high-pitched and panicked and mostly incoherent—but they're the ones that stand out now. The ones that twist a hot blade in my gut every time I open the forbidden grimoire, searching for a clue about her past. *Our* past. This unknowable thing inside me, crackling with a wild, potential energy that simultaneously terrifies and fascinates me.

The forest-green leather is warm beneath my palm, and I try to pick up a sense of Mom's gentle touch, her laugh, the scent of frankincense that always trailed in her wake…

Nothing comes.

Nothing *ever* comes.

They say time heals all wounds, but next week marks five years since I buried my parents, and I still wake up every morning to the suffocating press of grief on my heart. As far as I can tell, the only thing time does is march onward; all that's left for the living to do is try not to get trampled beneath it.

Another gust of wind buffets the rock, and a spiny lizard skitters across my blanket, smartly tucking himself into a crevice. Tamping down the simmering guilt, I slip the book into my daypack with the rest of my stuff, hop to my feet, and gear up for the drop.

Climbing shoes. Harness. Ropes. Chalk bag. Knife. Carabiners and hexes and cams… Check, check, check.

Tightening my fingerless gloves, I blow out a breath and step to the edge.

Darkness smothers everything in sight, casting shadows as far down as I can see. A strange, gray mist blankets the desert floor, the tops of the saguaros floating like the masts of a hundred haunted ships.

It's a long way down. A lot longer than it's ever felt before.

El Búho Grande—the big owl—is the largest of the three owl-shaped sandstone formations that tower over the Santa Clarita Desert, marking the southern border of their namesake town—Tres Búhos, Arizona. Three Owls. It's the only place I've ever called home.

The other two "búhitos" flanking me are significantly smaller—and much steeper, thanks to the protection of the big guy. But here on the Grande, where time has worn the top of the owl's head into a slab the size of an Olympic swimming pool, I can see my death coming from miles away.

Off in the misty distance, a streak of lightning splits the sky. I count to five before I hear the thunder—still a ways off, but not for long.

Goddess, let me be on the ground before the rain starts…

But even that's too much to ask, and as the first few drops darken the dusty red rock to a deep brown, I shoulder my pack, triple-check my knots, and begin the descent.

The ropes and anchors I set on the climb up are still in place, and at first, I make good progress. But it's not long before the rain picks up, soaking me to the bone and making everything I touch impossibly slick. Ignoring the drumbeat of encroaching thunder, I focus on my footing, wishing for once I *hadn't* ignored the NO CLIMBING signs posted at the bottom.

Fifty feet down, slow and steady. Sixty. Seventy-five. Another bolt of lightning flickers in my peripheral vision, the crack of thunder right on its heels, echoing across the eerie desert.

I need to hurry.

Shit. I hate the idea of leaving gear behind, especially since most of this stuff belonged to my parents—some of the few possessions I wasn't forced to sell after they died—but Mother Nature clearly wants me off this rock, and I don't have time to remove everything as I go. I'll have to come back tomorrow, hope that some bored park ranger doesn't take it down first.

Right now, it's all I can do to clip in and work my way down without slipping and smashing my face.

Wedging my toes into a horizontal crack, I release the slippery rock and reach behind me for the chalk bag, knowing I'll find a pasty mess, hoping it'll help my grip anyway. But I don't even find any paste—just a small, thin card, completely out of place.

It's a Tarot card. I know it before I even look at it.

Fear prickles across my scalp.

I've never had my own deck, but Mom did—one of the

few things she kept from her old life. Before I sold our house, I nearly tore up the floorboards searching for it, eventually concluding she had it with her on that fateful day, losing it in the tumult of the rushing water. But on the one-year anniversary of their death, the cards started appearing to me at random like this. Under my pillow, tucked into the spokes on my bicycle wheel, hidden in an old shoe. Last week the King of Cups dropped out of my sealed electric bill. Yesterday I emptied the washing machine and found the Fool prancing around at the bottom, bright and undamaged.

I can't say for sure it's Mom, but the cards always bring me a message, and they're never wrong.

I hold it up to my face now, blinking away the stinging mix of rain, sweat, and sunscreen.

The Tower.

At the center of the ominous image, a stone tower rises from a rocky outcropping at the edge of the sea. A bolt of lightning decimates half the structure and sends two people jumping out the highest windows, presumably to their deaths.

Not the most encouraging visual, given the circumstances.

I try to feel into the energy, to decipher whatever message is trying to come through. Usually I pick up on an impression, a general feeling. But this time the message feels more sinister, more urgent. I sense it in the tightening of my muscles, hear it like a whisper on the wind, straining to reach me through the rain.

Danger ahead, Stevie. Trouble and treachery. You're not alone...

Seconds later, the card vanishes from my grasp, lost beneath the clatter of some new threat. The prickling across my scalp turns at once to sharp, stinging pain.

Rockslide.

Instinctively I haul my pack over my head, shove one hand into a crevice, and tuck in close to the rock, toes still balanced in the crack. Dressed in a tank top and a pair of cargo shorts, I've got zero protection against the assault of tiny stones biting my bare shoulders and arms.

Stones? Scratch that.

Hail.

Lightning flickers behind me, making my shadow dance against the rock face as the wind surges with renewed force, whipping icy pellets at me from all directions. They clatter like gunfire.

Adrenaline shoots through my veins, my heart pounding so hard it hurts. Rappelling in this weather is much too dangerous, but I can't stay here. I'm totally exposed, and the storm is parked right on top of me now. It's only a matter of time before lightning zaps me like a bug, or a chunk of rock bashes my head, or my rope breaks and sends me careening into oblivion...

Come on, girl. Think. Think!

It's almost impossible not to picture the poor souls in that Tarot card, but I do my best to shove them out of my mind, refocusing on my own precarious predicament. I can't go back up—I'd be even more exposed up top. I'm better off descending, but I can't protect my head *and* manage the ropes and gear placements *and* mind my hand- and footholds. I can barely see a few inches in front of me.

I need shelter. And up here, there's only one possibility.

El Ala—The Wing.

It's a secondary route about twenty feet to my left and fifteen down, skirting the edge of the owl's "wing." It's the most dangerous route by far, but still bolted from when people used to climb here legally, back before a huge chunk of rock cracked off and killed three climbers in the early nineties.

Just inside the wing lies a deep fissure in the rock, big enough you can see it from the dirt road leading into town.

Big enough I can fit inside and wait out the storm.

Another bolt of lightning.

Another crack of thunder.

The hail intensifies, pinging off my pack. That shit's the size of gumballs now, their stinging bite turning into a bruising wallop.

El Ala? Here I come.

I re-settle the pack on my shoulders and lean back, propping my feet against the wall as the harness takes the bulk of my weight, providing momentary relief for my calves. My head and arms are prime targets for the hail and debris shooting down from above, but if I can't make the twenty-foot traverse climb to that cave, I'll have much bigger problems.

I lean close to the wall again, get a good grip, and gingerly step to the left, seeking a better toehold. But just as my foot finds purchase, the wind lashes out again, blasting me off the rock like a bug off a windshield.

Frantically I scramble for the ropes, but it's too late. I drop hard and fast, bashing my knee on the way down.

There's no time to scream, no time for panic. Suddenly the rope tightens and the harness jerks me to a hard stop, gear clattering, stomach leaping into my throat.

Blood leaks from my throbbing knee. My lines are hopelessly tangled. I'm suspended from Death's eager grasp by a rope that's less than an inch thick, and now I'm *below* the position of the cave, which means I'll have to climb over *and* back up.

Unless…

Fighting against the relentless wind, I kick my legs out and back, harnessing the momentum into a pendulum swing, rocking harder and higher, closer… closer… almost there…

My fingers graze the bottom of the wing, just a few feet beneath the cave floor, but I can't get a good grip.

I try again on the next swing.

Miss.

Again.

Again.

Again.

On what feels like the twentieth attempt, I finally hook it with the tip of my shoe, and let out a victory cry bordering on mania. The toehold is precarious, gravity doing its damnedest to suck me back in the other direction.

No way, asshole. You can't have me.

With every muscle in my leg screaming in agony, I pull myself in by my toe, fighting the wind, fighting fatigue, fighting mental anguish until finally I reach out with my hand and feel the rough, wet rock beneath my fingertips.

Quickly, I clip into one of the old bolts, sending a prayer of thanks to whoever put it there.

I climb the last few feet up to the cave and, with the very last bit of strength I've got, haul myself inside.

The clatter of the hail turns to a din, and a new warmth pulses all around me. Sprawled out on my belly, I give myself a moment to catch my breath, then slowly raise my head, peering inside the dark space of the cave.

I'm still here, mostly in one piece.

"Thank you," I exhale into the deep.

"You're welcome," comes an unexpected reply.

And there, from somewhere inside that gnawing blackness, a pair of glowing yellow eyes blinks to life, and a shadow in the shape of a man peels away from the wall and stalks toward the light.

Toward me.

What dangers and intrigue will Stevie face? Dive into the sexy supernatural world of Tarot Academy and find out! Grab your copy of Tarot Academy 1: Spells of Iron and Bone now!

ABOUT SARAH PIPER

Sarah Piper is a Kindle All-Star winning urban fantasy and paranormal romance author. Through her signature brew of dark magic, heart-pounding suspense, and steamy romance, Sarah promises a sexy, supernatural escape into a world where the magic is real, the monsters are sinfully hot, and the witches always get their magically-ever-afters.

Her recent works include the newly released Vampire Royals of New York series, the Tarot Academy series, and The Witch's Rebels, a fan-favorite reverse harem urban fantasy series readers have dubbed "super sexy," "imaginative and original," "off-the-walls good," and "delightfully wicked in the best ways," a quote Sarah hopes will appear on her tombstone.

Originally from New York, Sarah now makes her home in northern Colorado with her husband (though that changes frequently) (the location, not the husband), where she spends her days sleeping like a vampire and her nights writing books, casting spells, gazing at the moon, playing with her ever-expanding collection of Tarot cards, binge-watching Supernatural (Team Dean!), and obsessing over the best way to brew a cup of tea.

You can find her online at SarahPiperBooks.com and in her Facebook readers group, Sarah Piper's Sassy Witches! If you're sassy, or if you need a little *more* sass in your life, or if you need more Dean Winchester gifs in your life (who doesn't?), come hang out!